A SCANDAL HAS WINGS

GRAHAM
DONNELLY

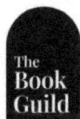

The
Book
Guild

First published in Great Britain in 2025 by
The Book Guild
Unit E2, Airfield Business Park
Harrison Road
Market Harborough
Leicsestershire, LE16 7UL
Freephone: 0800 999 2982
www.bookguild.co.uk
Email: info@bookguild.co.uk
Twitter: @bookguild

Typeset in 12pt Adobe Jenson Pro

Printed and bound by CPI Group (UK) Ltd, Croydon, CR0 4YY

ISBN 978 1835741 412

British Library Cataloguing in Publication Data.
A catalogue record for this book is available from the British Library.

MIX
Paper | Supporting
responsible forestry
FSC® C013604

For Roy and Robert

"A lie has no leg, but a scandal has wings."

Thomas Fuller 1608–1661

1

AUTUMN

LET US BEGIN WITH THE COLLEGE. AN establishment of learning, a society where tutors and students work together for the growth of knowledge and expertise and therefore the betterment of the nation. If we had approached the grand entrance to this particular college, we could have been in no doubt that its purpose was just that. Its architect, Sir Branwell Chivers, had avoided the concrete, sometimes brutalist, designs of so many colleges erected in the 1950s. True to his Palladian sympathies and love of the classics, he had designed something more in tune with the Royal Exchange in the City of London than the robust plainness of most of its contemporaries. The result was a building that would not have been out of place in Vicenza, the home of Palladio, or in the schools of learning of Ancient Greece. The façade of the building had been cleaned over the summer and the name of the college, The Thomas Newcomen College of Technology, was proclaimed in new silver block lettering in the pediment above the Doric columns.

Like all the colleges of further education in the 1950s, it had opened with an emphasis on engineering in all its

1

different branches: mechanical, auto, electrical, chemical and so on, but like the economy it served, it had later diversified into the service sectors: catering, hairdressing, business and management, the arts, social and health care, travel and tourism, etc. With this expansion came an ever-wider range of subjects and professions epitomised by the lecturers and students who made up this collegiate society: a place of learning, culture and progress. The college had grown rapidly in the last twenty years and many of the teaching staff were young, often only a few years older than their students; this was not an environment peopled by Mr Chips or Mr Crocker-Harris of *The Browning Version*. Like any place where the young and not yet middle-aged come together in large numbers; it would also be a playground where the immature become adults and adults might sometimes forget their claim to maturity; where for the teaching staff the prizes, ambitions and opportunities for aggrandisement invite competition, jealousy and corruption. For lecturers and students alike, innocent play and healthy rivalries may become something much darker.

It was the first day of the new academic year and one of the younger lecturers, Gillian Trevis, arrived punctually. She had driven into the staff car park in her racing-green Mini Cooper and pulled to a halt, the car shuddering slightly as if in anticipation. Twenty-eight with her black hair in a modern but not-too-exorbitant cut and dressed in a business suit with a cream blouse, she was aiming for a professional but not-too-severe look. She sat back in her seat and listened to the radio and the end of Showaddywaddy's version of 'Heartbeat', remembering with affection the original of Buddy Holly and thought how quickly the pop music of her childhood had come round again. Her reverie was interrupted by Carl Malcolm singing 'Fatty Bum Bum' and she wondered how there could possibly be two versions of a song with that name in the Top Forty. She smiled and turned off the radio, getting out of her car with a metaphorical spring in her step. There was something special about the first day of a new academic year and, though this was not an entirely new experience, she could not help but feel that quickening of the pulse and sense of expectation which for her always accompanied a fresh start: new courses, new students, new possibilities.

Gillian looked up and admired with pride the new block lettering of the college's name. Thomas Newcomen, as she had many times had to explain, was the inventor of the atmospheric engine, the first steam-driven engine to be produced. In the history of the Industrial Revolution, he had generally been overshadowed by later developers of his machine, like James Watt, Robert Stephenson and others. The college, though far from Newcomen's birthplace of Dartmouth, had as its first, and so far only, principal: a professor of engineering from an old university who had served in the Royal Navy and had a special reverence for the great man. He had convinced the local education authority to name the college after a person of significance, rather than go for a bland geographical title.

Gillian was not an engineer; she was an economist, the only female lecturer in economics at the college since, here, economics seemed almost as much a male preserve as engineering. She was unperturbed by this since for her a subject should be a matter of choice, not predetermined by gender. Anyway, she could point to notable women economists in the past: Millicent Fawcett, Mary Paley Marshall and others, when it really had been difficult to make a career in a man's world.

Reflecting on her sense of anticipation, not shared by all her colleagues or even most of them, Gillian supposed it was because she had a natural empathy with the academic year, which was itself derived from the agricultural year. Most professions had severed the connection between their working calendar and the agricultural cycle but the academic year remained inviolate and it shared many of the qualities of the agricultural one: a time for sowing in the autumn, nurturing and feeding of the crop of new students through the year, a harvest in summer and then the fallow period of the mid to late summer when there were no students. Then the lecturers could use the summer months from July through to mid-September to 'recharge the batteries' through the long holidays.

Her reflecting over, Gillian was now ready to face the future. She walked briskly up the stairs to her office, where she would undertake the first ritual of this bright new day: the renewing of acquaintanceships with her colleagues. Some of the conscientious ones would have come into college during the holidays to check the mail, prepare for new courses and update their reading. Others would have disappeared on the last day of the summer term, if not earlier, to their second home in France or their cottage in the country or, for an impecunious few, to casual work in the summer, none of them to be seen again until today. Gillian considered herself somewhere in between, though some of her colleagues thought she was too conscientious with her regular visits throughout the holidays, except when she was away. She called into the staff lounge to check her pigeonhole for mail and college circulars, waved hello to one of the admin staff who had worked through most of the summer, apart from a fortnight away, and went up to her office on the next floor. She shared this space with five others, all members of the business and management studies team. Two of them had yet to arrive but the others were settled at their desks and looked up when Gillian came in. They greeted her, two cheerfully with a smile and the other like a prisoner acknowledging another old lag who had returned to gaol after a brief period of freedom.

The one with the grim expression was Julian Wesley, a man in his early fifties who had forsaken long ago all hopes of progress in his career and had matched this lack of movement in his status with an equally moribund approach to the teaching of his subject. He was pleased to deliver his economics lectures to HNC business studies, A level and various other students, using the same notes he had used for well over twenty years without amendment. No texts since those of decades-old Samuelson and Nevin had ever impinged on his teaching aids and he avoided more modern introductions like the flip chart, case studies, the Banda machine and any other form of handout like the plague. He was witty and charming and generally admired by his students and, as his protégés changed each year or two years at most, none knew that they were receiving exactly the same well-delivered talks and being entertained by the same well-honed stories as scores of other students over the years. He would disappear to his villa in Portugal on the last day of the summer term, only to reappear on the first day of the autumn term, as he had now, scowling as he waded through the dozens of directives, memoranda and notifications from the principal or vice-principal, the welcome-back memorandum from the head of department and the copious letters, flyers and offers from professional bodies, educational publishers and other marketing media. From the limited information he divulged, he appeared to be happily married though the love of which he waxed lyrical was that for fine wines and their fortified relation, port. While staying at his villa, a trip to Oporto was always on his summer itinerary with a pilgrimage across the Luis I bridge to visit Sandeman's, Graham's, Calem, Taylor's and all the other great port houses.

Waiting on Gillian's desk was a good bottle of Douro, which Julian always brought back for several of the team.

"Thanks for this, Julian," Gillian said. "Very kind of you."

"That's OK," Julian replied. He picked up some of the papers on his desk. "There are three different versions of the VP's directive on work placement arrangements for HND students here," he added, waving them in the air before throwing all of them into the filled-to-overflowing bin under his desk.

Gillian smiled and looked at Bill Rendell, a lecturer in accountancy subjects five years older than her. He returned the smile. "Good break?" he asked, removing his reading glasses and running his hand through his sandy-coloured hair.

"Yes, thanks, two weeks roasting in Malaga. Tan's nearly gone," she added, looking wistfully at her arm. "You?"

"Usual. Cornwall."

Bill was a certified accountant and, probably more than most of the others in the room, earned far less educating future accountants as a lecturer of any grade than he would have done practising his profession. The question as to why he had chosen to teach when he undoubtedly was capable of actually doing the job was put to him at his interview and he answered that he believed in education and passing on his knowledge. Sincere or not, his statement of principle was of little consequence since a chartered or certified accountant in a college of further education is a rare prize to be savoured, evidence that, as in other subjects, accounting students might be taught by someone who knows more about the subject than they do. Consequently, Bill's students appreciated not only the knowledge he imparted but also what he had learnt from his professional experience through real case studies. Unlike Julian, he did keep up with the latest developments in his subjects, and not only because it was a requirement of his professional qualification. He had a pleasant if taciturn disposition and was always willing to help others but nobody at the college could say they knew him well. There was a wife and two children whom he occasionally mentioned and he enjoyed the solitary pursuit of brass rubbing, which took up many of his weekends and was a subject of which he was something of an expert. If an outsider enquired about him, that was the limit of any of his colleagues' knowledge.

The last person in the group was Roger Southwark, another economist, just turned thirty. "Hello, Gill, how are you?" he asked.

"Fine," she said. "Have a good holiday?"

"Went to the Hebrides. Weather was lousy but what you'd expect in the North West. I enjoyed it but no wonder the population is in decline."

"Inner our Outer Hebrides?" asked Gillian.

"Inner. I think I'll need to get into polar-expedition training before I take on Harris, Lewis and the Uists."

Gillian laughed and Roger, who could never make up his mind whether he found her attractive or not, but thought he probably did today, with her very dark hair, violet eyes and sparkling smile.

Like all the people in the room, Roger had worked in one occupation or more before coming into teaching. Gillian had been an economic analyst for an oil company while Roger had worked in banking in London and in Africa. Both had opted for a slower life or perhaps they had no longer been able to take the pace; only they knew the truth of that. Unlike Bill, neither were married nor had dependents, so their decision to take a lower salary was not influenced by concerns for others. Gillian always struck everyone as very committed, an avid reader of economic journals and papers and a regular attendee at study days and conferences, at Combe Lodge, the further education staff-training college, and conferences on economics elsewhere. Nor was she reluctant to revise and improve her lesson plans, unlike most of her colleagues who had only ever created a lesson plan to comply with a visit from an apprehensively unwelcome HM Inspector of Education. Gillian's lack of a husband or of any other known romantic involvement was a source of considerable speculation among some of her colleagues, whose interest ranged from curiosity to inquisitiveness, suspicion, pity and even envy. All such hypotheses were made all the more florid by Gillian's steadfast lack of comment to any fishing enquiries about her private life.

The paperwork of all four continued, interspersed with idle chatter or news about the likely intakes for the full-time courses in the new academic year; those for part-time and day release were always unclear until enrolment evenings.

Despite the usual comment that not much happened in August and that it was the so-called 'Silly Season' for the newspapers, the equivalent of *It's a Knockout* on the television, they spent some time discussing current affairs. The sporadic IRA campaign which had involved the bombing of the London Hilton earlier in the month and the death of two people got a mention but, though horrific, it was nothing new: as for most people in Britain, it was part of the backdrop to life.

"There'll always be another one," said Julian. "Somebody ready to be a hero if they can plant a bomb far enough away from them when it goes off."

There was silence for a few minutes. It seemed difficult to have a constructive conversation about a situation which appeared purely destructional.

From both a professional and a personal perspective, the economic situation was high on their agenda. The previous year, the government had increased the salaries of lecturers in further education by about twenty-five per cent in an attempt to make up the ground they had lost against comparable occupations over the last several years. All the people in the room were pleased to a greater or lesser extent at the time but the inflation rate, already accelerating, had now reached an annual rate of over twenty per cent.

"So, we are back where we started before the big pay rise," said Roger, having read out the latest inflation figures from the *Financial Times* opened in front of him.

"Except that we received a substantial rise before the government brought the pay policy in," replied Gillian. "Others will not have been so lucky."

"Six quid a week pay rise for everyone this time round," observed Bill.

"It's the only solution. It is our misfortune to understand how the economy works," said Julian. "We are aware of the damage a wage-price inflationary spiral will do and the futility of everyone chasing their own tail. That is our weakness as we will be inclined to be reasonable and moderate. Meanwhile, those who do not understand it or refuse to acknowledge they do, will be free to use whatever power they have to protect their interests, and, of course, they will."

"The government couldn't have done it without the support of the unions," said Gill. "I'm not sure all their members will be as keen."

"Good thing 'Red Robbo' isn't here," said Roger, referring to Robert Grainger, the politically very committed lecturer in sociology and politics who was based in another office up the corridor. Robert was quite proud of his nickname, taken from the indomitable union activist who had been for some time a key figure in industrial relations at British Leyland, the major British car manufacturer which had collapsed in the summer and been taken into public ownership by the government.

"Pity about British Leyland going under, but there it is," said Bill.

"Buses were good but would you buy an Allegro or a Marina?" asked Julian.

This remark was greeted with mournful laughter. All of them were old enough to remember when the vast majority of cars sold in Britain were built by companies based there. Now the last mass car producer in British ownership was on life support and their conversation became even more maudlin.

"What a tragedy, though," mused Roger. "A once-successful bus company brought down by its association with the British Motor Corporation."

"It's all Austin's fault," said Gillian, for whom economic history of the twentieth century had been one of her special subjects in her degree. "They were struggling with bad industrial relations and on the verge of going bust. Morris was pressured to take them over because he was successful and had good relations with his workers. But instead of Morris saving Austin, the drowning man pulled his rescuer down with him. William Morris must be turning in his grave."

"And now they've done it to Leyland as well," said Julian, "and with it, Standard Triumph." He thought wistfully of his much-loved Triumph Vitesse, now passed on to an impecunious nephew.

"Wait till the government gets hold of it," said Roger and they all laughed that laugh which is the only alternative to crying.

As they were lamenting the symbolic demise of Britain's mass car producer, morphing into a conversation of despair about the decline of most of Britain's major industries, the remaining two lecturers based in this office arrived: Rajeev Bhatt, a young, versatile lecturer who had joined the previous year and specialised in cost and management accounting, and

Una Jones, a woman in her late forties who had taught insurance and banking subjects at the college for over ten years. Her well-groomed fair hair and always impeccable clothes marked her out as the epitome of a sensible, professional business lecturer, and this did not belie the reality. Una was perhaps the best example of all of them in having practical experience since her husband was an independent insurance broker and Una kept her hand in at the weekends. She had married her husband three years before, moving from Miss Smith to Mrs Jones and was since referred to by her students with the nickname 'Alias Smith and Jones' after the TV series. A new round of renewing acquaintances occurred, followed by more clearance of the backlog of administrative and other communications, occasionally into a filing cabinet but more often to the wastepaper bin.

At half past ten the deputy head of department and one of the principal lecturers, Doug Jameson, came in to give them the rota of the enrolment evenings for part-time and evening-class students. Roger looked at his allocation then asked if anyone wanted a coffee. The others said they would come later, apart from Gillian and Rajeev, who joined him in the staff lounge.

"Well, back with a bang," said Rajeev, sharply dressed in a light-grey suit, a blue shirt and purple tie; one leg crossed over the other. "Two nights of hectic mayhem with hundreds of customers, some of them with not a clue as to what they want, then the dreaded totting up of numbers when we find out whether the courses we really like teaching are actually running and, if not, what we get lumbered with instead."

"The ones who are not sure what they want to do will have to watch out for Don Coppice or he'll hoover them up," said Gillian.

The other two laughed. Don Coppice was a senior lecturer in management who had developed an ingenious system for ensuring that the part-time courses he administered always had enough students to make the courses viable with virtually no students at all. He did this by offering many courses with overlapping syllabuses and then ensuring that the compulsory subjects of one group would be the options of other groups and so on. The process was made easier by the fact that Don was in charge of departmental timetables. Roger himself taught a subject on one of these courses.

"I like the enrolment evenings myself," said Roger.

"So do I," said Gillian enthusiastically. "All those people who really *want* to study and seeing people who come back year after year to develop their careers or just because they actually like learning."

Roger smiled at her enthusiasm. "Yes, it is a moment of near-perfection before the entropy sets in."

"Entropy?" asked Gillian.

"You know, the principle that order and harmony always give way to disorder and chaos. At the end of the enrolment process, the students have enrolled for the courses they either wish to do or must do from necessity for their career. Generally, they look forward to their courses and are optimistic about the outcome. Similarly, the lecturers look forward to a fresh start with a new cohort of students, some of whom will inspire us and make it all worthwhile. Then, term starts, some students have already dropped out by then and others leave when their expectations are not met. Most of the lecturers too are disappointed to some extent and the process of entropy begins as we settle into the typical year with something which is acceptable but never fulfils the promise we cling to today."

"Why do we do it, then?" asked Gillian, smiling.

"Hope springs eternal," Roger replied. "Anyway, it only lasts for a year and we get another fresh start."

Rajeev laughed. "I'll drink to that," he said, raising his cup of coffee.

"So will I," said Mark Harred, a law lecturer in their department who joined them along with Rob Grainger, the 'Red Robbo' of their earlier conversation.

"Yes," continued Harred. "Enrolment evenings: all those bright-eyed students you can give the once-over and pick the stars of the year and if you are wrong, what does it matter, move on."

"We know which ones you will be giving the once-over," said Rajeev with a smirk, the others smiling with a nod or a shake of the head.

Mark Harred did undoubtedly have an eye for the younger, but always over-eighteen, female students. It was not that other male lecturers were impervious to the physical charms of their students, rather it was the case that he was rarely one to view them in an abstract way or from afar. His interest in them was frequently reciprocated. With his slightly long, but well-coiffed dark-blond hair, his smart, rather flamboyant style of suits and ties, and his cheery, unthreatening demeanour, he cut the dash as an attractive, still-youngish man who compared favourably against the standard set by most of his colleagues. He came across as a not too serious, and definitely not creepy, sophisticate who had a good line in flattery and would be a bit of fun to get to know outside college. The fact that he had a wife would doubtless be a deterrent for some but a safety valve for others. At the age of thirty-two he was aware that, while the students were forever aged between eighteen and twenty-one, his relative youthfulness was a slowly fading asset that he was keen to make the most of before Father Time put paid to it. Of all the male lecturers he was the one whom the most promising students, in more ways than one, could be relied upon for the one-to-one tutorial or the occasional lift to an off-campus site. His reaction to Rajeev's comment was merely to smile, with a slight frown to illustrate his incomprehension.

Rob Grainger was of a similar age and, in his own way, equally attractive, perhaps to those of a more serious bent. His dark-brown hair was carefully tousled, his beard well-kempt and his NHS-style glasses added simultaneously an air of studious commitment and a disregard for ostentation. He wore a plain tank top under his tweed sports jacket which sported leather patches on the elbows, another sign of his 'make do and mend' frugality, never mind that the patches were actually a fashion accessory rather than covering worn fabric. Surely this man would appeal to a student whose education would be enhanced, not by prioritising a bit of fun, but in the company of an attractive man who could discuss the philosophy of Kierkegaard and Sartre, the films of Bunuel and Bergman, the novels of Iris Murdoch and John Updike and the art of Warhol and Rothko. However, Rob Grainger was not interested in using his well-crafted persona to develop closer relationships with his students at Thomas Newcomen College.

In fact, Rob Grainger was only marginally interested in his students at the college in so far as it gave him the opportunity to hone his political credentials by practising the espousal of his views and testing the quality of his arguments on the admittedly inexperienced students on his courses. This was because a lectureship in a further education college, even one as highly regarded and with prestigious courses like Thomas Newcomen, was not the target of his ambition. His aim, as it had been since he was sixteen, was to be a professional politician and to win a seat in parliament. In preparation for his future career, he had done all the right things. He had taken A levels in British constitution, economics and sociology, followed by a degree at a redbrick university in politics and philosophy. Then he had worked for a year unpaid as a research assistant for a demanding, but rarely generous, Labour MP, another year in residential social work and then three years in local government before becoming a lecturer at the college. Though he had a permanent appointment, he regarded it as merely as temporary staging post while he went about his real business of securing a parliamentary seat. Meanwhile, he had thrown himself into appearances at party conferences, notably the more cutting-edge ones. He readily agreed to sit on unpaid working groups and research projects investigating and helping to frame party policy, especially if it was chaired by a prominent member of the party, perhaps even a minister. He had perfected an admiring smile and a knowing nod while sitting through countless boring speeches of which he remembered barely a word and he cheerfully spent endless hours canvassing, putting up posters and attending rallies.

Unfortunately, Father Time weighs even more heavily on an aspiring politician than it does on any hopeful Lothario, even one who tries to do everything right to push his way up the potential candidate list, like Rob Grainger. The problem is that general elections came round only every four or five years and under twenty-five, unless you are a budding Pitt the Younger, you would not usually be regarded as having sufficient experience or maturity to be a candidate. On the other hand, you would rarely be selected as a new candidate, without experience, over the age of fifty-five, unless having an eminent background in some other field. This meant, at most, probably eight general elections to get into parliament. Since he had been trying to become a candidate, from the moment he reached the age of twenty-five, there had been three general elections. He had failed to be selected in 1970 and the two elections in 1974 he had been adopted for the same hopeless seat, as far as Labour was concerned, in Devon. However, he had slightly increased his share of the vote in the latter election and hoped to have a go at a more winnable seat next time, in 1979 probably. He would then be thirty-seven. With perhaps only four goes after that, he felt he had to win this time or be written off as a three-time loser. He had heard that an elderly MP with a safe Labour seat in the West Midlands was standing down at the next election and there had been hints that he might be given the nod and adopted as candidate next time. The distance from the college to the constituency was about an hour and a quarter's drive so he went over there most weekends and whenever else necessary to nurse his putative constituency. Anyone looking at him now, while the chatter went on in the rest of the group, would see that his mind was far away, thinking what might follow and what might yet be.

At half past eleven there was a full staff departmental meeting in the lecture hall. Fifty or so members of staff crowded into the tiered auditorium to be greeted by the head of department, Arnold Frost Ph.D., sitting in splendid isolation at the desk in front of the huge blackboard. A general glance round the room would show that several members of staff had a new appearance. A beard or moustache had disappeared here or there and new ones had appeared in one or two cases. Hair lengths had gone up or down, hairstyles changed or moderated or were completely new in the case of some female staff. Some staff were wearing exactly the same clothes they had worn at the staff meeting at the end of the last term while others exhibited new fashions or at least newer clothes in old fashions.

Yet, obvious to everyone was that the greatest makeover in appearance had taken place in Dr Frost himself. Gone was the greying, flat, side-parted hair, the pallid complexion, the dark pin-striped suit and narrow maroon club tie. In their place was a golden, the only word for it, slightly longer and blow-waved hairstyle, with a matching moustache reminiscent of the actor Peter Wyngarde in the character of Jason King, and his face wore a healthy, some might say too healthy, tan. He wore a large-check suit in brown with wide lapels and a kipper silk tie of a rather bilious green hue. Those who had already seen the transformation were no longer surprised; the others exchanged looks of incredulity, amusement or mild shock, but naturally none commented.

Dr Frost, now in his late fifties, was of that last generation of senior members of college staff who were always addressed by their formal title. Everyone else in the department from the principal lecturers down to the humblest lecturer, was addressed by first names or, occasionally, a nickname. Dr Frost welcomed everyone back and, almost as a challenge to his colleagues, given his own sartorial overhaul, referred to the change in appearance of one or two of his staff. None picked up the gauntlet. Gillian asked Una Jones if she knew why there had been such a metamorphosis in Frost's appearance and Una, who usually had an ear to the ground for all such news, whispered, "New woman."

The agenda of the meeting included introductions of two new members of staff, one in secretarial studies and the other in law, arrangements for enrolment, new courses introduced and details of liaison with other departments. There was a sprinkling of members of staff from other departments who contributed to business and management studies courses, such as English, foreign languages and psychology, partly there for information gathering but also to ensure that their areas were protected in any change of syllabus. For most of the people present, the meeting was purely a ritual to be endured, the rite of initiation to confirm that summer was truly over and the autumn term was here. For others, this meeting was the opportunity to stake their claim for a greater role for their subject or their course, or to lament the continued decline of a subject dear to them or to air grievances about matters that had been festering over the holidays or were a perennial gripe. Questions were asked about changes for the new academic year and dealt with efficiently by Dr Frost. Then came any other business and the opportunity for disgruntlement to surface.

Heidi Nachtnebel, a small woman in her fifties, square both in head and body, jumped to her feet. Heidi was a language teacher from Switzerland who, apart from speaking English, was trilingual in German, French and Italian. She also had more than a smattering of Romansch, the fourth language of Switzerland. Dr Frost rubbed the skin under his chin, a habit of his when he could feel a rise in tension. He was also aware that the skin was developing a sagging area that threatened to develop into a turkey neck, just like his late father's, and it was something he knew he was helpless to try to arrest.

Heidi breathed in and delivered her opening question. "Dr Frost, why have you cancelled the German option on the bilingual secretarial course?" she asked, her expression one of restrained fury. "As a member of the European Economic Community, Britain must have workers who speak European languages other than English if we are to play a full part in Europe and take up the opportunities working abroad offers. Furthermore, knowledge of each other's languages enables us to share more fully in each other's cultures and ways of life, as well as enrich our own languages. I am sure I don't have to remind you that the word 'avalanche' is a word we have taken from the Romansch language."

"I couldn't agree more," replied Dr Frost, in a conciliatory tone. "Unfortunately, there were not enough takers for the German option: there were barely enough for the French."

Heidi waved her hand in the direction of Dr Frost. "You have made me redundant," she said and marched out of the lecture theatre, head held high in dignified resignation.

Before Dr Frost resumed dealing with questions, there was a brief moment of silence during which most in the audience were grateful for Heidi's intervention, which had lifted the meeting out of its state of torpor. A few exchanged smiles or winks and none were surprised by Heidi's outburst, which was certainly not the first of its kind. In the calm that followed, Dr Frost answered questions as he saw fit and dealt with most matters requiring action with his two stock answers. He usually said that the issue would have to be 'kicked into the long grass' due to delays in college or local authority or examination board planning delays or departmental budgetary or staffing issues. Occasionally he responded with the answer that the matter 'needed to be looked into'. He then referred the subject to the relevant head of section, giving the questioner a glimmer of hope that it would see the light of day again.

The meeting closed with Dr Frost's mild exhortation to do sterling work at the enrolments in guiding potential students to the right courses and to have a successful and fruitful year.

The enrolment evenings didn't let the enthusiasts down nor give much respite to those who sought a quiet time. The usual stampede of delighted thirsters after knowledge, conscripted day-releasers and those seeking the key to unlock their door of ambition, all descended on the college for two evenings. Later, some would lose their thirst for knowledge, find the skills were not for them, suffer a loss of ambition or otherwise drop out of the registers but the vast majority would persevere and some would even enjoy their classes more as the course went on. Enrolment was supposed to finish on the dot at eight o'clock and, as always, there would be the valiant soul, dishevelled and exhausted, hot and out of breath, lurching through the front doors of the college to beat the deadline of entry by seconds. If the enrolment period was increased by half an hour that same person would arrive at eight-thirty. He or she is a member of that strange cult which arrives at libraries, polling stations, doctors' surgeries and almost anywhere which has a strict closing time, just before, never just after, the curtain falls. They are never asked and rarely give a reason for their cutting it fine. This person is not to be confused with those of a different cult which operates in cinemas, theatres and the like who always have a seat in the middle of the row and arrive to take it, carrying shopping and other belongings and treading on the toes of others, rarely apologising, just as the curtain rises. Of course, some people proudly belong to both groups, and all share the common belief that their time is more precious than that of anybody else so they cannot under any circumstance spend any of it being early or even on time for anything. They have taken to heart the epigram of Oscar Wilde that 'punctuality is the thief of time'.

The remaining days of the week were spent confirming staff members' core timetables and adjusting their other hours to take account of changes in the overall course offering. Few calamities for a lecturer can be worse than finding one's favourite course has failed to get the numbers and being required to top up their timetable with something nobody wanted. Within the department, the economists, lawyers and accountants provided business subjects to some of the secretarial courses, whose names were abbreviated for timetable purposes to intensive secs, advanced secs, A level secs, post-graduate secs, bilingual secs and medical secs, the humorous connotations of their titles staff generally kept to themselves. Some economists and accountants also lectured on management courses. Somehow, after negotiation and bargaining within the department and with other departments, acceptable timetables for every member of staff were always ready by the following Monday morning. Now, on Friday afternoon of enrolment week, with the final touches being made to the timetables by Don Coppice and his assistant and most of the other lecturers gone for the weekend, Roger and Julian had another task to perform.

Just before the end of the summer term, Julian had asked Roger if he was interested in a 'spot of part-time teaching'. Initially, Roger wasn't too keen, thinking it would mean private tuition which he had tried a few times but had found the students generally less enthusiastic than their parents. An hour, even half an hour, with a silent, uninterested student who didn't respond to questions, take part in a dialogue or show even a willingness to listen was one definition of excruciating. However, he was more interested when Julian revealed that it would be teaching in a private school. He agreed in principle and Julian had arranged for him to visit the school to speak to the headmaster at the start of the academic year.

Now, two months later, that day had arrived and they took Roger's car for the fifteen-minute drive to the school, situated in the nearby village of Twirleston Combust.

"That's two years you've done now, isn't it? Glad you made the switch to teaching?" asked Julian.

Roger smiled. "I'm enjoying it so far, by and large. The variety and the flexibility suit me more than the nine-to-five routine of the office."

Julian nodded. "That's good. It's not a bad life, once you get over the first year and lock into the routine."

Roger knew what Julian meant. The first year he had worked hard, every available free moment spent in preparation for his classes: writing notes, setting exercises and honing his teaching style which had begun from scratch. Then there was the marking and learning to adapt his methods to different groups. He had barely had a moment to think, except in the summer term, when he was on top of it and knew that much of the work was already done for the following year. Now he considered himself fully in the swing of his role. His thirty contractual hours, divided into ten sessions, included two evenings so that he had two daytime sessions which he could take off any morning or afternoon when he was not taking a class. So, there were days when he could pursue an interest or in the morning or afternoon just laze around if he wanted to. Coupled with the fact that when he closed the classroom door behind him, he was free from outside interference or direction, this meant he felt more in control of his day than he had ever done previously in his working life.

"Yes," he said, "it suits me just fine."

"You don't miss the old job?"

"Not really; sometimes the highs, when everything falls into place and you know you've pulled a big deal off or the excitement and a touch of fear when you have to get yourself out of a tricky situation. But I've done all that. I'm glad I can keep in touch with my subject in a practical way. Hopefully, there will be opportunities to develop my expertise and edge into new areas."

"You don't miss the money? That's quite a car you run."

Roger gave the question some thought, even though he thought it a little indelicate. During his banking career he had rarely been tempted to flaunt his salary and measure his self-worth by how much he could spend in an evening. He had used his bonuses wisely to build up his savings and provide himself with a flat in London and a cottage in the country, in one of those East Midlands/not-quite South-East counties which everyone fails to remember and where the college also stood. While working in the City of London, he had used the flat in the week and the cottage at weekends. As the cottage was only twenty miles from the college, he now used the cottage in the week and the flat at weekends to enable him to keep in touch with his old London social life. He had one special extravagance: a car purchased with his last decent bonus before the 1973 oil crisis and his decision to move on. It was a Ferrari Berlinetta Boxer, a source of envy, even bunches of sour-grapes comments from some of his colleagues, but the cause of much admiration for the car and, consequently, a measure of reflected respect for him from his students. While he had bought his two homes outright and had no borrowing costs, running them both, with two sets of cleaners and travel between, was another matter. That, and the expenses of his London weekends, when he tended to live up to his past way of life, much encouraged by two expectant girlfriends, fortunately expectant only in anticipation of a good night out. While he could manage on his salary, he had noticed a steady decline in the value of his savings, particularly now inflation was doing its worst.

In answer to Julian's question, he answered, "I wouldn't regard having a smaller salary as an advantage, but I can manage."

"But a few extra bob might come in handy, eh?"

"Tell me about this school we're going to."

"Twirleston Academy? It's a crammer school for the children of the very wealthy who have failed their exams. The parents hope that, away from the distractions of regular life, some of the spoilt brats will knuckle down and get through with a second go and indeed some do, though by no means all. They are split two-to-one between A levels and GCEs. The school employs a core staff, reinforced by retired teachers and they like to teach humanities and sciences. They also use some of us for business studies subjects, especially economics, law, accounting and so on."

"What subjects would they want me to take on?"

"Probably O level economics and A level British constitution. These were the classes Ian Baxter took on and his leaving left a vacancy. You can teach British constitution, can't you?"

"Yes. I did it last year for an evening class."

"Economics obviously no problem either."

"But is it OK with the college to do outside teaching?"

"There's nothing in our contract to prevent it and you have two evening sessions so you must have daytime sessions off in lieu. I've never had any problems fitting it in."

"What about expectations by the academy and the students?"

"The school knows that the student body is only here because they blew it at whatever expensive school they were at before. If a student fails, the school knows the parents half expect that already and the headmaster can do the sad head-shake routine if the parents ask what went wrong, which they rarely do. Some of the students try and a few get their act together but most of them are pretty blasé. Fact of the matter is that, unless the parents are prepared to send the kids packing with the curse 'Don't darken my door again', the little dears know they will pretty much be kept in the undeserved luxury to which they are accustomed for as long as they don't go completely off the rails. Just do your best and keep your nose clean and you'll be fine."

The school was up a long lane just after they passed through Twirleston Combust. They went through the open gates bearing the name Twirleston Hall and drove up to a mid-Georgian grand house with four windows to either side of the front door and a similar number above. The roof was hidden by a pediment and the date 1773 was visible in the centre of the building, above the main entrance. Clearly not large enough for all the needs of the school, this fine building was surrounded by several pre-fabricated single-storey buildings which presumably accommodated some of the classrooms. Two tennis courts, a swimming pool and various other amenities were scattered in the grounds. As they drove up to the house, Roger had his first view of some of the students. A group of adolescent boys with fashionably longish hair, were kicking a football around on a field with a small-scale goal but they stopped when they saw Roger's car arrive and watched as he and Julian entered the house.

They walked into a grand entrance with oak panelling on the walls and a central circular marquetry table adorned with a large vase containing a flower display. Julian knocked on the door bearing a nameplate inscribed JKL Mandeville MA (Oxon) and entered on the deep-voiced response, "Come."

As Roger and Julian entered the room, a black-haired, balding man in a well-cut navy three-piece suit, rose to greet them. "Mr Wesley. Welcome back." He looked over at Roger. "Mr Southwark, how do you do, Jocelyn Mandeville," he said, beaming. After shaking hands enthusiastically, he directed them to two occasional chairs.

Afterwards, Roger couldn't remember an interview taking place. Jocelyn Mandeville was friendly and courteous and discussed Roger's background and cultural interests without once referring to his academic experience or his proficiency in teaching any subjects. The conversation then shifted smoothly into the new academic year and the involvement of Julian and his colleagues in the work of the school.

"I am pleased to say, Mr Southwark, we shall be running classes in economics at both levels and Brit Con at A level, as usual. As well as Mr Wesley, Mr Harred from your department will be joining us for law, as last year, and Mr Brompton for accounts. Classes can run until half past five to assist in aligning our timetables."

Roger produced a copy of his college timetable which allowed them to slot in his classes at the academy with no difficulty at all. Julian had a clash with one of his classes but Mandeville quickly offered an alternative. Roger was impressed by Mandeville's efficiency and admired his no-nonsense approach.

The headmaster produced class lists for them: Roger had a group of six for economics and of seven for British constitution. "You have a number of foreign students but they all have a perfect command of the English language." He coughed with a deep, resonant sound like an idling elderly lorry and took a packet of cigarettes from his pocket, offering them to Julian and Roger, but both declined. Julian took the opportunity to produce his pipe while Roger noted the cigarettes were in the appropriately brown packet of Capstan Full Strength, a cigarette almost off the scale of tar and nicotine content in the Government Chemist report on the relative potential harmfulness of the main brands of cigarette.

"You can still get those?" he asked Mandeville.

The headmaster smiled as he lit one. "Yes, a relic of the old days when what you were inhaling into your lungs voluntarily was the least of your problems and was down to you. No doubt they'll be banned eventually; everything with a kick in it will be one day. Mind you, it's advisable to be seated when one inhales the first one of the morning." He laughed and coughed at the same time as he took a drag on his umpteenth of the day, producing a combined noise which resembled a steamroller going over a pile of gravel.

He went through the barest necessities of the school rules in so far as they affected Roger, produced a map of the grounds and the various facilities and allowed Roger thirty seconds to memorise it before putting it back in its drawer. He didn't ask Roger if he had any questions.

"Well, there you have it, Mr Southwark. I am pleased to welcome you to our team. Now, take no nonsense from any of these over-privileged wastrels. I'm sure you'll have no problems but if you do, send them along to me and I'll fire off a letter to their parents." He propelled his chair back on its wheels and leapt to his feet, signalling the end of their conversation.

The two lecturers left the academy and found Roger's car now being examined in detail by the student footballers.

"Is that your car, sir?" asked one of them, a spotty-faced boy with a Bay City Rollers haircut, as Roger went round to the driver's side.

"Yes."

"My old man's got one. He let me drive it once."

"But never again; even he's not got more money than sense," said one of his friends and the others laughed.

Roger smiled and he and Julian drove off, the boys watching until they reached the gates.

"Mandeville is well organised," said Roger on their drive back to college.

"Oh, he runs a slick organisation and has got it taped as far as results are concerned: the school takes the credit for successes and the parents accept that failures are down to the students themselves."

Roger smiled. "So, will we be paid in cash? If it's through the books, what do you do about declaring the earnings?"

Julian smiled. "Nothing. Mandeville assured me that part-time teaching fees are listed as an aggregate under costs and so we are anonymous. I've been doing this for five years and heard nothing from the Inland Revenue. It's small beer after all; you will never get into the millionaire class teaching at Twirleston Academy."

Roger nodded. He came from a working environment where the more one earned, the easier it was to avoid paying tax on one's income. Now at the mercy of the PAYE system, he was not perturbed by the thought that some casual earnings might not go through the usual channels any more than Charles Clore would be concerned about earning his wealth in Britain but being domiciled in the tax haven of Monaco.

THE LADIES' MAN

THE FIRST WEEK OF TERM: NEW FACES EVERY DAY as day-release and evening groups were introduced and the lecturers attempted to familiarise themselves with sixty or more new faces each day of the week, fewer if one was teaching mainly full-time groups. It would be some weeks before Gillian, Roger, Bill and the rest would be able to identify for sure those destined to be stars, those with promise and those who would struggle in each group. As the year progressed these rankings would occasionally move as early stars faded and late starters made dramatic improvements. The lecturers could facilitate, encourage and support them all but the students, especially the part-time ones, were largely the masters of their own destiny.

The weeks went faster as the term settled in to its regular routine for both teaching staff and students. Paradoxically, in this faster tempo, everyone, students and staff alike, seemed to have more time to spend on social and other activities. Both groups made use of the refectory; the main one for students and another for staff, though the menu was the same for both with such culinary delights as spam fritters, corned beef hash, sausage and mash and pilchard salad all making regular appearances on the table d'hote menu; there was no à la carte. For those prepared to lash out on a reasonably priced haute-cuisine lunch, there was also the training restaurant where the catering lecturers trained the kitchen and front-of-house service students to a very creditable standard worthy of customers from members of the public as well as staff.

To break up the routine and to get away from their place of work, some of the business studies lecturers would regularly go to a pub every Thursday for a convivial pint and a less mass-produced lunch from a freshly cooked menu. The pub in question was The Bellerephon, formerly The Revenge but renamed in honour of the First World War battleship during the 1930s by the landlord who had actually served on HMS *Bellerephon*. Some of the customers, if asked, thought a bellerephon was a form of dinosaur. Roger was ever-present in the group, as he avoided cooking for himself as much as possible. His usual choice was ham, egg and chips, a speciality of Peggy, the landlord's wife. Other regular members of the group included Bill and Rajeev, Mike Brompton, the senior lecturer in accounting and John Knowles and Tony Laycock, two management studies lecturers. Other lecturers joined them from time to time. On this particular Thursday, in mid-October, they arrived as usual in ones and twos but there was no Tony Laycock.

"Tony not joining us today?" asked Rajeev, twiddling with a horse brass hanging by his head.

"No, he's on 'chaperone duty' for Mark Harred," said John Knowles. John was a little older than most of the others, now in his late thirties. He was of a different generation only because, born in London just before the war, he actually remembered the tail end of hostilities. He had resolutely stuck to the same haircut he had sported in the 1950s and would have nothing to do with the wide lapels, loud checks and flared trousers of the current age, dismissing the fashions as too ludicrous to last for long. His only concession to changing taste was a wider tie than he was used to, under pressure from his wife.

There were smiles and raised eyebrows all round.

"Already?" said Roger. "He's been quick off the mark this year."

"There it is," said Bill as he went to the bar with their orders.

Everyone was familiar with Harred's chaperone duty as most of them had been called upon to do it at least once. If he was interested, in an extracurricular sense, in one of his full-time female students, Harred would invite her and a friend to a meeting with him and one of his colleagues which would be an opportunity for Harred to test the lay of the land. The fact it was a foursome enabled Harred to obscure the nature of the invitation so that he could pass it off as an opportunity for students to chat to their lecturers about how they were enjoying the course: a tutorial of sorts rather than a date. The true objective of the exercise would enable Harred to discern whether the young woman of his fancy reciprocated his interest. Over the years, this had proved a successful mechanism for the avoidance of embarrassment or misunderstanding in his relationships with his female students. It served to filter out those students flattered by Harred's attention but not regarding him as anything more than their teacher and those suspicious that his attention might prove to be no more than that of a scheming lecturer. Those which remained would initially be invited for an innocent drink after hours and become the object of his after-hours attention within that year's student body for as long as it suited him or her.

The pattern was always the same. Harred and his fellow lecturer would meet the students after classes for the day had finished or after lunch when there was a free period in the afternoon. They would go to a tutorial room, discuss a few generalities about the course and the various subjects in it and then Harred would suggest they have a drink to discuss it further. Sometimes the student who was merely a decoy would decline, sometimes not. Harred had so far never guessed wrong regarding the student to which he was attracted. Either way, after one drink Harred would offer to take the student/students home and the chaperone would depart, his duty done. None of his colleagues liked their chosen role and usually demurred, but Harred would catch them on the hop when they were least prepared and nearly always managed to talk them into it.

The only one of his colleagues who had bluntly refused to have anything to do with Harred's schemes was Mike Brompton. Mark had only tentatively asked him to accompany him on one of his quests and had certainly not tried to cajole him into it. This was because Mike, though pleasant and sociable, had a slightly unapproachable demeanour, the cause of which none of his colleagues could quite identify. His status as a senior lecturer carried some weight and Mark was aware of this when he presumed to ask him to act as a chaperone. But the lecturers did not generally hide behind their rank and Mike certainly did not. It was more something about him. As a successful chartered accountant, he had taken a considerable cut in salary when he first became a lecturer five years before but had soon made a good impression on his superiors and been promoted to senior lecturer two years before. With his well-regarded background and businesslike approach, he was considered a bit of a high flyer by his colleagues who saw him cutting a dash in the stodgy world of further education advancement. At thirty-eight he was still quite young, had reasonable looks with a fine head of black hair and a neatly trimmed moustache, dressed smartly in a fashionable, but not excessively so, style and a smooth drawl when he spoke. In addition, he was always courteous and obliging in his dealings with others. All in all, based on the impressions of his colleagues and his own sense of self-worth, he was a man of substance.

Mark Harred's behaviour with his students was a source of amusement for his colleagues but few of them criticised. Some thought his behaviour immoral and unprofessional and one or two were outspoken about it. Any comments made to Mark were dismissed as jealousy, as he thought, perhaps with some justification, that his severest critics were the sort who would never have the nerve or the charisma to hit it off with any of their female students.

At the very moment John Knowles was telling those in the pub that Tony Laycock was on chaperone duty, Laycock was indicating that he was having second thoughts to the persuasive law lecturer while they were waiting in the tutorial room for the arrival of the students.

"But why do you feel uncomfortable?" asked Harred, sitting back in his chair, his thumbs in his waistcoat pockets.

"It seems underhand, as if we are tricking them in some way."

"Not in the least, Tony," replied Harred, affably. "In fact, the reverse is true. One of the young ladies appears to have shown some interest in a social relationship of some kind with me and I just want to make sure that I am not misjudging the situation. Meeting in this way avoids her feeling under pressure since she has a friend with her and we are on college premises. If she doesn't wish to go for a drink there is no problem whatsoever and that is the end of the matter."

"What about driving them home afterwards?"

"Nothing sinister about it at all," said Harred, a slightly hurt expression crossing his face followed by a reassuring smile. "They can be dropped off together or apart but always to their home or back at college, as will happen today. If the student I am interested in wishes to see me again, I shall take it from there. Your role is purely to ensure that the students feel comfortable and under no obligation with the situation. I always tell my students that I am married so there is no misunderstanding of that sort. It's purely friendship, no more. Something to add a bit of zest to the teaching of the noble subject of jurisprudence to those who can rarely distinguish between morality and legality and don't much care."

"Well, I suppose…"

"Good man," said Harred, jumping up to greet the two students who knocked on the door and came into the room.

It was immediately obvious to Tony Laycock which of the two young women was the object of Harred's stated beneficent interest. Not from their physical appearance, as both were clearly attractive. Rather, it was in their demeanour; one a little flushed round her neck and a slightly shy, engaging smile on her face; the other smiling in an open, relaxed manner. A lecturer in human resources management himself, Laycock resigned himself to his role as an observer and hoped that what followed might provide useful material for his lectures on human behaviour, and so it proved. As he had come to expect from years of experience, nobody took any notice of him. He couldn't put his finger on what made it so but it was always the same, whatever the situation. He had noticed it first at school when he was never called to ask a question or give an answer, however long he held his hand up. Though a decent inside forward, he was inevitably the last chosen when teams were selected by captains from among his peers. When he began work in an aircraft factory, he would come forward with good ideas but they would never be implemented until somebody else came up with the same suggestion. It seemed that for most people he was just part of the background, indistinguishable from the furniture and fittings, inaudible if he spoke. He mused that it might be his dress sense. He was always drawn to browns and beiges and, when buying clothes, Dunn and Co was his default option since its muted colours and conservative styles made him feel at home. The resurgence of brown as a fashionable colour in the early 1970s allowed him a brief moment of being 'with it' but it made no difference to his impact on others: he was now merely a fashionable background to life but as drab as ever. He had met his wife at a dance, at which nobody had asked her to dance until Tony, and she was the only one who had accepted his invitation. Afterwards, they had shared a conversation in which neither heard what the other said but they took comfort in their compatibility. They had been happily married for ten years and there had never been a cross word between them, nor anything remembered which either had said to each other. He had been successful in his application for a position at the college after one candidate failed to attend for interview and the only other candidate was offered the post but turned it down. He would never be promoted on merit but would eventually become a senior lecturer because he lectured on post A level courses.

Tony was not bitter nor any longer hurt by his failure to penetrate the consciousness of others. He knew his students didn't pay much attention to his lectures and never asked him a question at the end of class but they were content to read the textbook and enjoyed his innovation of group discussions in which they participated enthusiastically, though they didn't hear his summaries afterwards. They completed their essays and projects and he gratefully gave them good comments, which they couldn't find the will to read. None of his students ever thought about him nor ventured an opinion on him but his line manager took silence as assent and he was regarded therefore as competent in his role.

Needless to say, when Harred asked the two students what they thought of the lecturers on the course, Tony didn't come to mind, even when he was sitting facing them. They were polite about the lecturers in general and both were fully of praise for Harred's classes. The conversation then gravitated towards his teaching in particular, and then onto tentative compliments about his qualities, which he was happy to reciprocate. Inevitably, though Tony was not aware of it, this discussion had reached what Harred named his 'blast-off point' and he said what he always said at this juncture.

"This is a very interesting line of thought and I'd like to discuss it further. What do you say we adjourn to somewhere a little more convivial and have a quick drink before we resume our college day? I find a fresh location always opens up new ideas to the subject at hand, don't you?"

The two students, Alison and Christine, both coloured a little as they looked at each other. Alison, the principal object of Harred's attention, looked encouragingly at Christine who smiled and nodded. "We'd love to," said Alison, immediately regretting that she had given away her true feelings.

"Great," replied Harred, nodding to Tony as he checked he had his car keys and picked up his coat. Tony followed, reluctantly, wishing he was having a pint and a pie with his friends at the Bellerephon rather than what he knew would follow. All four walked out to the staff car park and strolled towards Harred's sand-coloured Fiat 124 Special T.

"Oh, is this your car?" asked Christine. "Very nice, twin headlamps too."

"Yes, it's the rally model so it's got all the latest refinements as well as a top speed of over a ton: high-spec lights, rev counter, disc brakes all round, reinforced body shell, cloth seats, ultra-accurate warning light on the petrol gauge, etc."

"So, you can't pull the old fast one that the car's run of petrol miles from anywhere," said Alison and they all laughed, even Harred.

Tony was pleased that she wasn't in awe of Harred and he felt more comfortable about their possible relationship as she was obviously no shrinking violet.

"Take your own car, Mr Laycock, in case we have to leave separately. The Marquess," said Harred as he opened his car and the two students leapt in the back. He had already exited the car park by the time Tony had walked over to his own Hillman Avenger.

Tony made the ten-minute drive to the Marquess of Northampton, a rather grand public house on the main road built in the 1930s for the rising numbers of travelling motorists. Having checked the saloon bar and seen nobody he knew, he went into the large, wood-panelled lounge bar where the other three were already seated at a round table with padded chairs. Tony waved him over and indicated to a pint of beer waiting for him. Tony took his seat, raised his glass, though nobody reciprocated, and settled into his usual role of silent observer while Harred amused the two young women with witty comments about college life, the joys of being a lecturer and how much he enjoyed teaching their talented group.

They were only there for about forty minutes, enough time for one drink and a packet of crisps for the young women, and it was time to go. The two students went off to the ladies' and Harred watched them disappear before turning to Tony.

"Thanks for helping out today, Tony. Mission accomplished. You know, somebody, I can't remember who, said that the life of a college lecturer is the nearest we can get these days to that of a country parson in the nineteenth century. I have no idea what that involved but I guess it was a busy Sunday, couple of services and a sermon to write, perhaps a christening or a wedding and then the rest of the week prayer services twice a day and the remainder of the time free for doing what you fancy: reading, interests, bit of prayer or meditation if you feel like it."

"What about parishioners?"

"Just offer to pray with them and most will run a mile. Otherwise turn up at the parish fete and that kind of thing. Nothing too demanding."

"I still don't quite understand the analogy," said Tony, finishing off his drink.

"I suppose what the chap meant was that we are pretty much in control of our working lives. When we close the classroom door, we are generally free to do what we like, as long as we stick roughly to the syllabus; after all, we write the examination papers. Look at old Barnaby; he has spent the last ten years with the HNC business studies courses doing nothing but show films he gets from libraries and whatever, and then setting the economics exam paper on the films. I saw last year's paper with questions on the Aswan Dam, farming in the Kalahari Desert, Wartburg cars and the manufacture of nose flutes, and so on. I suppose if he was a law lecturer he would set examination papers on the Nuremburg Trials, the working day of a prison warden and a couple of episodes of *The Main Chance*."

Tony nodded, picturing Barnaby, the senior lecturer in charge of economics, with blackout curtains closed and he standing at the film projector with one of his documentary films. "Then there are those who use a different textbook to the one the students have and just read from their book while the students copy it down. But we are not all like that."

"Of course not; many of us take our teaching seriously. I'm just saying it's in our hands. Don't forget the time outside the classroom. We are contracted for just thirty hours a week, and at least eight of those are free periods for administration and preparation when we can do what we like. We don't even have to do research like those in the universities. On top of it all, a chance to meet all these interesting, overage students." He leaned back in his chair and folded his hands behind his head, a self-satisfied smile covering his face.

Tony shook his head, thinking Mark quite incorrigible. Personally, he did take his teaching seriously and liked working on new methods and exercises for keeping his subjects fresh for himself as well as his students. There were others in the department who did make use of their free time to undertake research, add to their qualifications and, best of all for those who had their sights on working in a poly, attempt to get published. Tony himself had been an external moderator for the postgraduate diploma in management studies at a polytechnic in London for four years. On every visit he had approved the programme being offered and suggested minor changes to improve the experience for the students. On every visit he was given a very good lunch with fine wines and his recommendations were noted but never acted upon. One day he would be more forthright but so far it had never been the right time. Maybe next year.

As they left the pub and walked over to the cars, Tony turned to say goodbye and, while Harred and Alison ignored him and walked to the Fiat, Christine called out to him, "Goodbye, Mr Laycock. It's nice to get to know you as a person, and not only our teacher. See you soon." She smiled at him sweetly before walking after the others.

Tony stood still for a few moments, stunned that somebody had gone out of their way to say something kind to him, about him. He was sure he could not detect a note of sarcasm or teasing in her voice. He found himself waving at Harred's Fiat as it went past him on its way out of the car park. Nobody waved back.

WITNESS FOR THE
DEFENCE

While Tony Laycock was waving off Mark Harred's Fiat, Roger Southwark was driving through the gates of Twirleston Academy for his weekly class in A level British constitution. Three minutes later, he was walking into the portacabin with its slightly echoing sound and decidedly bouncy floor. For once, all six students had arrived before him.

"Good afternoon," said Roger, receiving a few grunts in response.

Though a school, the ethos was more like a college, much as Roger was used to. The students of the academy were all over sixteen and the vast majority over eighteen and as adults, or near adults, were largely treated as such. They wore no uniforms, were not supervised outside class times and were free to come and go as they pleased. The esprit de corps, such as it was, consisted of a shared failure or underperformance at their previous schools in their GCE O or A levels, and a greater or lesser willingness to try to improve their grades at a second attempt in a less-constrictive environment. The one common characteristic of the student body was that their parents were almost all very well-off and willing to risk throwing good money after bad in paying for their children to have another go.

In this resit British constitution class, five students had sat the examination before, resulting in two failures and three Grade E's. The first of these was a medium-height, blond, freckled young man named Dean Wayne. Not content with his son being saddled with the surname of one American legend, his father had also named him after his own idol, James Dean. In both appearance and demeanour, the youth did not resemble either hero, neither a dominating figure of assertive masculinity nor an edgy, rebellious figure who would stand up to authority. Dean Wayne was a diffident, pleasant young man of reasonable intelligence who was hoping to improve his A level grade from an E to a C by dint of repetition.

The other male member of the group was a tall, dark-haired young man who suffered from the mixed blessing of thinking he was brighter than he was. This might have been partly due to the fact his name was Newton, though James not Isaac. His exaggerated belief in his own ability gave him the advantages of self-confidence and a willingness to express his views, coupled with the disadvantage that he not infrequently grasped the wrong end of the stick but was hard to convince this was the case. His failure in the examinations was, he remarked, undoubtedly due to the inability of the examiner to understand the finer points of his incisive answers to their questions.

The four young women on the course were all unique in their own ways. The first, in the view of Roger, was an absolute stunner: tall, long dark hair, fine features and a shapely figure, a Juno in all but name. Her actual name was also worthy of note. Her father had arrived in Britain after the war with the Polish army in exile. Having become a naturalised British citizen with a very successful business, he then decided to abandon his original surname and adopt an English one which would better suit his status and signify his family as being from the British upper class. Consequently, his daughter bore a name evocative of a Norman heritage: Antonia Mortimer de Courcy. She confessed herself rather embarrassed by her adopted surname, which she felt would have been slightly over the top had it been borne by her ancestors but, as an ersatz confection it was, she admitted, frankly ludicrous. On the third meeting of the class, she announced that she had decided to drop 'de Courcy' in everyday use and would now be known as simply Antonia Mortimer. She was not very interested in the subject of the British constitution but was agreeable and always polite during the classes. She was quite candid about her limitations and expressed the hope that through greater familiarity with the basics of the subject, she might creep up a grade on the second time around.

The second female in the group was a shy, almost invisible young woman of pleasant but unremarkable features, named Madeleine Grey. She had been absent from school for much of her last year due to an unnamed serious illness, from which she had recently finally recovered. The consequence of the interruptions to her studies had been that, despite her best efforts, she had been unable even to scrape an E in British constitution, though she had passed both sociology and English literature. She was working hard now and hoped to improve her grades in all three subjects and Roger was sure she would be successful.

Suzy Plunkett was definitely the most interested of the entire group in politics and constitutional matters. She was an outspoken holder of strong political opinions and labelled herself as a Trotskyist with pacifist tendencies and thus a supporter of Nuclear Disarmament. She put her failure to pass her British constitution A level down to her examiners being stooges of the bourgeoisie and therefore unable to support her critique of the British constitution, virtually all of which she thought should be abolished, as reflected in her answers to the examination questions. When she explained this to Roger, he suggested that perhaps she should study A level politics, where there might be more scope for her theories than in British constitution, which does require an acceptance of the basic precepts of the British political system. She had explained that 'politics' had not been offered at her school but surprised Roger by accepting his advice and resigned herself this year to doing what needed to be done to get into university. Once at college, in an environment conducive to freedom of speech and tolerant of most political ideologies, she would be able to give full vent to her attacks on the prevailing political system and this she intended to do.

The last member of the group was unique in several ways. Most notably, she was a member of one of the royal families of Malaysia and was entitled to the title of Tengku, translated approximately as 'princess'. However, she chose to be called simply 'Zara' with no reference to her royal status. Unlike the other members of the group, she had no particular educational ambitions. She was spending a year or so in England to widen her horizons and her time at the school was one aspect of this. Her studies of British constitution, geography and English literature would not necessarily culminate in her taking the examinations, as this was not the object of the exercise. Zara was polite, friendly and cheerful but she rarely spoke in class and Roger felt he never really got to know her. Perhaps his reluctance to ask her a direct question in class, which he couldn't explain, had something to do with this.

Suzy felt no such inhibitions and, during the course of the

year, it would be her challenge to the democratic credentials of Malaysia that caused the one and only show of emotion by Zara in all the classes she attended. A discussion about parliamentary democracy and its claim to true democracy had, as usual, led to Suzy attacking the western democracies. She had concluded her diatribe with the words, "I suppose, imperfect though it is, Western democracy does possess some traces of democratic behaviour, unlike the corrupt and autocratic regimes of the Asian monarchies."

"They are not all autocratic or corrupt," said Zara, smilingly.

"Name one," barked Suzy.

"Malaysia," said Zara, smiling again.

Suzy snorted derisively. "Malaysia's full of tinpot sultans and their wives lording over the proletariat. More sultanas than a Christmas pudding," she concluded, provoking some smiles from the other students.

Zara shook her head. "You don't know what you are talking about, Suzy. The constitution of Malaysia provides for a federation of the Malay sultanates and the other states. The states have sovereignty within their own jurisdictions but the federal government is a parliamentary democracy with a constitutional monarch, similar to the Westminster model. Mr Southwark will confirm that, I'm sure." She looked at Roger and smiled.

Roger was rather vague on the constitution of Malaysia but he answered as accurately as he could. "All the Commonwealth countries were equipped with parliamentary democratic models when they gained independence and Malaysia has not changed that situation, as far as I am aware."

Zara nodded, satisfied.

Suzy muttered, "It's not immune from corruption."

"But according to you all democracies are corrupt so what's the problem?" asked James, putting an end to the argument as he emptied half a packet of salted peanuts into his mouth.

This was a rare exchange of views, let alone there ever being a forthright discussion, heated or otherwise, among the students on Roger's classes at the academy. Both in this class and his economics O level course, the students were almost always silently quiescent, accepting without question and with little involvement the material he put before them. They rarely asked questions and few bothered to submit the optional essays he set them as homework. The one exception was Suzy with her frequently raised objections to some facet of the British constitution, usually met with looks of derision from her colleagues.

Roger was surprised and a little confused by the situation as he usually enjoyed his teaching at the college and, it *was* teaching even if his formal title was 'lecturer'. What made it worth doing was the interaction in the classroom and, using a variety of teaching methods, he was usually able to generate interest in and active participation from students in his classes at college. Of course, there was the odd day-release course where the group was there purely because their employers sent them and a culture of apathy proved difficult to overcome. If this had been typical of the groups he taught, he probably would have found his interest in teaching wane and re-examined his career choice. He put the attitude of the academy students down to a similar sense of conscription among them but he could do little more than shrug his shoulders and take the cheque. He was, after all, in the position of a guest speaker rather than a course tutor, without either power over or responsibility for his academy students. Nonetheless, he couldn't totally dispel a sense of underperformance. After a few weeks he mentioned his concerns to Julian Wesley and asked if there was something he might do with his approach to teaching at the academy.

Julian shook his head. "No, it's not you. I get the same

thing every year. It's very difficult to motivate people to study when they have done the course before. They feel they know it all already and you are just there to go through the drills, shake off the cobwebs and prepare them for another run. Of course, most of them will fail again and then their parents will give up and they will get on with their mollycoddled lives. Everyone knows that contacts will be approached and one or two might cadge a place at an Oxbridge college on the Churchill Premise."

"What's the 'Churchill Premise'?"

"Churchill was absolutely useless academically at Harrow but he turned out to be a brilliant statesman and won the Nobel Prize in Literature. So, a far-sighted academic might be encouraged to see past the mediocre academic record to recognise a person of great potential who will shine at university. Of course, Churchill himself didn't bother to go to university; he was too busy producing a life story you couldn't make up."

"What about those who can't squeeze into a university?"

Julian shrugged. "They will be found a sinecure somewhere until they marry into money or Grandma pops her clogs and their inheritance comes in, or both of the above. Our job is to make sure everybody goes through the motions so that they can be seen to have tried. We are in the business of flogging dead horses."

Those words of Julian's had once again come to Roger's mind one afternoon, after a particularly dreary session with the academy's O level class in economics. Delayed by a discussion with the head, he was in danger of being late back to the college for his next class there. Letting his Ferrari loose to do what it did best, he soon screeched into the staff car park and twenty seconds later was bounding up the stairs of the main staircase, two at a time. As he approached his office, he saw two of his OND students waiting and instinctively knew they were bound to want to see him.

As he approached them, they smiled and the girl said, "Hello, Mr Southwark. We were hoping to have a word with Miss Trevis. Has she gone home?"

Roger looked at his watch. "No, she should be finishing a class about now. I should hang on if I were you."

"Thank you," said the boy.

Roger didn't give the matter another thought but raced to his next class, where a group of twelve intensive secretarial students were waiting for their weekly session on commerce, a subject which introduced them to the myriad operations, practices, standards and regulations which could impinge on their role in a secretarial or administrative post in the great variety of organisations in which they might find themselves employed. Inevitably, some subjects, such as weights and measures, postal services and transport facilities, were necessary but not necessarily exciting and sometimes Roger would have a quiz on vaguely commercial topics for the last fifteen minutes of the class, which the students always enjoyed. On this day the topic for the class was the types of commercial organisations: joint-stock, public and private, partnerships, etc. and when Roger declared 'quiz time' it was not a moment too early for most of the group. As usual, the quiz produced some good and not-so-good answers, together with the odd amusing one, as this day when one student thought a stevedore was a kind of bullfighter.

Meanwhile, Gillian walked back to the staff room after a session with the HND students to find the students waiting patiently for her. She knew them both as students from the OND business studies course, on which she taught economics.

"Hello," she said. "Can I help you?"

The two students looked at each other, then the girl spoke. "Sorry to trouble you, miss, but we are having to attend a disciplinary hearing, and we thought you might be willing to help us."

"I see," said Gillian. She opened the staff room door and turned on the lights. "I'll be glad to help if I can. Come into the office; we won't be disturbed as most people have left for the day. Take a seat." She pulled up a couple of chairs. "So, what's this disciplinary hearing all about?"

The boy, whose name was Melvin, was sixteen or seventeen with longish black hair and a little acne on his neck. He was dressed in bell-bottom trousers and purple platform shoes which added to his height. Gillian had no idea what the boy was like outside his class but, as a student, he was generally quiet and attentive and did not seem the sort of person who would be either troublesome or rebellious. The girl, Janice, was about the same age but seemed older, more worldly and more confident. Gillian knew them to be friends, Melvin's interest in Janice occasionally indicated by a look or a brief note passed across, which she reciprocated. They looked at each other and again it was the girl who spoke.

"We have been accused of immoral conduct in the college."

"What sort of immoral conduct?" asked Gillian.

"Sexual relations in the refectory," she said, blushing a little.

Gillian thought the idea so preposterous in the well-lit, always-busy refectory that she had difficulty keeping a straight face. "Is there any truth in the accusation?"

"None whatsoever," said Janice.

"We weren't even on a banquette," said Melvin, exasperatedly.

"What *were* you doing?" asked Gillian.

"Just sitting, talking. We have witnesses who would testify to that," said Janice.

"No physical contact at all?" asked Gillian, raising her eyebrows.

"Well, we were sitting together and holding hands," replied Janice.

"Is that the whole truth?" asked Gillian sceptically but hoping she didn't sound too much like a headmistress.

"We did kiss once or twice," said Melvin, looking down.

"So basically, what you are saying is that you were being a little amorous in the refectory and somebody, for whatever reason, misunderstood what was happening and thought you were what? Going the whole way?"

Both of them now coloured considerably. "Something like that," said Melvin.

Gillian smiled. "I'm sure this can be sorted out. What is it you are being asked to do? Go to a meeting with the course tutor and the head of department? I'd be pleased to speak on your behalf."

"No," said Janice. "It's a disciplinary committee chaired by the principal, with witnesses and everything."

"Like a court," said Melvin.

"If that's the case, I think you should ask one of the law lecturers to help you; they will be more competent than me to represent you."

"We don't know them as well as you except for Mr Harred and we would prefer you," said Janice. "Please, Miss Trevis," she insisted, her expression that of a damsel in distress.

"Well, if you are sure," said Gillian, deferring to her judgement. "Do you know when this hearing will take place?"

"Next Wednesday afternoon at two o'clock," said Janice. She produced an envelope and removed a letter from it, giving it to Gillian.

Gillian glanced at the letter and passed it back to her. "I don't have a class at two o'clock but I have one at three. It shouldn't take long," she muttered, to herself as much as to the students.

"Do you want to meet again before the hearing to discuss it?" asked Melvin.

"I don't think that will be necessary. Just make sure your witnesses will be there on the day, in case we need them," said Gillian, with that clear-sighted understanding of the situation experienced by those who understand nothing at all.

The disciplinary hearing took place in the college's boardroom and was not at all what Gillian expected. She had envisaged a fairly simple meeting with the principal; Janice and Melvin asserting their innocence, Gillian herself being required simply to attest to their character and, the evidence debatable, a warning as to future behaviour being the end of the matter. Instead, when Gillian arrived for what was only her second visit to the boardroom she was confronted by what resembled a court of law, or perhaps a court martial. The principal, Professor Dunmore, sat at the boardroom table, moved for the occasion nearer to the wall. He was flanked by Dr Frost on one side and the chief administrative officer, the line manager of the catering manager, on the other. Dunmore's secretary sat at the end of the table. Behind them hung a portrait of Thomas Newcomen, his expression thoughtful as his head was tilted towards the viewer, a diagram of his engine sprawled out before him. Copies of paintings of industrial activity dating from the eighteenth and nineteenth centuries hung in several places in the room, some particularly well-known ones by Joseph Wright of Derby.

Facing the table were a dozen chairs, set out at the other end of the boardroom, for those who were involved in the hearing. Gillian took a seat in the back row, behind Janice and Melvin and two fellow students, presumably there to support them as witnesses. Gillian recognised in the front row the catering manager and another lady, dressed in the refectory uniform. There was also the students' course tutor, who took the group for business English, and a few other members of staff present, including Mark Harred, presumably out of curiosity or interest. Finally, there were representatives of the student union to ensure justice was done.

The principal called the meeting to order and the students stopped whispering. Professor Dunmore was in his early sixties with what had once been a mass of curly red hair, now reduced to an unruly grey adornment around the lower half of his head. His thick eyebrows retained their fiery colour and his light-blue eyes shone through his tortoiseshell glasses. His expression was serious but not unkind. He looked briefly at his notes before addressing those present.

"I have convened this hearing in public because it is a very serious matter, one of gross misconduct, which may have profound consequences for those involved and I do not wish there to be any hint of a kangaroo court or decisions being made without a true airing of the facts. We live in changing times and sexual freedom has been one of the hallmarks of these changes but what constitutes decent behaviour in public has not changed materially because what we do in public involves the sensibilities of others. Two students aged seventeen, Miss Laine and Mr Charles, are alleged to have behaved improperly in a public place, the refectory, which gave offence to others, and is a disciplinary matter of the highest order. We shall hear the facts from those involved and arrive as near as we can to the truth. This is not a court of law; there will be no fierce cross-examinations or intimidations of witnesses, though questions may be asked about statements made. Perhaps, Miss Davison, you would outline the reason for your complaint about the behaviour of the students said to be involved?"

Miss Davison was an elegant woman in her early fifties, her attractive face set off with a neatly coiffured hairstyle. She had been the catering manager at the college since it had opened. It was she who had brought the behaviour of the students to the attention of the principal. She stood and in a clear, quite deep voice, gave a short statement.

"One of my staff, Mrs Tufton, came into my office at about half past five and said that two students were apparently engaging in lovemaking in the refectory. They had gone beyond simple kissing and hugging and it was frankly lewd. I immediately went into the refectory, which was almost empty at this time. I saw two students at a table in an embrace and walked towards them: it was those two students, there." She pointed at Janice and Melvin. "As she saw me coming, the girl pushed the boy away and adjusted her clothing. When I asked what they were doing they both replied, 'Nothing.' I took their names and reported the matter to both their course tutor and Mr Milne and they are here today."

Mr Milne, the chief administrative officer, asked, "I'm not expecting you to be specific but I gather you did not yourself see anything to confirm your suspicions?"

"No. I think things may have, to some extent, calmed down by then but I have no reason to doubt the statement of Mrs Tufton."

"Perhaps she should be here," said the principal.

"Mrs Tufton is rather self-effacing and asked me to make the statement but she can be sent for if required." She looked at her colleague sitting next to her who nodded.

"We shall see," said the principal. Miss Laine and Mr Charles, would you like to say what happened in your own words?" he asked, turning to Janice and Melvin.

Gillian was pleased that both Melvin and Janice had dressed appropriately for the occasion: Melvin in a jacket and tie and Janice demurely attired in a black, knee-length dress.

Janice now stood up. "We were having a cup of tea and a bun in the refectory and Melvin started messing about, trying to drop a teaspoon down my neck. It was just horseplay. I think the dinner lady got the wrong end of the stick."

"You were not engaging in any canoodling?" asked the principal.

"Any what?"

"Canoodling: kissing and cuddling."

Janice looked surprised. "Certainly not. We are just friends," she said, glancing round at Melvin.

All those present looked at Melvin as he nodded vigorously.

The principal turned towards Dr Frost and then to Mr Milne, both of whom raised their eyebrows. Gillian did her best to remain expressionless but she was disappointed. She had hoped for a more nuanced statement by Janice and Melvin, which she was sure would have left it open to the principal and his panel to find the case 'not proven' or some such let-out involving a caution or a minor chastisement. However, the total denial by Janice of any amorous behaviour was bound to seem like a cover-up, as if there were something to hide.

"I know there are witnesses willing to corroborate the statement that the two young people have just made and we will hear what they have to say if necessary. I gather Miss Trevis has been asked by Miss Laine and Mr Charles to make a few observations on their behalf. Do you have anything to add, Miss Trevis?" asked the principal, looking over at Gillian.

Gillian stood, smiling and thinking quickly on her feet. "I think we have here a situation where the truth is there to be seen between two very different viewpoints: Mrs Tufton is perhaps, I'm sure quite unintentionally, exaggerating what she saw while Janice and Melvin, probably out of embarrassment, are understating their precise physical interaction. They are 'inaggerating', if that is a word."

Gillian's attempt at a joke fell on stony ground. The principal stared at her blankly while the course tutor muttered, "Etymologically doubtful."

Somewhat in desperation, Gillian took a more serious tack. "I feel it would be helpful if Mrs Tufton were present so that we can hear from her what she claims she saw."

The principal looked at Miss Davison, who nodded and said something to her colleague who went out of the room. The room was silent for a few minutes and then the door opened and in came Miss Davison's colleague and another woman in the same uniform.

"Thank you for attending, Mrs Tufton. Just one or two points of clarification, if you don't mind," said Professor Dunmore.

Mrs Tufton stood at the boardroom table, peering around the room, and Gillian noted that she was wearing quite thick glasses.

"Mrs Tufton," said Gillian, smiling, "standing where you are, would you look round the room and point to the female student you saw in the refectory, apparently misbehaving."

Mrs Tufton peered a little more as she scanned the people in the room and she pointed a finger at Gillian. "Her," she said, confidently.

There was stunned silence in the room for a few seconds and then the friends of Janice and Melvin burst out laughing, followed by Janice and Melvin themselves and one or two of the observers. Even Dr Frost smiled broadly. Professor Dunmore shook his head. "Thank you, Mrs Tufton, that will be all."

Mrs Tufton, appearing confused that her monosyllabic evidence should have been greeted with merriment, nodded and made a quick exit.

Professor Dunmore rose to his feet. "I think we can all

consider the matter closed." He turned and swept out of the boardroom, accompanied by his secretary and Dr Frost.

Mr Milne glared at Miss Davison and barked at one of the caretaker staff to get the room back to normal before following his senior colleagues. As the rest of those involved in the hearing went about their business, Janice and Melvin came over to Gillian.

"Thank you very much, Miss Trevis," said Janice. "You were brilliant."

"Yes, straight out of Perry Mason," added Melvin. He thanked Gillian and took Janice's hand as they walked off with their friends.

"It was rather good," said Mark Harred, coming over to Gillian and patting her on the arm.

"Hello, Mark. Why did you come? Of course, you know the students."

"Yes, I came to give the students a little moral support; ludicrous, trumped-up charge. I was pleased to see you in action, with the coup de grâce delivered brilliantly. Did you have a plan?"

Gillian shook her head and pointed to her one sheet of paper with only the names 'Janice Laine' and 'Melvin Charles' written on it. "I was hoping to get Mrs Tufton to back down and when I saw she was short-sighted I hoped she might pick out the wrong student but, what a farce! Time for a cup of tea."

Only when they had left the room and decorum could be relaxed, did Gillian allow herself a laugh.

IV

CHRISTMAS

THE LAST WEEK OF THE AUTUMN TERM WAS A TIME for parties celebrating the festive season throughout the college. Although Christmas was still at least a week away by the last day of term, the students tended to treat this last week as a rehearsal for the real thing. The day-release students, even if they returned after lunch, were at best relaxed and only marginally attentive in the afternoon. The full-time students had numerous parties to attend and most of their classes in the last few days reflected an end-of-term atmosphere. On most full-time courses, lecturers accepted they were fighting a losing battle and accepted a lighter atmosphere: revision competitions, quizzes, case-study discussions, a vaguely relevant documentary or TV recording. Mr Barnaby showed a film with a Christmas theme: the 1970 version of *Scrooge*.

Mark Harred, whose diary metaphorically overheated at this time, referred to this week as 'the days of holly and ivy': holly because there were always prickly situations and ivy because some students could stick and be difficult to get rid of. Some of his colleagues noted that he seemed more downbeat this year, less forthcoming about his plans for the festive season.

Whereas for Mark Harred and one or two others, the excitement was welcome, perhaps even craved, for the rest, the excitement carried its own dangers. The tendency for the office party season to get a little out of hand is well-known in all work situations, but in colleges, certainly this college, this tendency was magnified by some of the lecturing staff, particularly the younger ones, seeming to undergo something of a reversion to their own student days. Perhaps this was due to a reawakening of past happy times in an environment with echoes of their own college days, especially at the end of a long term and with the chance to relax after a period of intensive study. Then again, being in a working environment in which the majority of the people were in their late teens and were young adults with whom they could identify to some extent may have played a part. Who can say? Whatever the cause, most of the lecturing staff looked forward to the Christmas parties with frissons of excitement mixed with dread. The excitement came from the half-hoped prospect for some members of staff to get themselves caught in situations ranging from the amusing, enjoyable and mildly embarrassing, through the regrettable, humiliating and frankly inexplicable, to the eternally unforgettable misunderstandings and errors of judgement bordering on disciplinary causes célèbres. Such incidents, arising from a combination of an excess of alcohol, an unexpected situation and a lapse of prudence could expect to become part of departmental folklore and provide much amusement to those who witnessed the event. The dread came from the possibility, however unlikely, that any one of them might be the central figure in such a situation to be reminded of it each year when Christmas came round.

The previous year, under the category 'inexplicable', one of the accounting lecturers had returned from a party and walked into the wrong classroom in the afternoon to give a lengthy exposition of the difference between fixed and current assets in a business to a group of music students. The group sat politely silent, not asking the obvious question until he had finished his presentation. The most recent cause célèbre had been the case of a now-retired male member of the secretarial section who had been found by the janitor locked (from the outside) in the departmental stationery cupboard with one of his female students in a state of partial undress and with a rubber stamp mark on his forehead, reading 'Account Paid'. Remarkably, none of these incidents had resulted in a disciplinary action or even a reprimand. In some parts of the college, as in Ancient Rome during the days of Saturnalia, the normal order was, to some extent, suspended.

On the last day of term, full-time classes were cancelled in the afternoon and Dr Frost held an office party in one of the large lecture rooms. His secretary organised a whip round for contributions to drinks and light snacks, and Dr Frost added a large donation to round this figure up. Although this was seen as an act of appreciation and generosity, some of the department thought the gesture enabled the majority of staff to be corralled in a room where they would be less likely to fall victim to an act of recklessness or worse.

The party followed the last staff meeting of the year, which was usually not much more than a general thanks for all the staff in the department and those administrative staff who provided clerical support to the lecturers. Perhaps because of Dr Frost's supervision or the absence of some of the likely candidates for over-indulgence or just a more restrained atmosphere, there was a notable flatness to the proceedings this year and people began drifting away after an hour or so, once the drinks and nibbles were finished. Most went to clear their desks and leave for home but the principal lecturers went off to their own rather superior annual drinks party at a local hotel, to which some administrative staff were invited and where any infringements of decorum would be less public. Mark Harred, juggling several commitments, went to a student party at which he had promised to make an appearance and took another member of staff with him, though nobody could remember who afterwards, nor did anyone admit to being the one. A few drifted to the Bellerephon for a more relaxed farewell to the end of term, among them Roger Southwark, Gillian Trevis, Bill Rendell, Rajiv Bhatt and a one or two other usual suspects from the department. Even Rob Grainger looked in for a drink.

"Glad you could join us, Rob. Not dashing off to nurse the constituency?" asked Roger.

Rob was standing at the pub's fairly ancient pinball machine which the landlord had retained for regulars. Its screen featured a young woman in a one-piece bathing costume and stiletto heels, with long blonde hair and extraordinary eyelashes smiling innocently at the potential customer. The money slot, which had once taken threepenny pieces had been adapted to take a shilling or five-pence coin. Whatever the price, it certainly didn't pay the landlord much; most of the aficionados could make five pence last a lunchtime through winning bonus games. The income had risen recently when the film *Tommy* and its hit song 'Pinball Wizard' encouraged younger customers to begin to learn the gentle art of nudging the machine and mastering the flippers to keep the ball scoring, but not to the mastery of either Tommy or even the college lecturers.

"Parliament's already risen and everything closes down at constituency level," said Rob, his words coming out between pauses as he scored a hundred and caught the ball with the edge of one flipper to send it ricocheting with the other to the top of the table again.

Roger turned to talk to Bill Rendell. "What are your plans for Christmas, Bill?"

Bill was feeling decidedly queasy. He was not a great wine drinker and three glasses of Malbec at the office party followed by a second pint at the pub was bringing home to him the old adage 'Beer before wine is fine, wine before beer makes you queer'. *Well, there we are,* he thought to himself and eventually replied, "Same as usual."

"What, home with the wife and kids and your parents?"

"Yes. I am also taking the kids to see the Flying Wheelers in a pantomime."

"Another drink, Gillian?" asked Mike Brompton, noticing her empty glass.

"No thanks, I must go. I've got packing to do."

"Going away for Christmas? Skiing?" asked Rajiv.

"No, I'm going to Timbuktu."

One or two of the others laughed. "Seriously, where are you off to?" asked Rajiv, smiling.

"I really am going to Timbuktu."

"Is it a real place?" asked someone.

"Of course it is, you ignoramus," said Rob. "Free game won!" he called triumphantly as the pinball machine flashed all its lights to celebrate. He passed control of the game to Tony Laycock and took his vacant seat. "It's in West Africa, isn't it?"

"Yes, Mali," confirmed Gillian.

"What on earth are you going there for?" asked John Knowles.

"Well, I wanted a change from the interminable Christmas fandango and that is about as far away from it as I could go."

"There's Antarctica," said Roger.

"Hasn't Santa opened a branch there by now?" asked Rajiv with a wink.

"Too cold," replied Gillian, "Anyway, Timbuktu is a place worth visiting. It was the centre of an early Islamic civilisation so there are some ancient sites and much of it is still intact: buildings with a very early library and museums and so on. I just fancied going there." She picked up her bags and, with a cheery wave, left them to it.

"Do you think she's going on her own?" asked Mike. "She never mentions anyone close."

"Probably an organised tour," said Tony, cursing as the ball in the pintable evaded his desperate lunge with the flipper.

"Can't imagine going anywhere worse for a holiday," said John. "Wherever you go sand, nothing but sand, in your shoes, in your drink, in your ice cream. Like going to Scarborough in a gale without the sea."

"And you daren't drink the water," said Bill.

"I'm sure she's perfectly capable of looking after herself," said Roger.

An hour after Roger made this remark, Gillian was saying much the same thing to her parents. "Really, Mum, I am twenty-eight years old. I am perfectly capable of looking after myself."

"I have no doubt you are," said her father.

"Christmas is supposed to be a family occasion," said Gillian's mother, slightly imploringly but rather more assertively.

"Mum, I have spent twenty-seven Christmases in a row with you and Dad and Martin and I just want to do something different, for once."

"You could always go away after Christmas," suggested Gillian's father.

"It's too late. I've already booked the holiday," replied Gillian.

"Without even discussing it with us first?" asked her mother.

"I knew you would try to talk me out of going."

Mr Trevis took that response as his cue to pick up his newspaper and turn to the crossword page. He smiled slightly as he saw nine across read: 'Push an American young woman into extravagance (8)'. *Prodigal*, he thought with satisfaction.

His wife slumped back in her chair and was quiet and Gillian felt guilty, as she knew she would.

"I will be back before New Year. It will still be within the twelve days of Christmas and we can spend time together then."

"That's true," said her father, looking up. "The Three Wise Men don't get into the picture till the Epiphany."

"Yes, but Martin and Hazel and the children will have gone home by then and they will miss you," countered Mrs Trevis.

"I'll go and see them over the holiday," said Gillian. "Look, Mum, Christmas just gets to me. It's all the razzmatazz, all the steady build-up before it finally arrives and you can't get away from it. The shops with Christmas trees and tinsel in October and Slade and Wizzard non-stop in the background while you are trying to think what to buy for somebody you know won't like it, whatever it is. Then the television full of Bing bloody Crosby and Johnny bleeding Matthis and all the other sentimental dross and the Christmas specials of all the sitcoms and, of course, Morecambe and Wise. To cap it all, people who wouldn't be seen dead in a church for the rest of the year rock up to the carol services as if that's just another entertainment. Then suddenly it's Boxing Day, people start gearing up for the winter sales and it's all over for another year before you can sing Good King Wenceslas. Nobody cares about the other eleven days of Christmas when the pressure is off and you could relax and enjoy it. So, for once, I am going as far away from the Christmas climax and anticlimax as possible."

Mr Trevis smiled. "I see your point, Gillian but, however

fleeting the moment, the goodwill that Christmas Day can generate in the unlikeliest of people is surely a good thing. After all, it even stopped the fighting in the First World War."

"For one day," snorted Gillian. "If it had had a real effect and the soldiers, on both sides, had refused to fight each other, the war would have been over. But they were told to go back to their trenches and resume the fighting and they did. It was just another sentimental gesture and it didn't happen again because there was no room for sentiment after that. What's the point of being kind or generous for one day if the next you go back to your old ways? In some ways it's worse than being the same all the time; at least people know where they are with you."

All three knew simultaneously that the argument was over and silence like a pall settled over the sitting room as Gillian unpacked her bag of presents to all those whom she would not see open them. But Mrs Trevis broke the spell by opening the drinks cabinet and pouring them all a glass of Harveys Bristol Cream. They smiled and raised their glasses to each other with the compliments of the season.

"I do hope you have a happy holiday, Gillian," said her mother. "It is such a long way and on your own, too."

"Not really on my own, Mum. It's an organised trip by one of those companies who specialise in faraway places. You'd be amazed at some of the destinations you can visit on a planned tour."

"This one will be quite a trek, I imagine?" asked her father, topping up the glasses.

"It is rather. A plane from Paris to the Mali capital, Bamako, and then there will be a chartered flight to Timbuktu."

"Where will you stay?" asked her mother, keeping her extreme anxiety about the whole business, especially the question of accommodation, under control, like a boiling kettle refusing to flip its lid.

Gillian smiled. "Oh, it's all right, I won't have to sleep in a tent or anything like that. There are proper hotels there and we will be put up in a well-regarded one."

Mrs Trevis inwardly shuddered but maintained her smile.

"Just to stop your mother worrying, you won't go off on any trips on your own, will you, love?" said her father."

"Really, Dad! You'll be saying 'Don't take sweets from a stranger' or 'If a car stops, don't get in' next. I am neither a child nor stupid. I promise I won't talk to any strange men or hitch a ride on a camel." She leaned over and kissed her father and he smiled broadly.

Soon after, Gillian took leave of her parents and drove the twenty-five miles back to her flat. There she packed her suitcases and had an early night, though not much sleep, to make a prompt start the next morning. She went first to London to join the rest of the party, her guilt from the conversation with her parents evaporating in the warm feeling generated by the excitement about her forthcoming trip. There followed a coach journey to Dover, a ferry to Calais, another coach to Charles de Gaulle airport and a six-hour flight to Bamako. Despite arriving late in the evening, the heat hit her as she disembarked from the plane in a temperature twenty degrees hotter than she had left in Paris. The party were escorted to a nearby hotel where, exhausted, she fell into bed, barely casting an eye over her surroundings. The next morning, after a gurgling, occasionally boisterous, cool shower she enjoyed a French breakfast before a chartered plane took her party to Timbuktu, a flight of over an hour and a half. Once again, the tropical savannah heat hit her as she walked down the steps from the plane and, with mounting anticipation, strolled through the shimmering air towards the modest terminal building over which a banner was draped with the words 'Joyeux Noel – Merry Christmas'.

V

THE ITALIAN JOB

THE FIRST WEEK IN JANUARY AND THE ARRIVAL OF the spring term, spring referring to its official name rather than any evidence to support it. The Great Storm of 1976, as it came to be known, had carved a swathe of devastation across the country from Scotland through the North-West of England, the Midlands and into East Anglia. The college had not escaped entirely, with a large linden tree having been pulled up by its roots by the gales and thrown across the rugby pitch. On the first day of term, the tree still lay where it had fallen. Gillian saw it when she parked her car and walked over to it, an act of curiosity, or was it bereavement, as she experienced sadness as she approached it.

"Shame, isn't it?" she heard a voice say as she looked down at the roots, their work and life ended. She turned round to see John Knowles, his hands in the pockets of his trousers. She thought he looked impeccable as usual, in a dark three-piece suit. It was a mild day and he hadn't bothered to take a topcoat. Gillian nodded.

John looked down at the massive tree trunk. "Just like us, I suppose. A seed is sown, life bursts forth, you grow up, reach maturity, put on weight as you get old and one day, out in the wind you lose your footing, fall over and can't get up again. How was Timbuktu?"

"Oh, it was fine, thanks. Very hot but the buildings, libraries and museums were fantastic; a lost, great civilisation."

"I suppose the lot that took over weren't a patch on the former inhabitants. It's like Greece and Rome: great civilisations that dominated the known world in their time but the modern Greeks and Italians not really of the same calibre. We're on the way down ourselves: from Captain Scott to Norman Scott. So, you had a good time?"

"Yes, thanks," said Gillian, leaving John to his reflections.

Actually, though Gillian had enjoyed it, the trip had been something of a mixed bag. The culture had indeed provided a wonderful, unforgettable experience: the medieval mosques, the library of ancient scrolls, the architecture. The hotel, though Spartan in amenities and limited in cuisine, had been clean and the staff attentive. But she had frequently wished she had been alone, without fellow travellers. An Englishman on his own in his early forties, while not bad-looking, appeared to believe that she couldn't possibly be content to be a lone traveller, especially a female one, so far from home. Friendly and mildly solicitous on the first day in Timbuktu, he became something of a limpet. At first, he hovered around her when they were out in a group and he progressed to join her at table whenever the opportunity arrived, then sharing his view of the day's excursions, to eventually asking her to have drinks in the bar after dinner. She tried to be sympathetic, after all he might well be lonely and he had not yet made any physical advance, but she knew from past experience that affability can be mistaken for, or presumed to be, interest. When invited to drinks she said she had another engagement and, though she had to say exactly the same thing the next day, this finally did the trick. Her would-be suitor consequently ignored her for the rest of the trip. At dinner on subsequent evenings, she joined a pleasant, if rather uninteresting couple from metropolitan-line suburbia, who exchanged small talk most of the time and only became animated by reading the menu and recalling exotic meals from previous holidays in Asia and Africa. Most of the other members of the group either kept to their own company or merely exchanged the odd pleasantry with Gillian. The exception was a rather studious-looking young man from Edinburgh, Gillian's age or probably a little younger, who listened attentively to the guides and always had a notebook and pencil at the ready to jot down anything that appealed to him. After one excursion, he entertained her on the coach back with his knowledge of the Benin empire. She found his exposition very interesting for the first forty minutes but soon after realised that this earnest young man did not understand the concept of listener's boredom. As all her attempts to change the subject failed, Gillian sat back and nodded occasionally until the end of the coach journey back to the hotel gave her a chance to slip away. She was firmer in her resolve now to keep to her own company, not because she didn't want to be friendly but because she didn't want to be anything more than friendly. From now on she carried a book in which she could bury her head should the need arise to avoid being drawn into conversation. So, when she joined the regulars for a drink at the Bellerephon and was asked repeatedly how her holiday had been, she was able to say truthfully that she had thoroughly enjoyed it.

"What will be your abiding memory of Timbuktu?" asked Roger, after she had mentioned some of the highlights of the tour.

"I know this sounds odd, but actually it was the sand."

"I told you so," said John, looking over at Roger.

Mike Brompton laughed. "I'm sure there was plenty of it but that was just the background, surely?"

Gillian smiled. "It was but I was always conscious of it, blowing into the city and surrounding it. If the people left, how long would it be before the desert reclaimed it?"

"True, nature will soon move in if we move out," said Javeed.

"There it is," Bill said, nodding.

"Still, you avoided the usual Christmas hullabaloo," said Roger.

"Yes and no. It was a bit low key but the hotel put up the bunting and had a tree. Christmas Day there was a drinks party. Some of my fellow guests seemed to enjoy that."

"Changing the subject," said John Knowles, "I've got to go down to London for a meeting with the examining board about the new structure on the management diploma. "We've sent them our proposal and they have to renew our approval. It's just a formality but I could do with a management accountant for any queries about the financial bits. Anyone fancy a trip?"

"Ah, the joys of being a senior lecturer, John. I'll come," said Javeed, "Keep an eye on you." He grinned.

"Great," said John Knowles. "All-day job, so we'll sort out a good day for us both and I'll fix it up."

Two weeks later, John and Javeed took the London train for a meeting at the examining board, in their offices near Portman Square. On the train, John went through an outline of the day.

"Basically, we're going for a new model of the same product. Like going from the Cortina Mark III to the Mark IV: a few new features, bit more performance, more stylish but the basic product is the same for the same market."

"The Mark IV is less stylish than the Mark III," intervened Javeed.

"Yes, just an example, but you are right; with the changes in the diploma the basics are the same but more emphasis on style: less emphasis on the subject matter and more on the delivery and buzzwords all over the place. It's just a game to keep us on our toes and them in a job. I see from the letter that Doug Sanders has retired and we'll be seeing some new bloke today and another person, a consultant. Nothing to worry about."

Javeed nodded and looked through his copy of the college proposal, drawn up by John and his senior colleagues in the management studies section. "Can't make head or tail of some of these definitions used by the examining board. They seem to be turning verbs into nouns and nouns into verbs half the time. Why do these bods make everything incoherent?"

John laughed. "That's the idea. Change the language, use obscure or resurrect long-defunct words to make it look superior to what went before and bamboozle everybody into believing it's an improvement. All the new quasi-sciences are full of it in case it appears that you are merely stating the bleeding obvious. It's never challenged because the biggest fear of any academic is to be seen as ignorant or behind the times. The fact is that a spade is still a spade, even if you now describe it as a 'utensil for cleaving the earth for the process of circulation and installation.'"

Javeed smiled. "I shall say as little as possible but with a knowing smile."

John looked in his case and produced a thick, bound booklet of vouchers the shape of a raffle ticket book but on a much larger scale. Each voucher was brightly coloured and printed with the name of a restaurant.

"What's that?" asked Javeed.

"This, my friend, is our ticket to lunch. I went to a meeting the other week at the Chamber of Commerce, and this chap was giving a presentation to sign up people for a subscription which gives you discounts on lunches at good-quality restaurants. As I had organised the meeting, he gave me a complementary set of vouchers. He was supposed to send me a guest membership card to accompany the vouchers but it hasn't arrived yet."

"Surely you need the membership card?"

"Not according to the chap who gave me the vouchers. Some of the vouchers say specifically you must produce the card but others do not. As long as you produce a voucher and it doesn't mention the card you're fine. After all, you have to have effectively bought the vouchers already. Obviously, you need the card if you have used up the voucher for a particular restaurant already. Some restaurants ask to see the card as extra proof or to enable them to monitor usage and so on. I have selected a very nice Italian restaurant where there is no requirement to show the membership card. With our expenses from the college, we'd be lucky to pay for a lunch in one of those mass office workers' restaurants. We'll get fifty per cent off with the voucher, so we will have to pay something, but it'll be well worth it."

"Sounds great," said Javeed.

John put the vouchers back in his case and closed the clasp with a satisfying click.

They arrived at the unnoteworthy building ten minutes early and went up to the first floor where the examining body had a suite of offices. They presented themselves to an unsmiling receptionist who dismissed them to a couple of chairs and they waited. It was twenty past ten when they arrived and they waited, and waited, occasionally looking at their watches and the clock in the reception area as the minute hand climbed towards twelve and the hour hand crawled towards eleven.

John looked at Javeed. "They are keeping us waiting so we know who's in charge. Pathetic."

At five minutes past eleven the receptionist took a call and said to John and Javeed "You can go through now, room 231."

They knocked on the door and entered without waiting. A man and a woman sat at a desk and looked up at them as they entered. The man was in his forties with receding dark hair and a slightly lower parting than he would have had a year ago. He looked at them over his glasses. The woman was wearing a dark dress and had a short, businesslike hairstyle with dangling earrings.

The man smiled. "Take a seat. Mr Knowles and Mr Javeed? I am James Phillips, Senior Executive Officer on course approval and my colleague, Melanie Chambers, Implementation and Innovation Officer." He nodded towards the woman who also smiled. "Thank you for coming down. There are a few items we would like to discuss from your proposal."

John nodded but did not smile. He was not pleased that no apology for being kept waiting had been offered.

"We notice that there has been no change in the subject headings, despite the wide-ranging adaptations to the content of each module."

"The subject headings are quite broad and still incorporate the new material. They are familiar to the potential students and their employers," John said with a slight smile.

"I take it the teaching team have been fully briefed on the new material and have received tutorial assistance in the new approach?"

"Naturally," said John. "They all have considerable experience both in managerial roles and in teaching on the course and will have little difficulty in adapting to the new programme."

"All the staff have served on the course for some years. Is it not time to freshen things up a little?" asked Miss Chambers.

"This is one of our high-level courses and it already has the most appropriate people on the team. We consistently produce among the best results throughout the country on this course. I see little purpose in changing the team purely for the sake of it." John could hear his voice sounding a little peevish but half couldn't do anything about it and half didn't want to.

The two administrators looked down at their notes and then at Javeed. "Give us a flavour of your new approaches to delivering the course. We want to tease out signs of innovation and novelty in your approach."

Javeed moved a little in his chair. "I use practical exercises, case studies, teamwork, analysis and so on. As you know, this is a part-time course with a great deal to get through, so inevitably much of the learning must take place through guided teaching rather than discovery."

John thought that Javeed had given a good answer, especially when Miss Chambers had used one of those irritating phrases, 'tease out', so loved by educational administrators.

Miss Chambers was not so pleased with the answer. "So, basically a handouts-and-practice man of the old school."

Javeed looked a little uncomfortable but was momentarily stuck for an answer. Before Javeed could respond Miss Chambers moved to her next question.

On it went: interminable questioning, always with a slight edge and no positive feedback on the responses. John answered the questions patiently and avoided irritation, negativism or sarcasm in his answers but there was no let-up in the inquisition.

Suddenly, without premeditation and not triggered by any particular question, John stood up and said, "I'm afraid we are not getting anywhere and this is clearly a waste of my time being here."

He closed his briefcase and walked out, expecting Javeed to follow him. But ten seconds later he stopped in reception and Javeed had still not left the room. John sat down in reception, unable to explain his own actions, other than that the final straw must have activated him without warning. He noticed the receptionist watching him and presumably finding his neither coming nor going an unusual ending of the meeting. But he could hardly leave and he could definitely not return so he sat and waited. The next five, seven, ten minutes passed excruciatingly slowly and then he heard a door open and close and a few seconds later a beaming Javeed appeared in the foyer. John stood up and Javeed waved him over to the reception desk to sign out. They signed out and Javeed wished the receptionist a cheerful farewell and they hurried down the stairs to the exit.

As soon as they were outside the building Javeed laughed and clapped him on the back. "That was brilliant," he said.

"What happened in there?"

"I wish you had told me you were going to do that."

"I didn't know I was going to do it myself."

"Well, I was stunned. I didn't know whether to follow you or not but then I looked at their faces. They were shocked too and were staring at each other, mouths open. I was still trying to work out a strategy for what to do next and they probably wanted to have a chat about their position but were worried about me so nobody spoke for nearly a minute. I spoke first and said something like, 'This is a very unfortunate situation.' That loosened them up and Phillips said, 'Yes. Are you empowered to act alone?' I said I was and they both looked relieved and they were as good as gold after that. They said how much they valued our participation in the programme and that there were no hindrances to our approval. I have the documentation from them, signed and sealed. They were extremely grateful."

John laughed now, much to the consternation of passersby. There are few things more disconcerting to people going about the daily trudge of life than going past two or more people in a public place in good humour or actually laughing and not even drunk. Consequently, they were given a wide berth as Javeed, at John's insistence, went through the story once again and they were barely able to contain themselves.

"Time for lunch, I think," said John, as they recovered their composure. "Definitely a celebration drink. Let's go to our Italian restaurant."

It was a quarter of an hour's walk to the restaurant, near Grosvenor Square. They went down some steps to be greeted by a helpful head waiter who was able to find them a table after much scanning of bookings and the substantial numbers of currently empty tables. They were seated at a table with John on a banquette and Javeed opposite him.

"Nice place," said Javeed as he looked down the menu. "Spoilt for choice."

A waiter took their order for drinks and, at an appropriate moment, returned to take their orders for food and drink.

With their order, John presented the appropriate voucher to the waiter.

The waiter looked at it for a moment. "Do you have the membership card, sir?"

"No, unfortunately not on me, but as you see on the voucher it does not request that the voucher be presented with the membership card."

The waiter nodded and went off.

The restaurant was geared to an efficient turnround at lunchtime for the benefit of London workers and their starter soon arrived.

"Well, a satisfactory day all round," said John as they enjoyed their starters and savoured a glass of Montepulciano d'Abruzzo.

A different waiter took their plates away and they prepared for the main course of veal saltimbocca but the original waiter appeared first. "I'm sorry, sir, the manager says that the membership card must be presented with the voucher."

"But the voucher doesn't mention a requirement to have the card. Surely."

"I'm sorry, sir."

"But…"

As the waiter walked off, their main course arrived.

John shook his head. "What's the point of the man from the company telling me one thing and the people who take the vouchers saying something else?"

Javeed shrugged and the two ate in silence, the delicious food for John now having lost all its attraction. As they neared the end of it, John leaned over the table and said quietly, "You know, I think we are being swindled here and it's not good enough. I think we should finish our meal and just go."

"You mean without…?"

"Yes. We leave together and you go ten feet ahead of me. As we near the head waiter's desk, if you are stopped, say that I am paying, then go. When I get there, if I am stopped I shall say I thought you had paid. If neither get stopped, we walk up the stairs then speed up to the bus stop and get on the first bus so we can hightail it."

"Are you sure?"

"Yes," said John, sidling out of from the table.

Javeed got up and began to walk, in a rather stiff way that John had never seen before, towards the exit. Twenty seconds later they were running up the last couple of steps and saw a bus at the bus stop. But as they ran towards it, the bus pulled away.

They looked behind but nobody was running towards them.

"Quick, in here," said John, heading towards the nearest building.

They pushed the revolving door and found themselves in the reception area of a foreign merchant bank.

"Can I help you?" asked the smiling young woman at the reception desk. She was surrounded by the apotheosis of high-quality taste in walnut and marble.

"Erm," said John.

"Sorry, I think we've come to the wrong building," said Javeed and they rushed out the way they had come in.

Back on the street there was no sign of anyone looking for them and, once again in fits of almost uncontrollable laughter, they walked briskly down the road and went into the first bar they came to.

John ordered two double brandies from the barmaid, who ignored his high colour and rather stupid grin. They toasted themselves and, unable to recount the precise events that had just passed, referred cryptically to the most humorous moments of the last ten minutes or so.

"Have you ever done anything like that before?" asked Javeed.

John shook his head. "No. You?"

"No. I can't believe I have now."

"A one-off. I just saw red when, once again, I, the customer, think I am doing everything above board and correct but then the supplier or seller steps up with a veto under the dreaded heading 'Terms and Conditions' and we are stuffed."

Two more brandies later, and suitably, if artificially calmed, they took a gentle walk to St Pancras station and the train. Sitting opposite each other, they sat mostly in silence, often smiling as they reflected on the day. When they left the train, they cheerfully went their separate ways. John was in such a good mood that, though 'tired', he stopped to assist a young woman whose car had broken down. He failed to get it started, the only disappointment in a magical day, or was it that the spell had broken? A suspicion that was given some credence when he opened his front door, walked into the kitchen and found his wife mopping the floor after a malfunction of the washing machine.

Neither he nor Javeed mentioned what had happened that day to anyone else and Javeed gave it the name 'The Italian Job', which they used between themselves to describe the day they would never forget. The day when the normal way of the world had been temporarily turned upside down and the bureaucrats did not dictate the procedure and the customer was always right.

VI

O, TO BE IN ENGLAND

O, TO BE IN ENGLAND, NOW THAT APRIL'S THERE, thought Mark Harred, unable to remember the next line and not sure he had ever known it. But what did it matter? It was the joy of spring that was lifting his heart as he drove through the gates of Twirleston Academy then along the drive, surveying the freshly mowed lawns and the woodland areas ablaze with the colours of bluebells, tulips, late daffodils and early rhododendrons. He was no gardener so it wasn't the burgeoning activity of plant life below and above the soil which aroused such anticipation, it was what it symbolised: the drive of all life to go forth and multiply, the compulsion to let nature take its course, and for humanity to surrender to that delicious excuse, 'I couldn't help myself'. Unlike Browning's poem looking forward to a May of blossom and songbirds, Mark could see only the onset of warmer days, balmy in May, simmering in June and semi-tropical in July. April was just the beginning of the best months of the year and they would not be frittered away.

Mark would be the first to admit he was driven in his relations with women but it was not totally about sex, not even primarily about it, despite what his friends and his colleagues thought. He was not absolutely sure himself where his motives came from as he had neither the time nor the inclination for philosophy. He knew only what he knew: that the saddest day of the summer was the summer solstice, Midsummer Day, the longest day, after which the sun would begin to retreat a little bit each day and the march to winter would begin. The best day of the year was the winter solstice when the sun would begin to come closer. He liked Fridays better than Saturdays because the weekend had yet to begin, the last day of term because the holidays were intact. The best month was April since the summer lay ahead, untouched, full of promise. He had to make the most of each summer because the next one or the one after or at some time in the years ahead, there would be no promise because his peak would have passed and he would be past it, perhaps when he was forty. By then, he would be old enough to be the father of anyone he fancied. That's why he had to 'make hay while the sun shines' rather than thinking about the alternative, which was decline and ultimately death. He had concluded that most people don't think about death often enough, otherwise they would not waste so much of the lives they still have thinking instead of doing.

He got out of his car, waved cheerily to a student in his O level class and went into the main building where his classes were generally sited. He had convinced the headmaster, Mr Mandeville, that a subject as grave and grandiloquent as law needed a more suitable, a grander environment than a portacabin if students were to immerse themselves in the spirit of it. His classes were always timetabled for a wood-panelled room which had once been the morning room of this grand house. He was looking forward to his class today as he anticipated making plans for the final lesson of the term next week, which he hoped would involve a party of some kind. He hoped, rather than envisaged, since his usual self-assurance and belief that he was the master of any given situation had taken a knock the previous term.

His original idea of having Alison from HND business studies as his occasional female interest for the year had not gone according to plan. Not because Alison was unwilling to go out with him; she was happy to do so and was very pleasant and charming and neither demanding nor self-obsessed. Everything he could have wished for in fact. But she had told him after their first date alone that she didn't want an entanglement, especially in view of Mark's marital position, and hoped he wouldn't be too devastated if she made this a one and only night together. Always the one who decided such matters in his relationships and now confronted by a rejection which smacked of condescension, he was at a loss to think of a way to reassert his own status in the relationship. The ground cut from under his feet, he couldn't even face the offer of a consolation prize of a one-night stand given out of charity. He dropped Alison off at her home early, driving away while she waved the way he suspected she would have done to a pet.

His ego, having convalesced over the winter, was now recovered and, with spring beckoning, he was prepared to give his previously successful routine another outing. This time he would explore an opportunity at the academy, away from the college where everyone knew your business and any malfunction of his dalliance was bound to spread around the student body like wildfire. His students at the academy covered a narrow range of wealth but from past experience he knew they constituted a wide spectrum of characters and personalities, from the sophisticated, worldly wise and down-to-earth to the spoilt brats, dysfunctional and frankly psychologically disturbed. As a generational cohort they possessed one great quality in that they were the first teenagers who had come of age after the sexual revolution of the 1960s. When he had been eighteen, the '60s had barely got going and few of the girls he knew would have discarded their virginity lightly and retained quite strict protocols regarding sexual favours. The present members of that age group had a more open perspective and for this he was grateful as he felt he still had more lost ground to make up.

The subject of his interest for a summer adventure was the beautiful, nineteen-year-old Antonia Mortimer. She appeared to be at the down-to-earth end of the behavioural spectrum, was interested and participative in his classes and more mature and polished than the other female students. In Antonia, he thought he had found someone who would be willing to enjoy an easy-going, light relationship which she would be pleased to wind up at the end of the summer. Nonetheless, the unfortunate misunderstanding with Alison still haunted him and he was determined to tread carefully. Indeed, as he walked towards the morning room, he experienced, not for the first time, that gnawing sensation of wondering if all this business of attraction and proposition and enticement was really worthwhile. But he patted his impeccably coiffed hair, adjusted the one strand which had fallen over his forehead, straightened his Windsor-knotted shot-silk tie and marched into the room. Antonia looked up as he came in and smiled at him and his doubts faded.

At the end of the class, Mark asked if the students were looking forward to the end of term. They smiled. "That's a leading question, isn't it, sir?" said one of the girls.

Mark smiled, "Very good, Jane. Are you having a celebration or all clearing off to a holiday of some sort?"

"The headmaster has something arranged," said Jane. "He says we should have a function but everything fizzles out at the end of the summer term so the end of this term is better."

"Not at Whitsun?" asked Mark. "Warmer then."

"We will have started the A levels by then," said one of the boys.

Mark nodded.

"Teachers will be invited," said Jane. She smiled at Mark and he realised that she was prettier than he had thought before and that gave him food for thought.

At the end of the class, Mark went down to the secretary's office where the mail he never bothered to check would be waiting for him.

"Hello, Mrs Raglan," he said breezily to the middle-aged woman typing with some force on a stencil.

"Good afternoon," she replied, without looking up.

"Just thought I'd better check the mail." He walked to the pigeonhole with the most mail in it, which he instinctively knew was his. Most of it had already long passed its applicability date and went straight into the wastepaper bin near Mrs Raglan's desk.

Mrs Raglan looked down as the papers slid into the bin. "Glad you popped in, Mr Harred. You have just confirmed what I've always believed; that most of what I do is a complete waste of time, typing letters and circulars which go from my typewriter to the dustbin without being read by anybody."

Mark laughed. "I'm sure that's not true. I've just been a bit slack on my post lately. Working on something important now, no doubt."

Mrs Raglan's eyes were firmly on her stencil; one slip could spell disaster and more work. "You'll see in good time," she said, raising her glasses and checking what she had just typed.

Mark walked behind her and saw the heading on her piece of work, 'Easter Gathering', and smiled to himself. He left the room, clutching the last three missives from his pigeonhole to spare Mrs Raglan's feelings and then threw them in the wastepaper bin at the end of the corridor.

He was about to head for the front door when a voice called out to him. He turned to see Ben Townshend, one of his O level students.

"Hello, Ben, what can I do for you?"

"Could I have a word in confidence, Mr Harred?"

Mark was instinctively sure this spelled bad news and thought it best to have the conversation out of earshot of anyone else. "I'm just leaving. Appointment back at college. Shall we have a walk out to my car?"

Ben nodded and they walked in silence until they were outside, clear of the main doors. There were other students around but they paid them no attention.

"Well, Ben?"

"The thing is, Mr Harred, the thing is that I have a copy of the summer examination paper."

"What? How have you got hold of that?"

"I'm not allowed to say."

"Well?"

"I wondered if you would go through it with me; point me in the right direction with some of the questions. My father would make it worth your while."

They had stopped walking. "I can't do that, Ben," said Mark. "It wouldn't be right."

"I have to get this subject, Mr Harred. I need it for my future."

"I understand that but I wouldn't feel comfortable about being involved. Look, if you have the questions, you have ample time to look up the information and put together the answers. If you don't pass with that advantage, you probably wouldn't pass if you had my help." Mark started to walk towards his car.

"You won't tell anyone about this, will you, sir?"

Mark shook his head. "No, Ben. You took me into your confidence and I won't betray you."

"Thank you, sir." Ben walked away with his head down and Mark thought no more of it.

The next time Mark was back at the school, two days later, the latest circular from the headmaster was in his pigeonhole. The proposed 'Easter Gathering' of staff and students had been arranged for the Friday afternoon of the following week, the last day of term. It would begin at two o'clock and end at four-thirty. The school would be officially closed for the end of term at six o'clock, by which time everyone was expected to have left the premises.

"How did this come about?" asked Mark, waving the circular in the direction of Mrs Raglan. "I don't recall anything like this before."

Mrs Raglan looked up from her work. "It has something to do with the Board of Governors."

"The Board of Governors? I didn't realise there was one but I suppose there must be?"

"Oh, yes. The Chairman of the Governors, Sir St John Sunstream, actually founded the school in about 1950. This building was going cheap as the family that owned it couldn't manage the upkeep. Originally, there were to be lots of places for the less well-off, subsidised by scholarships, but gradually the rising costs meant we had to concentrate on paying guests. Anyway, the school was supposed to be more than a crammer, with a social side, perhaps a bit of culture and, every once in a while, one of the governors, usually the chairman, asks about that kind of thing. At the governors' meeting at the start of term, Sir St John suggested there should be some sort of reception to build esprit de corps, as it were, and Mr Mandeville thought this might be quite suitable."

"So, the old boy's still going? Where on earth did he get a name like Sunstream from?"

"I think it's originally Swedish but corrupted over time."

"Anyway, good for him. I think it's a great idea," said Mark, his thoughts brimming with potential scenarios. Glancing at the other pigeonholes, he noticed that invitations had been given to all the college lecturers who taught part-time at the school: Julian Wesley, Roger Southwark, Mike Brompton, Lesley Hornbeam, a sociology lecturer and even Rob Grainger. Rob had taught sociology the previous year but had dropped out this time, thinking it wise not to teach in private education once he was in line to be a prospective parliamentary candidate.

The day of the reception arrived and when Roger and Julian drove into the school entrance, they were surprised to see Mr Mandeville dressed in his graduate gown and hood while greeting the guests. The venue was in the grounds where trestle tables were laid out with white cloths, on which four catering staff in white tops and black skirts or trousers were laying out a buffet. Another table acted as bar and was well stocked with wine and soft drinks and even a dozen bottles of champagne.

"It's more upmarket than I expected," said Roger to Julian.

Julian smiled. "I think the head has an annual allowance for social events but he hasn't used it for years, so he's got a decent surplus to make use of and he had to put on a bit of a show for the chairman of governors. That's him, talking to Mrs Raglan."

Roger looked over at a tall, distinguished-looking man, dressed in a double-breasted suit with a fob watch in his breast pocket. He was smiling as he chatted to the school secretary. He appeared younger than Roger had expected, no more than sixty, his hair still dark in places and only thinning a little at the temples.

ⁿ️️

"I thought he would be quite elderly," said Roger.

"He was only in his thirties when he started the place, with money inherited from his family. He's an old-fashioned Tory; you know, paternalistic, duty to do one's bit for the lower classes, that kind of thing."

"He must have done something useful to be knighted."

"Not a knight, a baronet, the fifth generation. Let's get a drink."

"No students here yet?"

"No, they were given a starting time half an hour later than the other guests to ensure we all get a drink before the stampede to the trough begins."

"Very sensible idea."

They walked over towards Mandeville, who was talking to a couple of the part-time teachers who were not based at the college.

"Glad you could make it, gentlemen," said Mandeville, nodding to them both. "May I introduce Mrs Bland who teaches history and Mr Rouse, geography? Mr Southwark and Mr Wesley, two lecturers from the college."

Roger and Julian reciprocated courtesies with Mrs Bland, a lady in her thirties, and the elderly, nondescript, Mr Rouse before heading to the bar table. Julian cast an eye at the champagne and was politely informed it would be served for the toast, so opted for a glass of Madeira. Roger settled for a glass of Muscadet and they rejoined Mrs Bland and Mr Rouse, Mandeville having now begun circulating among the guests, his basso profundo cough providing an occasional low-key sound track to the proceedings.

"Have you worked here long?" asked Roger, for nothing better to say and to no one in particular.

"Since I retired, ten years now," replied Mr Rouse. "I've enjoyed keeping my hand in but this is my last year. I've explained the difference between stalagmites and stalactites and between Guinea and New Guinea once too often. Not had one of these events for several years, have they?" He drained his glass and went to the bar to refresh it.

Roger thought Mr Rouse less boring than he appeared but now turned his attention to Mrs Bland. She was dressed in a flowery summer dress with a dark-blue cardigan draped over her shoulders. Her hair was dark, parted in the middle with a fringe and shaped above the shoulders slightly under her chin. She wore a necklace with a single pearl and her elegant hands had a bright-pink nail polish. He thought her extremely attractive.

Mrs Bland smiled effervescently, pulling her cardigan over her goose-pimpled, bare arms, the consequence of her optimistic choice of a summer dress for the occasion. "I've only been teaching here a couple of years, since the youngest started school," she said, in answer to Roger's question. She sipped her gin and tonic. "I hope it warms up a bit."

Julian laughed. "Yes, difficult month to predict, April. March comes in like a lion and goes out like a lamb but when it comes to April, lambs have built-in pullovers," he said, glancing at her bare skin.

"You were a full-time teacher before you had a family?" asked Roger.

"Yes, at the local comprehensive."

"How do you find the students here, compared to the school you worked at?"

She smiled. "They're all right but I miss the outstanding students, the ones who show you they really get it and make you think. Obviously, they don't come to a school like this because they don't need to."

Julian asked to be excused and wandered in the direction of Sir St John Sunstream. Roger looked at the background of people talking, joking, teasing, laughing, posing, strutting, fawning and mildly flirting around them and wondered if he wished to spend the time to come primarily in the company of Mrs Bland or whether he should strike out on a tour of the whole assembly. But one look around and he knew that there was nobody to whom he particularly wished to speak and what was the point of making the acquaintance of a series of other people just to indulge in the same small talk over and over again? Anyway, Mrs Bland was easily the prettiest woman there.

"Another drink, Mrs Bland?" Roger asked.

"Please call me Ann. Yes, I'd love one, thank you. It's a Bacardi and Coke, plenty of Coke." She laughed, passing him her glass.

Roger's thoughts were being replicated elsewhere as those who taught at the academy circulated among themselves, trying to avoid being trapped by a crushing bore, even the crushing bores themselves who never realised they were. The college lecturers had an advantage as they knew each other, at least while the part-time teachers had to tread more carefully.

The mood changed when the students arrived. Apart from Princess Zara, who always dressed quite smartly, as became her position, almost all the other students normally turned up for classes in casual clothes. But today, the male students were dressed quite formally in smart shirts, often with a jacket and most wearing ties. The females had more than matched this standard and all were wearing attractive dresses, smart platform shoes and full make-up. As the younger male lecturers watched them troop out from the main entrance, the age gap between themselves and their female students suddenly seemed bridgeable, at least in the abstract. Of course, Mark Harred had, through his past record, shown the gap was merely a chronological fact of trivial importance by his well-constructed displays of low-key, mildly complimentary conversation with his female students. Today, he took his time, waiting until he received eye contact from a couple of the students and then sauntered over to Jane, from his A level law class, and engaging her in a light-hearted conversation as she stood on the lawn, taking in her surroundings. Jane, who was used to Antonia being the primary object of Mark's attention, was pleasantly surprised and flattered, that without hesitation, Mark had appeared more interested in her. He could tell instantly that his little ploy had worked.

Queues soon formed for drinks and the buffet, as is the British way. Soon, most of the guests were armed with a glass in one hand and a plate and fork in the other. For the more sensitive the socially tortuous task of attempting to appear cultivated and well-mannered while chasing food round the plate with a fork and holding their glass in the same hand as the plate now followed. Simultaneously they might also be expected to say something of interest to a relative stranger. The wiser, and those old hands at this ludicrous way of organising a meal, found a patch of table to put down their drink or did not attempt to eat and drink at the same time. The students were the least comfortable; they were in danger of being judged gauche or immature while most of their seniors had long ago cleared those hurdles of potential personal embarrassment.

For the young and youngish male teachers, the risk of embarrassment lay mainly in the possibility that they might make an error of judgement in their conversations with their students. They had to strike a balance between not being so relaxed or friendly that they weakened their perceived authority in the classroom and not being so formal and reserved that they came across as stuffy and boring. This was especially problematic when dealing with the young women on whom they might wish to make a good impression without actually appearing to be trying to make a good impression. On the whole, with the drinks flowing and a growing sense of relaxation, a party mood developed. The lecturers were pleased to have a more informal interaction with their female students than they were used to, just as the young women enjoyed the attention and more serious conversation of these mature men, a change from the callow youths that pestered them with their clumsy chat-up lines and infantile jokes.

The male students were mainly left to enjoy their own company. They shared humorous, mostly derogatory, comments about the people at the party. They gave attractiveness ratings to the females, and shared their sexual ambitions, if the opportunity arose, towards the most attractive ones. They commented disparagingly on the probable virility of the male staff currently chatting to the women and fancied their own chances with Mrs Bland but did not actually have the nerve to speak to her. Some of them drew imaginative, if far-fetched scenarios of events which could bring the party to a more exciting climax or cause a chain reaction resulting in a complete standstill or even a disaster worthy to be reminisced over in the years to come. One of them took these ideas more seriously but couldn't conceive of how they might be put into practice.

Conversation and daydreams were temporarily interrupted by the arrival of glasses of champagne, sadly not a first for any of the students so they treated the matter nonchalantly. Mr Mandeville called the party to order as Sir St John wished to say a few words.

Sir St John had a strong voice and made a pleasant speech in which he applauded the efforts of the students and quoted the words popularised by Edward Hickson and repeated, poignantly by Neville Chamberlain in 1938: *If at first you don't succeed, try, try again.* He referred to it as a proverb for the whole of one's life and career, as well as for their studies. He then toasted the school and all connected with it and received a round of enthusiastic applause.

After that, the party began to break up. Sir St John, having shared a few words with different members of staff, took his leave in his Bentley T and he was followed by Mrs Raglan and several of the teachers. The party was about to wind down and, at four o'clock the headmaster bade farewell as the remnants of the buffet were cleared and the choice of drinks rapidly diminished.

"I suppose I ought to be going," said Ann Bland.

She and Roger had, largely through inertia, not bothered to circulate as the party went on. Occasionally they were joined by others for a greeting or a short conversation but for long periods they were left on their own. Now, two hours later, having exhausted the usual small talk and exchanged minor details to enable them to paint a thumb sketch of each other, they had found they actually liked each other and had an interesting conversation, ranging from education, through cultural interests and even into the pricklier area of current affairs.

Roger looked at his watch, "Yes, I should too. Can I give you a lift?" he asked, with a friendly smile. Having thought her the most attractive of the mature women at the party when it began, he hadn't changed his mind. Indeed, he now found her very pretty, vivacious and witty and was in no hurry to finish their time together.

Ann had left her car at home and accepted a lift to the academy from a friend, expecting that she would be offered a lift by somebody. Failing that she would get a minicab. "That's kind of you but I don't want to take you out of your way."

Roger shook his head. "No trouble, it's on my way. Well not far out of it.

By the time she had retrieved her coat and was ready to go, the numbers still present had diminished to less than twenty.

They cast their eyes around and waved at one or two. Mark Harred gave Roger a knowing look and winked; Roger, expression sphinx-like, ignored both gestures. They walked over to the car park and Roger stopped by his Ferrari.

"Lovely, isn't it," said Ann, also stopping to admire it. Then she saw Roger produce the keys and unlock it. "It's yours!" she said, her eyes widening.

Roger opened the door for Ann and she climbed in. "You are the first teacher I've ever met who has a Ferrari. In fact, it's the first time I've sat in one." She ran her fingers over the cream leather and adjusted her position on the rib-patterned seat.

Roger smiled, experiencing for the umpteenth time the reflected glory of the inanimate object in which he sat (he did not give his cars female pronouns). He was also amused by and did not disapprove of the greater attractiveness he had acquired because of the car. "When I bought it, I wasn't a teacher," he said. "Some describe it as the consequence of my ill-gotten gains from working in the City." He started his fashion accessory up and it made the appropriate sound.

"How fast does it go?" asked Ann.

"Over 170, apparently."

"You won't be able to do that in Britain."

"Not anymore. Actually, I've never done more than 140, even in Germany and that was only for a few minutes. It's a bit scary if you round a bend in the fast lane and somebody has moved into the lane to overtake but is going seventy miles per hour slower than you."

"So, the extra speed is really for sex appeal. It certainly has that," she said, stretching out her elegant legs and undoing her cardigan buttons. "I'm glad you're not a speed maniac, not with the roads round here, but I would like a little trip in it rather than go straight home, if you have the time?"

Roger nodded and they drove out of Twirleston Combust and took the straight B-road which went diagonally northeast rather than the winding road north towards their respective homes. Roger took the car through its gears and cruised at sixty or so, his foot well above the floor, then slowed and pulled into a lay-by.

"Would you like to have a go?" he asked.

Ann smiled. "I don't think I should. I've had a few drinks and if anything happened, I'd never forgive myself."

Roger nodded and they set off again.

"I wondered what you had in mind when you pulled over," she said, a mischievous smile on her face.

He didn't reply, as he was unsure what she'd meant. At the next junction he turned left and a few minutes later they drove through his own village.

Ann pointed to a thatched building next to the green. "I haven't been here for ages. That's a great old pub. I remember, when I was a child, it still had an earth closet in the toilet and the landlord had to, you know, sort it out after someone went in there. Not recommended." She shuddered.

"Ah, The Stag. Yes, modernised a bit since then but still has an old-fashioned feel about it. I sometimes pop in of an evening but I don't think it's open yet."

"Pity," she said.

"My place is just over there, if you fancy a drink." He pointed to the small, white, rendered house, standing in the lane just off the main road.

She smiled and he drove over to park outside his cottage.

"Lovely house; is it very old?" asked Ann, taking Roger's hand as she climbed out of his car.

"Late eighteenth century." He unlocked the front door which opened into the main reception room, quite well-lit despite the small windows.

"How lovely," said Ann. "You've made it look just right." She looked admiringly at the structural beams and then at the then-fashionable reproduction Jacobean furniture: a settle with cushions, a large sideboard and a cupboard above with bulbous supports and a dining table and chairs with twisted legs. "Modern furniture never looks quite right in these places, does it?" she added.

Roger shook his head. "No, beams clash with G-Plan. What would you like to drink? Bacardi and Coke?"

"Yes, please. I'd better stick to that."

She sat down on the cushioned settle and looked at the framed prints of Hogarth's *Rake's Progress* on the walls. "You like Hogarth?" she asked, gesturing at the prints.

"Not particularly but it's a reminder not to get too sure of yourself."

He had intended to have a soft drink but found himself with the same as Ann as he looked again at the Hogarth prints.

"Do you get too sure of yourself?" she asked, as he sat down beside her.

"Occasionally," he said. "Cheers."

"Cheers!" she raised her glass and, after taking a sip, she put the glass down and looked at him, waiting.

He smiled. "Would you like to see the rest of the house?"

"Oh, yes, please."

They stood up and he led the way into the room behind this one; a modernised kitchen with a large fireplace and off that another small reception room, which Roger used as a study.

"Is that where you do your marking?" she asked.

"Yes. Worst bit of the job."

She nodded. "Yes, how to find thirty different criticisms of the same mistake. You could always throw them down the stairs and give the best marks to those which fall furthest."

He smiled. "Would you like to see upstairs?"

He led her up to the two large bedrooms and bathroom. "The upstairs needed such a lot of work when I moved in. I had the walls sorted out. I don't like a bedroom with lopsided walls and crooked beams; it makes me feel like I've always got a hangover when I wake up in the morning."

She laughed and put her hand on his arm.

The bedrooms certainly looked modern, in sharp contrast to the ground floor. The spare bedroom had been decorated in a pale-blue and light-grey wallpaper, neutral and able to appeal to either gender, but the main bedroom was quite masculine, even severe, with its functional furniture, dark-blue sheets and plain coverlet. An armchair, bookcase and record player revealed something of Roger's varied use of the room.

"It's all lovely," said Ann as they stood in the main bedroom.

"It was in quite a state when I bought it but it suits me now."

"Mm, it is very sweet," she said. She looked at him and at the bed and smiled and he knew her thoughts but chose reluctantly to ignore them.

"Well, guided tour over, let's refresh our drinks," he said and turned to lead her downstairs. He didn't wait to notice if she was disappointed.

They sat on the sofa and talked over a last drink for twenty minutes or so but a spark had gone out for them both.

"Well, I suppose I should be going," said Ann. "I can get a taxi to save you having to take me home."

"I wouldn't dream of it. I have really enjoyed spending this afternoon with you and I'd like to drive you home."

In not much more than five minutes they were in the car. The journey to her house in the next, larger village was less than a quarter of an hour drive and they spent most of the journey in silence. When they arrived at Ann's house, an Edwardian villa with great bay windows and stained glass in the front door, Roger came round to open Ann's door.

She smiled. "Thank you for a lovely time, Roger. The day went much better than I could ever have expected thanks to you. I don't think we will but I hope we bump into each other again sometime."

"Me too."

They embraced briefly and she kissed him on the cheek, staying to wave him off as he drove away.

As he waved, he sighed at an opportunity missed though not regretted. He had found her very attractive and was more tempted than she would ever know. But where might it have led? "Complications, complications. Who needs them, old chum?" he said to himself as he turned the car for home.

Parties, even relatively formal events like the one being held at Twirleston Academy, can sometimes go off in directions the organisers could hardly have envisaged, seeming almost to have a mind of their own. Or perhaps it's merely a reflection of the characters and tendencies of those who make up the parties. It was certainly the case that the academy function took a turn not anticipated by most of those present after Roger and Ann left.

As the stock of drinks at the bar steadily diminished and the dignitaries began to disappear, Mark Harred became concerned that the party might come to an end before his personal ambitions for it had been realised. Always a man of action, he went into the office and telephoned the business and management department at the college and managed to get hold of John Knowles. He asked John to bring whoever might be interested to come to the party and to be sure to bring a few bottles. John was quite keen to see the academy he'd heard so much about and thought it would make a pleasant change to do something different at the end of term, so he readily agreed. The only other person still left in his office was Tony Laycock and he wasn't particularly interested in going but John talked him into it. They left for the local off licence and ten minutes later they had set out for the school with several bottles of medium-quality white and red wines and bottles of port and Scotch for those who were intent on getting a hangover.

"Who is paying for all this?" asked Tony Laycock, pointing at the clanking bottles in a wine box at his feet. He had found himself settling the bill at the off licence as John Knowles had insufficient money on him.

"Mark Harred, I suppose," said John, leaving Tony feeling slightly uncomfortable.

They took Tony's car as John was a bit short of petrol. By the time they arrived at the school, at about half past five, the catering staff had left, most of the students had packed their bags and gone and all that remained of the get-together was Mark Harred himself, Rob Grainger, Mike Brompton and eleven students: James Newton and Suzy Plunkett, the most outspoken members of Roger Southwark's British constitution class; Antonia Mortimer, Jane Stride and two female students of Mike Brompton: Fiona White and Ursula Seymour. There was also Max Jacobs, a pleasant, gregarious young man; Rory Marnoch, a science student; Jeremy Hyde, a friend of Max; and another boy and girl who, though still at the party, seemed preoccupied in their own private conversation. Keeping an eye on proceedings was the janitor, a burly main nearing retirement who saw his role of that as a gatekeeper rather than a doorman. He was holding a drink given to him by Mark in one hand and a bunch of keys in the other.

"Ah, the cavalry has arrived with reinforcements. Great!" said Mark, as John and Tony turned into the drive.

The janitor looked alarmed as the two lecturers emerged from the car with a box of wine and the bottles of Cockburn's port and Johnny Walker Scotch.

"Here, now," shouted the janitor. "This party has to finish soon. I have to lock up."

Mark, feeling he was owed a favour through his gift of a free drink, smiled amicably and called back, "Why not leave the keys with me? I'm a responsible adult. Take the evening off."

The janitor responded with the cliché beloved of those who wish not to comply. "No, I can't do that. It's more than my job's worth."

Mark ignored the janitor's hackneyed response and was about to remonstrate further when one of the boys, Max, whispered, "Don't worry, Mr Harred, there's another way out."

"OK," called Mark. "Come back at half past six. We'll all be gone and then you can lock up."

The janitor hesitated, weighing up the risks of leaving his jurisdiction in the hands of these irresponsible academics even for an hour. "I'll be back at six and expect everyone to be winding things down."

"Very well," said Mark.

The janitor shrugged, drained his glass and walked off to his home, the gate lodge to the old house.

Mark turned to the student. "What other way?"

"There's a disused gate down by the old stable block. It's always closed but left unlocked. I've got in through that way at night when the main gate was locked. The stable block is sometimes used as a classroom; we could go down there if you want to continue the party a bit longer." The young man smiled at him mischievously.

An idea began to form in Mark's mind; an idea he considered exquisite in its possibilities, its simplicity and its dash of conspiracy. "Will we be able to drive out that way?"

The student shook his head. "That drive is gone but if you park your cars in Back Lane you can walk to them from the gate. Just turn left out of the main gate and then first left onto Back Lane. It's a bit narrow but the verge is wide enough to park on."

"An excellent plan. We don't want to be locked in or anything." He patted the student on the back and turned to his colleagues. "Right, get your cars and follow me, gentleman. Boys and girls, we reassemble in the stable block. Pack up your belongings and bring them with you. Make sure you have a corkscrew and some crisps in case we get peckish. If any of you have a car, join the convoy." He took the bottles of drink from John and Tony and gave them to Max and Jeremy. "Guard these with your life," he said, and the students grinned.

To Rob Grainger's surprise, this adventure appealed to his imagination and he had no hesitation in following Mark over to the cars. John Knowles thought he might as well go along, as he'd only just arrived and Tony Laycock hadn't been paid for the drinks yet so he was not going anywhere. Mike Brompton hesitated for a moment or two but thought he ought to show solidarity with his colleagues and he felt a sense of responsibility too. They got in their cars and soon Mark Harred led a small motorcade out of the main gate and round to Back Lane. A solitary student, Rory Marnoch, followed in his car. They drove slowly until Mark came to a long-disused and overgrown turnoff with gates set in the wall a hundred yards or so in the distance. They parked their cars on the verge and began walking intrepidly through the wild grass, meadow flowers, thistles and nettles to the gate. The sun had gone in and one or two of them looked up at an ominous dark cloud.

A raindrop fell into Tony Laycock's eye and, before he could finish saying, "It's raining," the heavens opened and that large-dropped rain which drenches almost instantly was pelting down on them.

All of them started running, no longer trying to evade the nettles, the brambles or the thistles and in twenty seconds they reached the gate. Leading the expedition, Mark tried the latch. It didn't move. "Blast, it's locked," he said, trying again without success.

John Knowles looked at it with the eye of a former mechanical engineer then picked up a stone and gave the handle a sharp bang. The bar moved. "Just stuck," he said and pushed the creaking gate open.

They ran through the gate and twenty yards in front of them stood the old stable block and attached carriage shed. It did not look at first glance an attractive venue for anything: paint peeling, or completely gone, windows cracked, some missing, stone sets in the yard pushed up by brambles and other plants and one of the doors hanging off its hinges. But at the end nearest the main house the windows were intact and an attempt had been made to smarten it up with a new coat of paint and a sign reading Stable Block Classroom. The figure of the attentive student, Max, appeared from the door and waved them over. Five men in their thirties were vaguely aware that there were on the threshold of something new, an increasingly rare occurrence for all of them as they slid gently down the hill towards middle age. But foremost in their minds at that moment was the thought that they were soaking wet. They ran over to the open door and entered, taking off their jackets and shaking them, looking down at their grass-stained trousers and muddied shoes and cursing the weather, gradually becoming aware of the amused expressions of the students present. The lecturers' sour expressions were replaced by sheepish smiles.

Then the female students took pity on them and hung up their jackets and Antonia took off John Knowles's tie saying, "Your nice tie, we ought to hang that up too."

"Isn't anyone going to take off my tie?" asked Mark Harred expectantly and, to his satisfaction and the irritation of his colleagues and the male students, Jane stepped forward and did his bidding.

Tony and Rob took off their own ties and the lecturers, without their jackets and ties, the symbols of their status, thought they did not look so different to the male students. Max plugged in a couple of electric fires and the lecturers stood by them and the room was filled with the smell of damp clothes drying.

The classroom was a decent size, thirty feet by twenty, and the space was made roomier by the desks and chairs being stacked up against the wall. The students, led by Max and Antonia, had found some glasses and two large bags of crisps and had put these on the table at which the teacher usually sat. There were also bottles of Perrier and soda water. Bottles of wine of both colours had been opened and the students had helped themselves to drinks. Some of them looked rather flushed, perhaps through the drinks they had already consumed or the anticipation of the shape of things to come.

"This is all rather good. Well done, everybody. Did you bring all your stuff over? By the time this party ends we won't be able to get back into the house," Mark said breezily.

The students smiled and nodded.

Over drinks, the party soon settled into small groups of twos or fours. The boy and girl who had been holding hands at the party were now sitting together, hands joined, talking quietly, their lips occasionally touching. Meanwhile, talkers by profession, the lecturers had little difficulty in conversing about any subject the students had in mind though they tended to guide the conversation towards their own interests. So, Mark, John, Tony and Rob and Mike entertained their more youthful party guests with their own knowledge, experiences, opinions and achievements, not all of them exaggerated. John Knowles, who had been a national serviceman in Aden in the early 1960s, told a vaguely interested group of some of his more hair-raising experiences in the late colony. Rob Grainger gave some of the girls, and one boy, insights to the world of politics and recounted his experiences meeting Harold Wilson and other prominent politicians. Tony Laycock listened patiently to the career ambitions of Max and one of the girls. Mike Brompton kept a watchful eye on everybody, prepared to deal with any delicate or indelicate situations while engaging in small talk with one of his students. Only Mark concentrated all his time with one girl, the rather bemused Jane whom Mark assured was getting prettier every day and that he would soon find her irresistible, such had been the extent to which she had swept him off his feet. Previously attracted to Mark but thinking she had made little impression on him, she now found herself adoring him.

Though the party had been initiated by the school and then led by the lecturers, as it went on the students were beginning to feel more relaxed and less inhibited by the status of their teachers. Without making a conscious decision, they were treating it more as a social gathering of equals. John Knowles was the first to notice it when his listeners were less reverential in their reaction to his stories as a soldier in Aden.

"Although it was not great for you that served there, I have to ask why we were there in the first place; it was their country and they saw the British as an occupying force," said Rory Marnoch, a shortish young man with a rather pugnacious expression.

"Yes, Aden was just a useful port for protecting British shipping. We didn't care about the place and you can tell that because it's gone communist now," added one of the girls, Fiona.

John Knowles smiled, slightly uncomfortably, not used to students being so forthright in challenging his view. "It was part of Britain's role as an imperial power to keep the high seas free from privateers and pirates so that trade can go on and innocent people are not captured and press-ganged or held for ransom. That role has come to an end now but we left the place better than we found it," he answered defiantly.

"All depends what you mean by better," said Rory. "Conquering a country and destroying its culture to supplant it with your own doesn't seem to make it better to me."

"That assumes the original culture enabled the inhabitants to thrive and progress more than the subsequent one, which might not be always be so," said John. He smiled, more confident now that he was getting into his stride. "The Ancient Egyptians were undoubtedly civilised but eventually were conquered by the Greeks and the Greek civilisation was one of the greatest ever known but the Roman Empire eventually conquered Greece. Whether the supplanting culture was better for original inhabitants is a matter for debate. The Romans conquered half the known world but most of what they built ended in ruins. For the Romano-British, the invasion of the Saxons probably seemed a backward step but ultimately the civilisations fused so it's an argument that now gets us nowhere. When the British Empire, already pretty well finished, has faded from living memory and joins the dustbin of history, it will cease to be something anybody goes on about. How often do you hear people moan about what the Romans got up to in Britain or someone telling a Norwegian he should be ashamed that his Viking ancestors came over to England, pillaged the place and crunched a few heads in? The Turks conquered most of Southeastern Europe and held onto it for hundreds of years, repressing much of the native culture but I can't remember the last time I heard someone complain about that, even though I don't suppose the Greeks or Bulgarians thought it was particularly great."

"You're not saying that you agree with all those things?" asked Fiona.

"Of course not. I'm just pointing out that throughout history it has gone on but the further back you go and the less directly relevant it is to us, the less we relate to the event, however dreadful it was."

Fiona nodded. "You know a lot about history. Is it your subject?"

"No, I'm an engineer by profession who moved into organisation and methods and then management and that's what I teach now. History is an interest. Let's have another drink, shall we?"

Fiona smiled at him and accompanied him over to the drinks table. John poured the drinks, more in his glass than hers, conscious of her tender age. They raised their glasses to each other and the thought flashed through his mind that she was technically young enough to be his daughter, a consideration instantly dismissed on the grounds that any interest in her looks were purely aesthetic. He did like the way her shortish mid-brown hair was straight on the crown but then fuller and curlier at the edges. She was wearing a plain dark-blue midi dress with a scoop neck and matching shoes. The combination of youth and elegance he found quite charming.

"It's a shame you don't teach at the school. I'm sure you are very interesting and informative in your classes," Fiona said, breaking the silence.

John smiled. He liked the flattery but wondered if it was mere politeness from a young woman to her senior. He would not put it to the test; better to let the conversation peter out when they both thought it right. But he enjoyed this brief practice in the art of pre-courtship and he turned the conversation to Fiona. "Where do you live when not boarding here?"

"My family lives in Derbyshire, not far from Bakewell. I am staying with a family friend tonight; she lives locally."

While John was enjoying the company of Fiona, Rob Grainger was engaged in a more serious conversation with Suzy Plunkett and James Newton.

"Mr Southwark told us you are a prospective parliamentary candidate, Mr Grainger," said James.

"Well, that hasn't been confirmed yet. The current MP has three years to his retirement at the next election but, yes, I am hoping to be adopted in due course." Rob was slightly annoyed that Roger had informed his students, it being rather premature. Having witnessed many a promising career in politics come unstuck at the first fence, he was guided by the proverb, 'Many a slip twixt cup and lip'.

"For the Labour Party?" asked Suzy.

"Yes, how did you guess?" asked Rob.

"You don't look like a Tory and if you were a Liberal, Mr Southwark probably wouldn't have bothered to mention it as you'd be a no-hoper."

Rob smiled at Suzy's succinct statement of the realities of politics. "I suppose you are both very interested in politics," he replied.

"Suzy is. She's a right Rosa Luxemburg," said James.

Rob laughed and was impressed that James knew of Rosa Luxemburg. He looked at Suzy. She had a deadly serious expression and he realised he should have guessed from her clothes that she expected one's dress to reflect their political viewpoint. Suzy was wearing a boilersuit and a white tee-shirt peeking out at the neck, with Doc Marten boots. Her dark hair was short and the cut slightly on the brutal side. He would describe it as a worked at 'I'm too serious to be bothered with what I wear' look. However, past the image he could see she was quite pretty and she had youth on her side.

"You know where I stand on the political spectrum but where do you sit in the Labour Party?" she asked, a little threateningly.

"On the left wing," replied Rob, an answer subject to adjustment, depending on what he gauged the questioner's own position to be.

"Insofar as there is a left wing in the Labour Party," snorted Suzy.

"Left wing is relative so even the Conservatives and even Fascist parties must have a left wing of sorts," said James, triumphantly.

Suzy merely snorted again. "Yes, but that's meaningless when you get to the very right wing because even the least extreme would be beyond the pale. The Tories aren't much better."

"What about people like my grandfather," said James. "He's very rich, had his own business and would never vote anything but Conservative but he's generous to a fault, supports loads of charities and was in the army in both world wars, absolutely hating the Nazis: how can you lump him in with them?"

"His type still exploits the working class and holds back women from equality. They still use force to suppress the poor, just more subtly," said Suzy, rolling a cigarette and lighting it with a Zippo lighter.

"What to do you think, Mr Grainger?" asked James, feeling he was unable to do justice to his beloved grandfather's reputation.

"I think the whole spectrum of right and left is treated too simplistically these days. In the past it generally meant reactionary versus progressive; the right wanted to keep things as they were or even looked back to the past and the left wanted to change things, presumably for the better. But in this century, we use the term right in both the old sense of Conservatism and also to describe people who have quite radical ideas but not necessarily agreeing with the views of the left or even with Conservatives."

James nodded, thinking he couldn't have put it better himself.

Suzy frowned, wondering if Rob was an apologist for James's grandfather and the like. She wanted to respond but Rob was now in full flight.

"One could make a case for describing both Nazism and Fascism as not being right wing in policies at all. After all, Nazism is short for what?"

"National Socialism," said James.

"Precisely," said Rob, taking out a cigarette of his own and lighting it. "If you look at Nazi policies, they are certainly not Conservative. Hitler had no truck with the Germany of the Kaiser. He wanted a new *Reich*, in which everything was subject to the state: the army, workers, big business, all directed by the will of the people in the form of the Führer. Hitler liked to use traditional German archetypes of male strength and women as mothers as part of the myth he wished to create but he was not Conservative. As far as its policies went, Nazism was a dictatorship more of the centre than the right."

Satisfied that his grandfather's honour had been protected, James went off to get another drink and talk to Rory Marnoch, who had been abandoned by John Knowles and Fiona.

Suzy was still frowning. "But the centre can't be as brutal and dictatorial as Nazism."

"We must separate beliefs from methods. Karl Polanyi argued that the principles of freedom and democracy are incompatible with the modern complex society. He said the liberals deny the reality of society and live with the illusion of freedom, the fascists accept the reality and are willing to abandon the concept of freedom."

"What about socialism?"

"Socialism believes in a planned, controlled economy and does not allow freedom to prevent that. The difficulty is that socialism cannot always win the hearts and minds of the whole people and then it can sometimes have to resort to similar methods as those of the fascists but the motives are always good. Once the people are at one with the new economic system and work for the greater good of all, the state will no longer have to direct and control society. The people will be free to live in harmony."

"You believe in *Clause IV*?"

"Absolutely and literally. It is the only way for socialism to beat the capitalist system."

Suzy smiled and nodded. She thought he was quite good, better than Mr Southwark with his wishy-washy, vaguely liberal views.

Rob offered to get her another drink and she gladly accepted. She watched him walk over to the bar and thought how pleased she was to meet him. At last, someone who understood the truth as she did; that fascism suppressed freedom to uphold a state-run oppressive capitalism while state socialism was on the side of the working classes and the ordinary people and any controls were for the greater good. Of course, there were bad people in any system and some evils were perpetrated but the system itself was good. Rob understood that. She watched him pour the drinks and thought he was quite good-looking: pleasant features, thick hair and a fine beard, and with the glasses she reminded him a little of Trotsky, only more attractive. She had never heard of Polanyi but she would not admit to that. She would look him up at the library when she had the opportunity.

Rob came back with the refreshed drinks and saw that the frown had disappeared and Suzy was smiling at him. She looked younger, he thought, but not too young. She was quite a bright girl and serious too, someone who could comprehend what he was talking about when discussing politics and she hadn't switched off as so many people did when he explained political theories. Of course, he didn't believe that people like Brezhnev and Honecker were paragons of virtue and the thought of living under communism filled him with loathing. But it was not good to crush the ideals of youth while the flame burnt so brightly in her. She would learn the need for compromise in due course. He thought again about Brezhnev and Honecker and, much to his horror, he suddenly remembered the famous photograph of Brezhnev and Honecker greeting each other with a full mouth-on-mouth kiss and shuddered.

"Well, cheers, Suzy," he said, raising his glass.

"Cheers," she said. "Thanks for your analysis of left and right in politics. I realise my understanding was a bit simplistic."

"The media and the political parties are to blame; they use labels without ever bothering to explain them properly."

"Still, I wish I'd had you as a teacher to explain it for me before."

Rob smiled benevolently. "Do you study politics here?"

"Not exactly. British constitution with Mr Southwark."

"Ah. It wouldn't really be in the syllabus of British constitution. Mr Southwark couldn't be expected to cover it."

Suzy said nothing but nodded.

"Still, it gave us the chance to talk about it, which I've enjoyed very much."

Suzy's expression was brighter again. "Me too," she said. "Would you like a roll-up?"

Rob's mind went back momentarily to his student days, which had ended only fourteen years before but seemed such a time of innocence now. "Yes, thank you," he said.

Suzy rolled two cigarettes expertly and put them in her mouth, lighting them both before handing one to Rob.

"Thanks," said Rob, "Very *Now, Voyager.*"

"Pardon?"

"Nothing, just an old film in which cigarettes play a symbolic part."

Suzy looked puzzled but merely smiled. "I suppose the party will have to finish soon."

Rob looked at his watch. "Not seven yet and there are plenty of drinks left. Are you in a hurry to go?"

"No. I'm staying with friends. How about you?"

"Normally I go back to my constituency at the weekend but nothing happens in the Easter recess. I probably shan't go."

"Where is your constituency?"

"Staffordshire, East Staffordshire."

"Oh, that's not far from where my family lives, Bosworth."

Rob nodded. He thought that if he did go back to the constituency, he could give Suzy a lift but he didn't say anything. "Well, let's have another drink, shall we?" he said, picking up her glass. "What would you like?"

"Could I have some red wine, please? Not the port, it gives me a headache."

Rob went over to the drinks table and poured them both a drink. He looked round the room. Apart from the young couple, who seemed to have disappeared, everybody else was still there. Mark Harred was now sitting down with Jane, who appeared to be captivated by his every word, her hand resting on one of his knees as she stared into his eyes. Rob thought he could hazard a guess as to where that relationship was going. A relaxed Max, no longer burdened by the duties of party organiser, was chatting to a pretty girl whose name Rob didn't know; John Knowles was recounting a story which Fiona found very amusing and, much to Rob's surprise, Tony Laycock, of all people, continued to be enjoying the company of the beautiful Antonia. He was laughing and telling her a story of some sort and she appeared to be having a great time. Mike Brompton was leaning against the wall, chatting to one of the girls and Jeremy. Only Murdoch and James were having a private conversation, standing in the corner of the room, their backs to everyone else.

Tony was as astounded as Rob that he had not yet bored Antonia silly. From that moment when she had removed his tie and undone his top button, he had been enraptured by this young woman. Usually, not that there was anything usual in her approach to him, he would find himself tongue-tied, even speechless, in the presence of a young, beautiful woman. Yet the unknotting of his tie had somehow unlocked his self-consciousness and banished his sense of inadequacy and he found the conversation flowed. He had one great advantage in any discussion in that he rarely spoke about himself. Consequently, people found that he was more interested in them than himself, a quality they found quite charming, even though they weren't interested in prolonging a conversation with him. Having spent some time listening to the career aspirations of some of the students, particularly Antonia, he did not feel uncomfortable when invited to talk about himself, and the wealth of personal reminiscences, rarely revealed over the past few years poured forth with freshness and a newly found fluency. That would have been enough for him, but the fact that Antonia seemed to enjoy his stories, he would put it no stronger than 'seemed', was an added and unexpected bonus.

Mike Brompton was soon wondering why he had not left the party when it moved to the stable block. He had been talking to a couple of his students when the big move was decided and they had clearly expected to continue the discussion after the move. It had seemed churlish not even to stay for a few minutes more and he did have that sense of responsibility of his. But now he was feeling cornered by Ursula. She was undoubtedly very striking: pretty with a full figure, Pre-Raphaelite red hair and a self-confident forwardness which belied her youth. But it was these very positive qualities that made him feel slightly overwhelmed and defensive when he liked to be in command of any given situation. She now had him to herself and embarked on a tour de force of charm, witty humour and erudite storytelling, within a wrap of coquettishness, that left him both entranced and alarmed with hardly the chance to put a word in edgeways. Unwilling to be rude and seek escape in an abrupt departure, he quietly surrendered to what was not an entirely unwelcome defeat and let himself be wafted into her web of light-hearted entrapment while he listened, drank and occasionally refilled their glasses, interjecting the odd comment of approval, agreement or even flattery. Though he had no intention of engaging in any flirtation or seduction of any kind, he soon acknowledged to himself that if he did have ideas of that sort, she would be the ideal target. He even allowed himself the odd imagined scenario while in silent contemplation of her performance.

As the evening wore on, several half-attempts were made to leave by one person then another but for some reason they never managed to go. There would be one more story to tell, one more drink to take, one more farewell to make. The party had its own volition and it would end in its own time. The next day, few who had been at the party could remember when or how it did end.

VII

DAY ONE

THE MAN WOKE. THE FIRST SENSATION WAS THE smell: a musty, unpleasant odour surrounding him and invading his nose. The second sensation was the pounding headache which forced him to close his eyes and made him feel sick. The third sensation was a numbness in his arm, an arm he couldn't move that seemed to be stuck in the air. He forced himself to open his eyes and look above his head to the arm, hanging from a rail of the bedhead and which he found unresponsive to his attempts to move it. The fourth sensation was of a disorientation, a fear that nothing was right and he did not know where he was. He looked down at his body: he was lying on a bed and he was naked, except for his underpants, his watch and his socks. The bed had no sheets, just old, damp-smelling, rough, brown blankets, and he was not alone on the bed. A young woman lay at the far edge of the bed, in a foetal position, also with one arm fixed to the railings, her back to him. She too, was wearing only her pants and socks. The sensation of disorientation gave way to a realisation that he had no idea of what was going on; he was trapped and he was afraid. Briefly, he convinced himself that this was one of those dreams when you eventually realise it is a dream and then awake. This thought was fleeting and he was now trying to make some sense of his predicament.

He looked again at the young woman for a few moments, her back spotless except for a bruise near her right shoulder. Then he felt insecure and tried to cover his body a bit with the smelly, repulsive blanket. He looked up at his arm on the railing: he was handcuffed to the bed and, although the arrangement was tight, he could slowly slide his arm down. There followed the return of feeling in the arm, welcome but excruciating at the same time. He looked round the room, taking in its features. It was a plain space with tongue-and-groove clad walls varnished long ago and now dull. Apart from the bed, there was an old wardrobe, a chest of drawers and a washbasin built into a small cupboard. The floor was also wooden with an ancient, patterned rug visible when he sat up, slowly to avoid waking the girl, an experience he was not yet prepared for. He guessed he was in an upstairs room, but where? Then he remembered the stable block from the previous evening. Perhaps this was a staff bedroom in the stable block. But he didn't know for sure; he didn't know anything for sure, except that he was tied to this bed and he was extremely uncomfortable, both with his situation and on what he was lying.

The man eased himself up slowly and was able to swing his legs round until he sat up on the edge of the bed. There were two issues: one paramount, the other urgent. The paramount one was the need to free himself, the urgent how to relieve himself. The first would require time to work out, the second offered no immediate, decorous options. His feet could touch the floor and, with his handcuffed left hand at full stretch, he could just about stand completely upright. As he stretched with his right foot to assess the limit of his reach, his left foot swung back a little and he kicked something hard just under the bed. He reached down with his free, left hand and felt a round object and smiled grimly. What followed was neither elegant nor straightforward but it achieved his objective and, thankfully, without waking the girl. He lay back on the bed and tried to remember the last time it had been before it was like this; yesterday was already rather fuzzy. He looked at his watch: it had stopped at two-thirty. The sun was out and quite high in the sky but he couldn't remember which way the stable block faced. His head hurt too much to think and he was thirsty. He wound his watch: at least he could measure the passage of time.

The young woman stirred a little and rolled over onto her back. He knew her; she had been at the party and they had spoken together for some time. He liked her and her company. He could not help looking at her semi-nakedness, her beauty, and wondered if they had been intimate in some way. He half-hoped so but then felt vaguely guilty; if he could not remember, how could it have been appropriate? He carefully took a piece of blanket, lay it over her and waited.

While lying there, he tried to assess the situation. He looked over at the basin. If the water supply was connected and he could reach the tap, they could have water to drink and you can survive on water alone for days while they waited to be released or he found a way out. He chided himself for such melodramatic thoughts because they were sure to be out before long. He heard the student groan in her sleep. He looked round at her, bringing the blanket back over his legs and, as he did so, she opened her eyes.

She stared for perhaps two seconds and then she cried a sound of anguish before her hand went to her mouth and she looked up at her other cuffed hand.

"What have you done to me?" she cried out, glancing at her lack of clothes and again at her tied hand, which she tried, without success, to free. Because her wrist was smaller than his, the handcuff slid more easily down the rail and she endured the return of feeling in her arm. She looked away from him, muttered a plea for help from nowhere specific and began sobbing.

"I haven't done anything, I promise you. As you can see, I am as much a prisoner as you are." He surprised himself with his calmness but it would do no good to lose control.

She looked round at him as he pointed to his cuffed hand. "Oh God," she cried. "How do I know this is not some elaborate plan that you are part of?"

He had anticipated the horror in her eyes and the cry of despair but not anything as complicated as this suggestion. "I assure you I have no memory of what could have happened last night to put us in this position and I only woke up about half an hour ago. I certainly wouldn't put myself through this to get some sort of advantage over you."

"Why would anyone do this to us?" she pleaded, rattling the bed as she again tried to free herself.

"I don't understand. I suppose we all had quite a lot to drink at the party and someone thought it was a good idea to play some sort of prank on us. They'll probably be along soon to free us."

"What sort of person would play such a disgusting trick on anyone?" She inwardly shuddered at the thought of some sweaty-handed man of any age undressing her while she was helpless. Though his protestations of innocence had a ring of logic about them, how could she ever be sure it was the truth? "I'll kill them for this," she vowed, then added prosaically as she saw his watch, "what time is it?"

"I don't know. My watch stopped. I wound it up again but I have no idea of the correct time." He thought how pathetic the average modern man was; only able to tell that there was daylight, which any bird could do just as well, while an average Ancient Babylonian would have been able to be much more precise. His watch showed three o'clock now.

The girl didn't reply. Her head was splitting and she was very thirsty. She didn't consider herself very precious but everything was not only cruel and nasty; it was so humiliatingly disgusting: the filthy bed, the feeling of being molested and the consequent lack of clothes even to protect her privacy. She was just realising the extent of her inability to do anything that would improve the situation and a fear that rescue might be delayed and this nightmare endure for more than a day. Yet she had stopped sobbing now and was determined to be like her mother who had served as a pilot in the Air Transport Auxiliary during the War and had seen and been involved in great acts of bravery at an age not much older than herself. Her mother's motto was 'Never lose your head, and cry in private'. She was annoyed with herself that she had cried a bit but she wouldn't do it again. She looked around the room and came to the same conclusions as the man. It was a dump, a room long discarded for normal use and this bed was not for the faint-hearted. She looked in vain for a glass of water of any age and colour and saw the basin, even more out of reach than it was for the man. "I could do with a drink of water," she said firmly.

The man nodded. "I've been thinking about that. I can get my feet on the ground but I can't stretch my hand as far as the basin."

"Could we move the bed?" she asked. "If I get off I could…" and she stopped.

He was aware of her dilemma. "It's all right. I don't need to look behind me. I'll pull the bed, if you can get off it. That will help, and if you can push that will help too." He quietly cursed the absence of casters on the bed legs.

As he began to get up, it crossed her mind that he might not have any clothes on but she didn't care, as long as she could get some water. As it happened, he was wearing blue underpants. She threw the scratchy, stinking blanket off herself and managed to turn her shackled hand so that it lay almost flat on the bed. She was able to get on tiptoe on the floor and she said, "Ready," as she put her weight against the filthy mattress. She realised that with each passing moment, every ounce of fastidiousness was slowly being squeezed out of her and wished for the time when none was left. She pressed her body even more firmly against the mattress.

The man pulled at the bed with the one hand he could get on the bedframe. He was aware that the laws of physics were against him with part of his weight actually adding to the drag on his progress and, at first, the bed refused to move. But while he was pulling against his own weight in his attempt to make progress, the young woman's weight and force was all pushing in the same direction and, after a few seconds, they began to move in the direction of the basin. After what seemed an age but was just a few minutes, the man reached the basin edge.

"We're there," he said and reached for the cold-water tap. He turned the tap but nothing happened, not even a gurgle or a sound, nothing. He sighed but tried to convince himself that he had expected this all along so was prepared to use his initiative.

The young woman had come to a halt with her toes against a partly filled chamber pot which had protruded into sight as the bed move over it. She found herself laughing and hoped she wasn't becoming hysterical.

The man was also concerned that she might have cracked but, unlike Euridice in mythology and Lot's wife in Genesis, he resisted the urge to look back at his accomplice. "Are you all right?" he called behind him.

She stopped laughing, remembering her mother's strictures in a crisis. "Yes. I don't know why but I seem to be seeing the funny side of all this. Perhaps it's the sight of two semi-naked people pulling a bed across a room in a futile attempt to obtain some water."

"I wish I thought it were funny," he muttered. He dropped to one knee and grimaced as a piece of grit stuck into his skin. Ignoring the pain, he could see there was an isolator screw on each pipe up to the basin taps. "Do you remember if the water was on downstairs during the party?"

"Yes, the toilets were operating normally."

He nodded. "I could do with a screwdriver."

She was tempted to make a facetious comment but managed to restrain herself.

The strain on his arm and the pain in his knee reasserted themselves and he rose, looking round for anything which might do the job of a screwdriver. "Can you see anything which might be of use?" he asked.

"There's a piece of metal on the floor over by the wall, to your right. It might be too thick."

He looked over at the wall. On the floor was a piece of steel about six inches long and an inch wide. She was right, it might be too thick but there was nothing else. "We'll have to move the bed again."

He began to move the angle of the bed and she followed, carefully avoiding the chamber pot. The pushing and pulling recommenced and this time, more competently, they moved the bed towards the wall and the piece of metal. He picked the metal strip up. It was a piece of steel plate, rusty in places, presumably an offcut from a previous job in the stables.

"Back we go," he said, giving the young woman time to turn round before he turned. This time the progress was faster as all his weight was now pushing, the girl pulling as best she could. When they had returned to the basin, he tried the piece of metal on the head of the isolator screw of the cold-water tap. It was too thick for the groove so he began to widen it by laboriously filing at the indentation.

"What are you doing?" she asked.

"Trying to widen the groove of the screw so I can get some purchase on it, otherwise the screw won't turn."

She sat on the bed. Her head was still pounding, she was so thirsty and now she realised she needed to go to the toilet, a prospect that made her inwardly quake but had to be addressed.

"I need a pee," she said eventually.

He stopped filing. "I'm sorry," he said, aware of the difficulty but unable to find an acceptable solution.

She looked at the chamber pot and felt the tears drop from her eyes.

"I'm sorry," he said again. "I'll empty it." He silently cursed himself for not doing it before as it was so far from where he was now.

"Don't bother. You are too far away. We'll do it later."

"I won't look." He resumed his filing and began whistling something.

She accepted the inevitable and somehow managed, to the accompaniment of the filing and the whistling. When she had finished, she sat on the bed and the whistling stopped. She watched him filing away, every minute or so trying the groove and she felt a certain warmth towards him. He was trying and he wasn't complaining and it helped her not to complain either.

Finally, after a quarter of an hour or twenty minutes, he stopped and the end of the piece of metal squeezed into the groove on the screw and he tried to turn it. Nothing happened and he restrained the urge to curse. He tried again, holding the metal strip so tightly he felt it cut into his hand, and again nothing.

"Any luck?" she asked encouragingly but doubtful.

"Not yet. It will come, I'm sure." He hit the screw head a couple of times with the piece of metal, hoping that something might give and then he tried again. This time there was a tiny fraction of movement and then a bit more. He straightened up and prayed under his breath to nobody in particular then he turned the tap. After a belch and a splutter some brownish water shot out of the tap and, after a few seconds, the water began running clearly.

"Oh, well done," she said.

He turned the water off for a moment, suddenly and irrationally worried about using up this precious supply. Looking round for something to drink from, he saw the chest of drawers on the opposite wall. "Shall we see if there any cups in the chest of drawers?" he said.

"Yes," she said and turned towards the chest, pulling the bed but aware that she was being propelled by the man. She opened the first drawer with difficulty, using the one free hand and found nothing. The second drawer contained some horse blinkers and bits of leather which she, not being a horsewoman, could not identify. The bottom drawer, deeper than the other two, contained a water jug and four glasses, some old magazines and a torch.

"Glasses," she said triumphantly and took out two and the jug. "God, it's tiring, humping this great bed around," she said as she turned round for the return journey, forgetting her state of undress but pleased that he had not and already had his back to her.

He ran the water for a couple of minutes and rinsed out the dusty but not dirty glasses and jug and then poured them both a full glass of water.

They sat on the bed, covering themselves with blankets, and drank the water. It tasted slightly odd but they didn't care; they chose not to care and took a second glass before their thirsts were quenched. He didn't say anything but noticed the water still had the odd taste.

Their immediate needs satisfied, they turned to their situation. Both were aware their wrists, the ones that were handcuffed, were very sore from the straining and the stretching but neither mentioned it. They did not want to dwell on that in the face of the bigger picture.

"At least we won't die of thirst," she said.

He smiled. "We are not going to die. Someone will rescue us."

"If they know we are here."

"The ones who put us here know."

"But what if they don't come?"

"We'll find a way," he said firmly.

"Do you remember coming here?" she asked.

He shook his head. "I remember the party, the conversation with you and other people, the drinks but not leaving the party. What about you?"

"No. It's the same for me. I did have more to drink than I'm used to but surely not enough to blackout."

"I didn't have a lot; I don't remember feeling drunk. But…" He paused.

"What?"

"Just a vague memory of going to bed feeling very dizzy, or was it a dream? I just don't know."

"Do you think anything happened?"

"How do you mean?"

"Us, on this bed."

"I think we would have remembered as it is not that easy being handcuffed apart."

"I mean before they did this to us."

"I would not take advantage of you or anyone."

She smiled sadly. "But if you were drugged in some way, you might behave differently."

"I believe that even under hypnosis, we cannot be forced to do something we would not normally do with our free will. I would not force myself on anyone under any circumstances."

"I'm sorry to have raised it but you understand?"

"Of course. But I am sure nothing happened between us, rest assured."

She smiled but knew she would never totally rest assured. She opted for an acceptable alternative: if she didn't know, she would believe nothing happened.

They left the bed where it was, near the water, and rested for a while, not sharing their thoughts with each other. Then the man took the piece of steel and began to file the handcuff on his wrist.

She watched him with appreciation for his positivity.

After ten minutes, he took the steel away from the handcuff. The steel had worn away a little; the handcuff was barely marked. "The handcuff is made of sterner stuff than this," he muttered.

"No use then?"

"We'll get through it eventually. If water can wear down a stone, we'll do this."

She smiled. It went through her mind they didn't have the time that water requires to wear down a stone. She wanted to say she was hungry but did not want to add further to his worries. She watched the muscles in his arm flex and relax as he patiently worked on his handcuff and admired his tenacity. As she watched him, she thought that for a man who was nearly middle-aged, probably well into his thirties, his body looked quite good: not exactly rippling with muscles but not bad.

After another five minutes or so, he stopped filing. "It's no good, I'll have to find something else."

She smiled encouragingly. "You have done so well already. How did you become so good at finding tools out of bits of old metal?"

"My dad is a carpenter. When I was a kid, I used to marvel that he had a tool for everything but if he was stuck, he'd find a way with any problem. Could do with him now." He smiled.

"Perhaps there might be something useful in the wardrobe," she said.

"Good idea."

Once more they moved the bed, more efficiently than previously and soon he was unlocking the key in the wardrobe. He prepared himself for it being empty. Their story was not to be like that of *Robinson Crusoe*, flotsam bringing ashore useful tools and other items to make life easier. As he opened the doors, he was not surprised, therefore, that it was empty; at least empty of clothes. On the floor there was a pair of wellington boots, size to be determined. On the shelf at the top of the wardrobe there was an old suitcase. He pulled it down hopefully but it was light and when he shook it the only noise was the squeak of the handle as it swung to and fro. He resisted the temptation to throw it but placed it back on the shelf. Apart from the old case there was only a couple of folded sheets, once white but now yellowing. He pulled them out and smelled them. They smelled of mustiness but he thought they might be better than the blankets and certainly less chaffing.

"No tools," he said, "Sorry."

She wanted to cry but couldn't, mustn't. "We shall have to wait," she said, turning her sad expression away.

They left the bed where it was, in the middle of the room.

"You must be hungry," he said.

"Not really. I tend to lose my appetite when I get a bit worried." She smiled. "I am only a little worried. What I really need is a smoke."

He smiled and nodded. He felt the same; a cigarette to calm the nerves, or to help him think or to give some little pleasure: all these things. He sat on the bed and looked up at the top of the rails where they joined the cross rail. With his free hand he pushed at the cross rail but it didn't move. The handcuff lay on the bottom horizontal rail so it wasn't going anywhere. He said nothing but wondered to himself what options were left.

"Anyway," she said brightly, "the body will adapt if we can't eat; it will slow down the metabolism and tell the body it doesn't need food, at least for a while. That's why people who go on crash starvation diets don't lose weight as quickly as they want to."

He smiled. "We can last for days on water. They'll be back by today or tomorrow."

He opened the first sheet. "It's a bit smelly but softer than those blankets. I'll air it and it will not be too bad."

They pushed the bed towards the large casement window and, much to his surprise, it opened without difficulty. He hung the sheet out in the sun. "We'll do the other one later," he said.

She nodded encouragingly.

He sat on the bed, aware that he was no longer self-conscious about his semi-nakedness. He lay back, his hands acting as a pillow. The day was much warmer now and he felt more positive that all would be well. He decided that, as long as they were released today, he wouldn't insist that the students, presuming it was students, were punished for their juvenile prank. After all, it had been a great party and lots of bounds had been, if not crossed, certainly stretched a little. One day, he would look back on this episode as an adventure.

She wanted to lie back too but wasn't sure how that might be interpreted. She remained sitting upright.

"Would you like something to read?" he asked. "There are some old magazines in the cupboard."

"What sort of magazines?" she asked.

"*Horse & Hound, Country Life*, that kind of thing."

"No thanks, not my cup of tea. God, I'd love a cup of tea."

They were both silent for a while then the young woman said, "I need to talk to you about something."

"Oh, what's that?"

"I think I may have to go to the lavatory soon, not a pee, and I just don't know how it can be managed. It's all so humiliating and disgusting. Why couldn't they have thought how vile it would be before they played this cruel joke?" She started crying and buried her face into the mattress.

He looked over at her heaving shoulders and wanted to reassure her but did not know how. He wanted to touch her but was that too intimate? But she was right; this was a terrible trick to play on anyone. "Please try not to be upset. I'll sort something out," he said, deciding he could touch her shoulder with a firm grip.

She stopped crying and he felt moved that she had faith in him, even if it was misplaced.

"Look, we have the paper from the magazines and the chamber pot and the basin. It will work and I won't think any the less of you for having to deal with this. In fact, I will be proud of you because you will have triumphed over a fear of embarrassment and shame by exposing them as mere facades. Perfectly natural human functions are nothing to be ashamed of and, in an emergency, we must be permitted to set aside some of the normal conventions. We shall arrange matters so that you will feel as comfortable as possible and know that your dignity and my respect for you will be unchanged. No, it will be greater."

She turned half round and held out her hand, which he held for a moment. Then he sat up and planned what had to be done to spare her discomfort as much as he could. She was grateful and a little ashamed that he cleared away afterwards but he neither commented nor sought her thanks.

Later, she appreciated his solicitude and she willed it that she would not let him down but would keep her head high so that he might admire her fortitude, though she wanted to curl up in a corner and die. However, like most experiences which damage one's pride, it was never as hard to bear again.

The sun began its slow downward curve and the earlier achievements of adapting to life in their strange confinement, though giving a brief lift to their morale, were exposed for what they were: mere moments of comfort which did nothing to improve their overall position nor to bring escape any nearer. Though a plentiful supply of water helped reduce the pangs of hunger, it could not halt a growing desire for some form of sustenance, especially now their hangovers had eased and other pains could push themselves into their consciousnesses. More serious was the failure of the perpetrators to appear. Neither shared their growing sense of alarm, each assuming the other was blissfully unaware of their own concern and not wanting to spoil their optimism.

They tried to keep busy with whatever came to hand, airing the sheets and then making the bed less uncomfortable, if not much cleaner. They read each other articles from twenty-year-old magazines and tried to do the general-knowledge crosswords, though they had no pencil or pen to fill in their answers and the girl was not even born when the events referred to in many of the questions took place. As the afternoon wore on, the man returned to his labour of filing at the handcuff round his wrist with the piece of metal.

She watched him in silence for a time then could not prevent herself blurting out, "No one will come, will they?"

He stopped filing and turned round. "We can't say that. We have to be positive."

"Then why bother to file with that useless piece of bloody tin?" she said. "Stop trying to humour me," she cried out, her eyes filled with tears and her modest piece of blanket thrown to the floor.

"I'm sorry," he said. "It's all I can offer."

The silence resumed, the silence of resignation. But after a minute, he resumed his filing, a thin groove now visible in the thick handcuff on his wrist. Angry with herself for losing her temper, she tried, for the hundredth time, to try to squeeze her small hand through the smaller gap in her cuff and wondered how thin she would need to be for it to slip through. She stared at her hand for a moment and tried to imagine it being crushed so that she might be free. She had read about a man who had cut his foot off to save his life when he was trapped on a mountain so could she not bear a crushed hand that might in any case be reset?

"Penny for your thoughts," she heard the man say.

"You haven't got a penny," she replied, smiling, though she couldn't think why when there was nothing to smile about.

"Actually, I was considering the possibility of my hand being squeezed enough to get out of the handcuff."

"How d'you mean?"

"Well, if you could break it."

"The handcuff; I very much doubt it."

"No, my hand."

"I don't know if it is possible, even if we had some tools. In any case, I couldn't bring myself to do that to you."

She shrugged. "Just an idea."

"If they don't come today, we will be missed and a search

will start. They'll find us; it's not as if we are in the middle of nowhere. This is the last place we were seen so they are bound to start here."

She nodded, comforted a little. "At least it's not cold," she said.

The sun went down and the light began to fade. He tried the light switch and mercifully the central ceiling light flashed into action. It was a dull under-powered bulb and any inclination either had to read one of the old magazines was swiftly expunged. The man set his watch to a time of eight o'clock, which he seemed a good approximate, given the approaching gloom.

"Eight o'clock. Do you think that's about right?" he asked.

"Close enough. We are not going anywhere," she replied. "Are you hungry?"

"A bit. I'm trying not to think about it."

"I suppose we'll end up eating the wellington boots; isn't that what they do in stories of people who are starving?"

He smiled. "The leather would be tastier. "Don't worry, it won't come to that. What shall we do?" He regretted the ludicrous question as soon as he asked it.

"There aren't many things two nearly naked people handcuffed to a bed can do."

He felt himself flush a little. "I meant would you like to talk for a while? You could tell me a little bit more about yourself; your childhood, that kind of thing."

"If you will do the same."

"Of course."

She sat up and took a sip of water. "Well, I was born on the 3rd of September 1957 in Market Bosworth. My parents still live in the same house where I was born. I have a younger sister. My mother doesn't work but she was a prep school teacher. My father is a doctor, a consultant with a private practice. I seem to have been at school forever, since I was four. I loved school when I was little but I fell out of love with it when I got to about twelve." She stopped for a moment. "I suppose it was because prep school seemed to be about doing what you wanted, you were encouraged to develop your interests and explore. Later, it was about choices, giving up some subjects I loved and having to concentrate on examinations in subjects I wasn't particularly interested in and always discipline: do this – don't do that. At least at this school we have a bit more freedom."

"What about sports and interests?"

"I liked athletics at school: high jump, long jump, running. I don't do it now. I like art, I draw a bit and I like reading, especially history, politics and literature. I'm boring, I suppose. I've not lived long enough to have done anything interesting."

"Most people don't do anything that most people would find interesting."

"I expect you have."

"Why do you say that?"

"You are a lecturer so you have been to university and have a good degree."

"Polytechnic, and I got a third, actually."

She smiled, admiring his honesty. "You were young in the 'Swinging Sixties' so you probably had a great time."

"It sounds like you think my best years are behind me," he said, laughing.

"Not really, but they were great times."

He nodded. "They were, I guess, but not for everyone, not for the less well-off. I believed then that we would be entering a time of greater economic progress and as the economy grew, more and more services would be paid for by the state so, although tax rates might be higher than some would wish, all the money you did keep would be yours to enjoy. Health, education, travel, social care, decent pensions, etc., all the necessities would be provided by the state and the working day would be shorter too, so people would have more free time to enjoy their lives."

"That might still happen."

"Yes, but I am less confident now. The economy is less stable: inflation, rising unemployment as many traditional jobs start to disappear, more social unrest. There's less sense of a common purpose and of fairness in the system." He laughed. "I'm probably just getting middle-aged and cynical. You must keep your ideals and it's always a great time if you are young. If you can't enjoy your youth, it's a sad thing."

"You are avoiding the subject. Get back to yourself," she said, pulling the sheet and blanket a bit more over her.

He grinned. "I did enjoy my time at school and then at the poly; it helped me know what I wanted to do and enabled me to set a plan for achieving it."

"So, you have always had your heart set on that one goal ever since you were my age?"

"Pretty well, yes."

"I have no idea what I want to do."

"There's no need to rush into a decision. Wait until you go to university and see what opens up. Anyway, people often have several careers in the course of their working life."

"You sound like my careers teacher at school, or my father." She laughed and he did too.

They were both lying on their backs now, feeling oddly relaxed. They had learnt how to put their manacled hands in the least uncomfortable position and their hunger pangs were bearable and only to be expected. Best of all, they had, to a greater or lesser extent, put to one side the feelings of uncomfortableness they felt in their forced intimacy.

"Tell me about your home and family," she said.

"I was born in Chingford, North-East London, a few years before you."

"More than a few," she said.

He laughed. "Yes, more than a few, fourteen in fact. I've got an older sister who is married with two children and a younger brother, also married, but no children yet. My sister works part-time in an estate agent's and my brother is a sales rep. My mother was a secretary at a sweet firm until she had children. My father is a carpenter, as I told you, and works for the railways. He has worked for fifty years for the same division on the railways, the LNER when it was private and the successor part of British Railways when it was nationalised. He will retire next year and get the regulation gold watch."

"Gosh, that's a long time to work in any job."

"People of his generation experienced the high unemployment of the1930s and job security and a pension were their main aims when looking for a job."

"What will he do when he retires?"

"He will keep his free travel so he plans to ride around on the train, with my mum, more than he has ever done while on the railways. They finally went abroad last year, for the first time." He suddenly felt emotional about his father, whom he didn't see that often, and whom he felt sad for and proud of, both at the same time.

The conversation went on for perhaps another hour, each sharing some details of their background but holding back on their own private feelings and judgements on themselves and their families. Neither was quite ready for that yet. Eventually they tired of the exchange of titbits and lay in silence as the darkness deepened and the feeble light above them could not prevent a growing sense of gloom.

"It's strange, isn't it?" said the girl eventually. "I thought it was time to get ready for bed but there is nothing to do, except for a pee, and all that involves. I feel so dirty or unclean, whichever is the worse; I think it's unclean. I don't think I've wished I could have a bath more in my entire life. Turn away for a minute."

He did as he was bidden and she used the pot and emptied it down the basin before rinsing the bowl. She used a glass of water to gargle and swill water round in her mouth as a gesture of oral hygiene before placing the pot on the floor and sending it sliding to his side of the bed. Then she got back into bed and waited for him to do whatever he wanted. They were already developing their own system of ergonomics: the bed within easy reach of the basin and only moved for specific tasks like opening and closing the windows or turning the light on or off.

"We are going to have to move the bed to turn off the light," he said.

"Shall we leave it on? I find it a comfort."

He was about to warn her of the risk of the bulb not being up to a lengthy period of action but thought better of it; she deserved to have her way. He took a magazine back to the bed and offered to read an article on the Hickstead International Horse Show of 1959, an offer which she accepted. Five minutes later she was asleep and he read quietly without much fervour until sleep finally came for him as well.

VIII

DAY TWO

He woke and looked at his watch; it said nearly six o'clock. It was light but the sun had only just risen so he guessed his watch was probably a bit slow, but not enough to worry about. His cuffed wrist hurt but otherwise he felt better than he had done the previous morning, except for the hunger, which was not abated in the least by a gulp of water and the need for a cigarette, which nothing would abate.

The tortuous process of his sitting up and reaching down for the glass on the floor disturbed the girl and she turned over in her sleep as much as she could, her one free arm unconsciously reaching out towards him. He watched her asleep for a minute or two and felt tenderly towards her. He lay back slowly and as quietly as he could while the bedsprings played a chord from a piece of experimental modern music. He rubbed his stomach in the hope of easing the feeling of hunger without success and he idly wondered how many mornings like this he would have to endure before they were rescued.

After some time, perhaps half an hour, she stirred again and opened her eyes, looked at him and closed them. Then she opened her eyes again. "I thought for one second that it was all a dream but we are still here," she said, resignation in her voice.

"You'll be missed by today, surely."

She shook her head. "My parents have gone on holiday over the Easter period and I told them I might see some friends before I came home. Nobody will worry about me. What about you?"

He didn't answer but got up and produced for them a breakfast of a glass of water and they commenced their unusual pattern of behaviour again: the water, the pot, the light switch, the shifting of the bed to complete each task. The girl splashed her face and under her armpits with the cold water and dried herself with a corner of the sheet and the man did the same in solidarity with her attempt to maintain a semblance of freshness.

"I know it won't come to it but how long do you think we can last without food?" she asked calmly as they sat on the bed, drinking a second glass of still odd-tasting water to placate their nagging stomachs.

"Water is the important factor. Without that, we would dehydrate quickly and the kidneys would shut down. We'd last no more than three or four days. But with water you can keep going a long time. Mahatma Gandhi fasted for twenty-one days and survived and he was very thin so had hardly any reserves. At first, the body will use up our reserves of glucose and so on and, after a few days, when food is not forthcoming, it will adjust our metabolism to eke out our reserves. We'll be fine, especially if we don't do any physically demanding things."

"How do you know all this?"

"I recently read an article about it, can't remember where, probably in *National Geographic* or *New Scientist*, one of those they have in the college library. I didn't think it would ever come in useful."

"Well, you've cheered me up a bit, even if it will be hell waiting to be rescued. Perhaps you had better not exert yourself trying to file through the handcuff."

He smiled. He didn't tell her he had already given up on that plan. The piece of metal would wear away long before the handcuff would be open.

When they were not talking, the girl was aware of the silence that pervaded their room. She had noticed it yesterday but now it seemed worse, more absolute, more oppressive. She was scared she might scream to break the silence, this deafening silence. But then she heard the village church bells ringing, calling the parishioners to Sunday service. She hadn't been to church for a long time but now she wished she could respond to this *Summoned by Bells*, as John Betjeman had put it.

"Can we open the window?" she asked.

"Of course."

They push-pulled the bed the few feet to enable her to fling open the window and she felt an unexpected joy as the muffled sound was replaced by the peal of the bells in their full glory as the bell ringers went through their rounds.

"Aren't they lovely?" she said.

"What?"

"The church bells." She got as close as she could to the window and it was as if she breathed in the sound of the bells. Then a robin alighted on the gates opposite and sang for a few moments before flying off and she felt a smile on her face.

"Yes, they are all right."

"I haven't been to church for years, not since I was confirmed."

He laughed.

"What's funny?"

"It just reminded me of that old joke. One vicar says to another vicar, 'I have a terrible problem with mice in the church; I've tried everything but nothing gets rid of them.' The other vicar says, 'I had the same problem so I confirmed them and they've never been near the church since.'"

She laughed too and her mood improved a little more.

He liked seeing her more relaxed; he regarded it as his responsibility to hold things together until the release came and that she was bearing up well gave him one less thing to worry about. He had been thinking about her parents being on holiday and her being unlikely to be missed over the next two weeks and whether they would be found before their nerve failed them. He looked at her staring out of the window and thought how well she had managed so far and that he was proud of her. All they had to do was survive for two weeks at most. The school would reopen and surely they would be able to raise the alarm if nothing else. But what of tomorrow and the next day and the next ten days, when the fear and the hunger gnawed away at them? Would one or both of them crack? He would have to find another way to free them, just in case no help came in time. But the realities of their situation provided no insights; he would have to apply his imagination, which he felt was not his forte.

Lying there, he had an idea. Not the handcuff, the railing. Pleased with himself, he took the piece of metal and began trying to cut through the brass rail. The metal made an impact but it was slow and still it made little progress; was the rail definitely brass? Even if it was, he had no idea what its strength would be. After a while, he realised the piece of metal was just too soft even for this. He stopped trying and wanted to throw it at the wall but the girl was watching.

"It takes time," he said. "I'll have another go later."

She smiled in return and went back to listening to the bells and looking out at the garden. The robin had moved on but a couple of blackbirds were having a look round the area near the gate, a quick scurry then a stop in that particular way blackbirds move. After a few minutes, with nothing worth their while, they disappeared into the grounds and onto a bush. She saw a car drive down Back Lane and waved in a half-hearted way to gain the driver's attention, knowing it was futile. The car passed a parked car and she called out to him, "What colour is your car?"

"Pale blue, why?"

"It's still there, in Back Lane."

"Glad to hear it. Not much use at the moment, though," he answered, slightly tetchily.

"Sorry, stupid comment."

"My fault. I didn't mean to be ratty."

He joined her at the window and she smiled at him. "Let's play 'I-spy'. I-spy something beginning with L."

"I haven't played this game for a long time."

"Even longer than it is since I went to church?"

"Definitely. Larch?"

"I'm not good on trees. Is there one out there?"

"I'll take that as a wrong answer."

"You are close."

"Latch?"

"Very good."

They played the game for a while until they were bored but agreed to try to think of games that they could play to fill the boredom and take their minds off their situation. "We must both come up with at least one new game to play each day," he said.

"I think you've just made up a new game of coming up with new games," she said.

IX

DAY THREE

ROGER SOUTHWARK WAS HAVING A LIE-IN ON THE
first Monday of the Easter holiday. He had been in London
at the weekend and met up with some old friends and had
returned rather late the previous evening. He had seen Delia
this weekend, but not Helen, and it would be the opposite
next weekend so neither could become too possessive. He
was planning to do some spring cleaning in his cottage and
preparation for the summer term but this morning he had
turned off the alarm on his bedside clock and had no plan to
get up before nine at least.

The telephone rang and Roger looked over at the clock;
it said ten past nine. He resisted the first three rings then
reluctantly answered it.

"Mr Southwark?"

"Yes."

"Jocelyn Mandeville here. I am so sorry to disturb your
vacation but something rather urgent has cropped up and I
would very much like to have a chat with you. Do you think
we might meet for half an hour over a coffee?"

"Today?"

"If at all possible. At a time of your liking, of course."

"At the school?"

"I'd rather not reopen the school. I thought perhaps somewhere mutually convenient. How about at The Stag? I believe it opens at eleven o'clock and has a private bar."

"Shall we say half past eleven then?" said Roger, reluctant and curious at the same time.

"Splendid. See you then."

Roger took his time getting up, showering and shaving and having breakfast. He dressed last of all and, at twenty-five past eleven he strolled over to The Stag. He walked into the saloon bar, greeted Jack the landlord and turned the battered knob on the door with the title 'Private Bar' in the centre of its stained-glass window. Jocelyn Mandeville was already there, a pot of coffee and two cups in front of him on the round table.

"Good of you to come," said Mandeville, shaking hands. He pointed to a chair and poured them both a cup of coffee.

"I apologise again for interrupting your leave," he said, "but there was a tragic incident after the school party last Friday."

"I have been away for the weekend so I don't know what happened," said Roger.

"Two of the male students were involved in a car accident on Friday night, nowhere near the school, and both of them were seriously injured. They were taken by ambulance to the nearest cottage hospital and once their conditions were stabilised, they were taken to the county hospital. They both suffered head injuries apparently."

"Are they going to be all right?"

"The parents inform me that one of them is in a coma and the other has no memory of any of the events of that day. The hope is that they will pull through, though in what state is another question."

"I'm sorry to hear that."

"Naturally the parents are very upset. Both sets have approached the school for information regarding the party. They are concerned that it might have gone on later into the evening and was unsupervised. Obviously, they are bothered if the events at the party played any part in what happened to their sons afterwards. You will appreciate that I have to ensure that the school is not in any way compromised by what took place or its repercussions."

"I was at the party but left before the end, and everything seemed fine then. Who were the students involved?"

"James Newton and Rory Marnoch."

"I know James, he's in my British constitution class, but not Rory. As I left early, I don't know if I can be much help as to what happened later."

Mandeville nodded and folded his hands in front of him on the table. "I quite understand that but I have had some difficulty identifying and contacting those members of the staff and student bodies who *were* there when the party drew to a close. Any information you do have would be helpful in trying to get to the facts."

Roger thought for a moment. As he had left the party, he had been concentrating on Ann Bland and hadn't really taken much notice of anyone else. "There were Mark Harred, Rob Grainger and Mike Brompton still there when I left but I don't remember seeing any other members of staff. As to the students, there were Antonia Mortimer and Suzy Plunkett, two of my students, James Newton you know about and quite a few others whom I know only by sight or not at all."

"I have spoken to the caretaker and he says two other men he didn't recognise turned up at the end of the party. By this time there were no more than twenty people left there. The two newcomers were known to Mr Harred so they may have been colleagues from the college. It was quite out of order for the caretaker to allow uninvited guests to the party and he has been reprimanded but he was in a difficult situation, challenging members of staff, as it were. The presumptive behaviour of Mr Harred and his friends leaves a lot to be desired and was quite unprofessional. In any event, everyone had left the school by about six-thirty, when the caretaker locked up the premises and the gates. I have been unable to get hold of either Mr Harred or Mr Grainger nor any of the other students named. Consequently, at the moment, I have absolutely no idea what to say to the parents regarding events after six-thirty."

"Surely, if the students are over eighteen, they are adults and not the school's responsibility outside of school hours."

"I agree but the whiff of scandal can penetrate the sweetest smelling of institutions. If we cannot answer questions satisfactorily and there are doubts as to our version of events our reputation is in danger. In any case, I am reluctant to fall back on the Pontius Pilate, not my business, routine. I have a favour to ask of you."

"Oh? What's that?"

Would you mind using your contacts at the college to see if you can get in touch with one or other of the teaching staff who were at the party and find out exactly what happened at the school after you and I left?"

"I wouldn't know where to start," said Roger defensively, thinking all this was well outside his remit as a part-time teacher at the academy.

"But if you could at least determine who was at the party when it came to a conclusion, we might be able to piece together the events of that evening."

"I take it you don't want to involve the police?"

"As far as we know, there has been no crime, just an unfortunate accident, probably the result of a misjudgement by an overconfident but under-competent driver. Even the mention of the police adds a sinister note to the proceedings and implies a crime has been committed and that is of no benefit to anyone. I am only asking you to use your connections at the college to help me get in touch with those staff who might be able to give me the full story of events later in the evening, without rancour or judgement."

Roger still thought the request for help a little unreasonable but was unable to conjure up a reason to decline and reluctantly agreed. "Well, I'll do my best but I can't promise anything. The college virtually shuts down during the Easter break."

Mandeville's face lit up with a smile. "Thank you, Mr Southwark, that is extremely kind of you. You won't mind my saying that the matter is of the utmost urgency."

"Perhaps the boys could shed some light on all this when they are feeling better?"

"Maybe later, but we don't know how long it will be before that is possible."

"Do you know which ward they are in?"

"Yes." He took a piece of paper from his inside pocket. "Howland Ward; I arranged for some flowers to be sent to them. Too early to visit at the moment, I'm sure you'll agree. But later a personal visit from a member of staff would be welcome."

"I'll play that by ear."

"I know I can rely on your discretion."

Roger nodded. Now that he had overcome his unwillingness to be put upon, he could see some interest in the task at hand, especially as the predictably egotistical and salacious Mark Harred was potentially involved and could be guaranteed to have had a hand in the way events panned out.

They finished their coffee and Mandeville made his excuses and left. Roger thought the matter could wait another twenty-four hours and carried on with his own, admittedly limited, plans for the day.

The next morning Roger drove to the college, arriving at about half past ten. As he expected, the staff car park was almost empty. He recognised Dr Frost's car in its reserved place, as was that of the principal and those of several of the senior staff. He left his car in a prominent position where it was sure to be seen and might secure a few brownie points then bounded up the stairs to the general office.

This office had its full complement of staff present and none of them gave him more than a cursory glance, presuming he had popped in for his mail.

"Hello, Maureen," he said to the administrative assistant who acted as Dr Frost's secretary. "Have you got a list of the whereabouts of departmental staff over the Easter break?"

Maureen looked at him as if he had taken leave of his senses. "Well, Mr Southwark, I certainly don't have your whereabouts over the Easter break as you haven't given them to me."

Roger noticed that everybody else in the office was listening with a variety of amused expressions on their faces. He waited for the coup de grace he knew was coming, especially as Maureen had used his formal title.

"It may surprise you to learn that you are not alone. In fact, in all the fifteen years I have been in this job, nobody below the grade of principal lecturer has ever given me a clue as to where they might be during the holidays. The only thing I can be sure of is that we are unlikely to see any of the lecturing staff, except your good self on this occasion, anywhere near the college premises until the Easter break is ended. Was there anyone you had in mind?"

Roger smiled. "On the off chance, Mark Harred?"

This suggestion led to a barely suppressed wave of tittering among the administrative staff.

Maureen smiled. "Mr Harred never comes in the college during the holidays. He has to recharge his batteries."

There were more sniggers from the office staff and Roger smiled himself.

He collected his mail and wandered along to his staff room with the extremely slight hope that there might be somebody around. He opened the door and, to his surprise, saw Gillian Trevis at her desk. She was dressed casually and Roger thought she looked younger than usual.

She looked up. "Hello, Roger. Didn't expect to see anyone else in today."

"Nor me."

She smiled. "I wanted to catch up with some of the magazines and journals while the library is empty. I've been asked to give a talk on rising levels of international debt."

"I know this is a silly question but you don't happen to know where Mark Harred or Rob Grainger or Mike Brompton have gone over the Easter period? I would like to get in touch with them."

She shook her head. "Sorry, I don't. Is it important?"

Roger hesitated for a moment, not sure how private his conversation with Mandeville was supposed to be. "You know the party at Twirleston Academy last Friday? Apparently two of the students were injured in a car crash after the party and the headmaster would like to speak to any of our lecturers who were at the party and might know what happened at the end of the evening."

"You weren't there at the end?"

"No, I left quite early and the only three lecturers who were still there were Mark, Rob and Mike and the headmaster has not been able to get hold of any of them."

"So, unless you can find one of them you are stymied?"

"Probably. According to the school two other lecturers turned up after I'd gone but I don't know who they are."

"What about the other students that were there? Can't the school get in touch with them?"

"Apparently not."

"Perhaps they haven't tried hard enough. Quite intriguing. I'll help you, if you like."

"I don't want to interrupt your reading."

"I'd welcome the distraction." She took a sheet of A4 paper from her desk drawer and drew a line down the middle of the page. "Right, people there when you left, teachers: Rob, Mark, Mike and two additions unknown, X and Y." She wrote the list and turned to the other side of the page. "Students?"

"There was another teacher from the school. I don't know his name but as the caretaker didn't mention him, I guess he'd gone by the time the party broke up. As to the students there were Antonia Mortimer, Suzy Plunkett, James Newton, Rory Marnoch, Max, I don't know his surname, Lisa somebody and another nine students, none of whom I knew."

She wrote down the names he had given and added the letters A to H under the list and Z under the staff list. "If there were about twenty people left at the end, we know there were five lecturers and perhaps twelve students. You've named six."

"Yes, but they may not be the ones who stayed until the end."

"I think we should concentrate on the five lecturers. Why would two men turn up to a school party where they are apparently unknown?"

"They must have been invited by someone at the party."

"By whom?"

"Presumably, Rob, Mike or Mark. It must have been Mark.

Rob isn't even teaching at the school this year and Mike tends just to turn up for his classes and then disappear."

"Mark is at the centre of all of this. Let's go round his house."

Roger was taken aback. "What? We can't just turn up in the holidays."

Gillian laughed. "I know the holidays are treated as sacrosanct but honestly, why does everyone get so precious about them? We are not talking about the average holidays of a typical working person: we get fourteen weeks a year. Surely we can spare the odd hour if it's an important matter."

Roger thought she was right and shrugged. "OK, let's do it," he said.

They looked up Mark's address in the college contact register and drove straight there, a drive of twenty minutes to a nearby small town, Crobbleton. Mark lived on the outskirts in a modern detached house, surrounded at the front by trees.

"Do you think we should both go in?" asked Roger, as they parked.

"I don't know. I could wait in the car, if you prefer."

"Perhaps it would be best. I don't want him to feel investigated."

Roger walked up the crazy-paving path and rang the doorbell.

There was no answer. He tried again. This time he heard footsteps in the hall.

The door was answered by Lorna Harred, Mark's wife, whom Roger had met once at a summer party hosted by Dr Frost. She looked tired and puffy-eyed. "Yes?" she said.

"Hello, Lorna. I'm Roger Southwark, from the college. We met at a garden party at Dr Frost's last summer. You probably don't remember me. I'm sorry to bother you but I wondered if I might have a word with Mark?"

Lorna ignored Roger's polite niceties as her eyes widened. "God, what's he done now? Mark's not here; I haven't seen him since Friday morning. Why do you want to see him?" Her expression was hostile.

"Well, there was a party at Twirleston Academy on Friday afternoon which went on into the evening and Mark was there. After the party broke up, there was a serious car accident and two students were injured. There is nothing to associate Mark with the accident itself but the academy headmaster would like to speak to staff who were present at the party to help find out exactly what happened."

"Wouldn't we all like to know? I'm not quite sure what your role is."

"I was at the party but left before the end. I agreed to help the headmaster try to get a better picture of the sequence of events because I know some of the lecturers who were there. From what you say, Mark is away at the moment?"

"You had better come in."

Roger followed her into the hall and then to the living room. There was a baby grand in the room on which were several family photographs, one lying face down. The room was bright and stylish but not too formal. He sat down on a sofa. "Who plays the piano?" he asked, making small talk in what was already an uncomfortable conversation.

"I do. Or did. Not much time for that now. You asked if Mark is away. I don't know where he is. He was at the party, as you say, but he didn't come home that night."

"Oh, I didn't realise. Have you heard from him?"

"No."

"You must be worried. Did you raise the matter with the police?"

"I am not exactly worried. This is by no means the first time Mark has disappeared for a couple of days, especially where a party is involved. I agree, three days is unusual and I have spoken to the police but they said to give it a little while longer, given the fact that most people turn up within a few days and also because of Mark's wayward tendencies."

"Surprising he hasn't rung you though."

"Yes and no. Mark is above all a coward and tries to avoid awkward conversations."

"Well, I'm sorry to have troubled you. I hope he turns up soon. Let me know if I can be of any help," he said, hoping that she didn't take him at his word.

He rose and she stood up too and saw him to the door. They said goodbye, she coolly and he uncomfortably. He walked thoughtfully back to his car.

"How did you get on?" asked Gillian.

"Mark has disappeared."

"Really?"

"Well, his wife hasn't heard from him since Friday. She did say that he sometimes does go AWOL but not usually for such a long time. She has been to the police but they are not interested, as yet."

"Apparently it's more common than we might think for people to go missing, and most don't want to be found. Still, blimey, I wasn't expecting that. I think he has children."

Roger nodded. "Two, as far as I know."

She shrugged. "So it does seem strange, just walking out on her without a sign he was going."

"It's certainly out of character. He has had a string of overage female students and none of them mattered at all. I can't see him giving up home comforts when he can have the best of both worlds."

She smiled. "We'll see. Where next?"

"Good question. I have tried to ring Rob Grainger a couple of times but he seems to be away. Haven't had any luck with

Mike Brompton either. We don't know who the other two lecturers were at the end of the party. Basically, I can't get hold of anyone. I don't think Mandeville is keen on chasing up the students too much in case that stirs up more trouble. We are a bit stuck."

"Do you know any of the students who were most likely to be there when the party ended?"

"James, but he's in hospital, and Antonia Mortimer. Mandeville said he couldn't get hold of her but it might be worth another go." He looked at his watch. "It's nearly twelve. Fancy a pint?"

Gillian grinned. "Yes, we can map out the next move."

They stopped at the first pub they saw and went through the public bar with its bar billiards table and dart board to a quieter saloon bar which had seen better days. An elderly man sitting at the bar ignored them and a couple of businessmen gave Gillian an evaluating glance but ignored Roger.

Gillian did indeed have a pint of IPA with Roger and they briefly chatted before getting down to the topic, which was becoming more interesting, especially to Gillian.

"You know Mark better than I do, Roger. From what you said about him, the scenario doesn't make sense; the one who should be going off is his wife. So, what could have led him to go off like that?" asked Gillian.

"Mark is very successful with women. In any given social situation, he gravitates towards members of the opposite sex and they do to him. He has a pretty straightforward modus operandi; plenty of charm, flattery and chat up and he tests the water carefully before making his play, and he is usually successful."

"Then what?"

"A no-strings-attached friendship with the person, and it finishes when he moves on to the next one. My guess is that, as he has done before, he's having a quick fling, probably with one of his students at the academy; she will probably be nineteen, certainly over eighteen."

Gillian looked contemptuous. "It might be technically legal but that is so immoral, using his position to exploit his students, presumably to satisfy his carnal instincts. He might think it's a laugh but really."

Roger looked uncertain. "He has never bragged about his conquests and has told some people that the relationships are purely platonic. I just don't know, but I get the impression that the conquest is the thing."

Gillian shook her head. "A trophy hunter; how puerile. Still, I suppose this spares the lions and the tigers."

"Of course, we don't know for sure that he made a play for one of the students on Friday night, though he was surrounded by them when I left."

"But does his disappearance have anything to do with the car accident?"

"We have to find someone who was there. You wouldn't think it was so difficult."

"Odd, isn't it? I'm sorry but I have to get back to college, you know that paper. Thanks for the drink. I enjoyed it."

"Me too."

Roger took Gillian back to the college and said he would keep her informed of his progress. "I'll give you a ring tomorrow."

Gillian went back to her reading and making notes for her paper but progress was slow; her mind was in too many other places.

X

DAY FOUR

THE GIRL LAY ON THE BED, WHERE SHE HAD SPENT the greater part of three days. With her index finger she touched her xiphoid process, that tiny bony at the bottom of the centre of the ribcage. It had always been a little prominent as she was quite lightweight but this morning it felt more obvious than ever. She looked at her wrist but couldn't be sure if it was thinner. Not that it mattered; her hand would never shrink to that of a child so she could squeeze it through the cuff. She looked at the other cuffed wrist. It hurt, it always hurt now, and it was bruised where she tried, time after useless time, to perform some sort of Houdini trick and wriggle out of it. She smiled at her irrepressible and futile optimism.

At least she wasn't hungry. She looked at the man sleeping beside her and thought how right he had been when he explained what would happen. The first three days had been hell but then the hunger pains had eased and now there were none. By now the body had used up its reserves of glucose and was now burning fat in a process called ketosis or something which slowed down their physical decline. Obviously, they were losing weight but he thought they'd be all right for at least a week, perhaps two weeks, by which time the school would be open and someone would find them. She felt optimistic again and didn't let her thoughts stray to what happened if all their fat was burnt up as he assured her it wouldn't happen for a long time.

She could hear him breathing deeply and she felt fondly towards him. His hand was open and still bore the scars of the metal which had cut into him while he had tried to file down the handcuff and then the rail, without much success at either. He had never complained nor even mentioned it to her but she had seen the spots of blood on the sheet.

She knew it was bizarre but she had grown to feel pleased that she was trapped here with him, rather than anybody else. He had been understanding of her embarrassment that first day and now they had made what they could of this miniature world of theirs and she was used to it. Even the horrible embarrassments seemed less awful now and she could cope with them. She had long since stopped covering herself at all costs when in front of him. Of course, she longed to be free but he had made it bearable, with even the odd moment of humour. He was kind and thoughtful and had maintained both his decorum and his respect for her at all times. It was that which helped her keep up her own sense of self-respect, even though now she felt disgusting without a bath or at least a shower. He had looked the other way when she had removed her pants and given herself a one-handed strip-down wash without soap or hot water. It was totally inadequate but she assumed this is what people meant by 'keeping up appearances'. He had done the same but never lamented the lack of hot water or soap. Lying there she felt caringly towards him again and wanted to touch him, just a touch, but was afraid he might, probably wouldn't but might, get the wrong idea. She reached out and stroked his arm but withdrew her hand when he stirred. She closed her eyes and pretended to be asleep.

He awoke and looked at her. How did she sleep on her back without snoring? He never could. He thought she looked thinner in the face but assumed it was his imagination. He knew he'd lost some weight, but a few pounds would do no harm, probably do some good. He looked at her in admiration and affection. After the early shock of their predicament, she had never once complained or berated him for failing to get them out. He found that inexplicable and frankly miraculous and thought her quite heroic. He heard the church clock strike seven and checked his watch was keeping to the right time. He still believed they would be rescued but now found it hard to understand why it had not happened before. Though he did his best to quell the thoughts, he repeatedly found himself plagued with doubts: that somehow their disappearance, even if registered, had not been investigated and never would be. His inability to explain how that could possibly happen made him unsure of anything but he would never reveal his concerns to her; what would be the point?

She opened her eyes. "Good morning," she said.

He smiled. "Good morning, did you sleep well?"

She smiled. "I did, actually. God knows why, considering the situation. I suppose we just sleep, like those people in *Invasion of the Body Snatchers* who knew they would be taken over if they fell asleep and still couldn't stop themselves from nodding off."

"You've seen that film! It's a bit before your time, isn't it?"

"It's a classic. I love all those old science-fiction films, especially the more subtle ones."

"You didn't like *The Blob*, then?"

She laughed. "That was just silly. But I did like the old *Frankenstein* films when they were on television a few years ago and the *Quatermass* ones and so on. By the way, you must have noticed that the people in horror films never say, 'This is like being in a horror film,' so the characters make the same mistakes over and over again: going down into a cellar or up to the attic where there is bound to be something creepy, running upstairs where there is no escape and all the other things they do while people in the audience are thinking, 'Don't do it.'"

He smiled. "I suppose it would break the tension for the audience if the characters were to be too aware of their plight."

"I suppose so, but it makes them seem rather stupid."

He smiled.

"It's just that sometimes I think it," she said.

"What?"

"That what has happened to us is a bit like something in a horror film."

"In what way?"

"Two people trapped without food in a prison and apparently no one knows they are there or, if somebody does know, they are doing nothing about it."

"I suppose you are right. Fortunately, we don't have to follow a script or worry about breaking the tension of the audience. We will get out all in good time and I shall be perfectly happy if it ends, not with a climactic, last-minute-to-midnight ending, with the flames licking the bottom of the bed or the monster about to grab you, but boringly with someone saying, 'Hello! There you are!'"

"I would, too," she said. "For you, what's the worst thing about the waiting?"

"Oddly enough, it's not our restricted diet and lack of variety, which I thought it would be. I suppose it's being shackled and unable to move properly. What about you?"

"There are so many. Obviously, the handcuffs and the movement are horrible. But the fact is that we can't stop the decline and make ourselves feel better whether it's by washing or exercise. What state will we be in tomorrow and the next tomorrow? Sorry, mustn't get self-pitying."

"I think you are entitled to be self-pitying, even though you haven't been. Don't ever apologise for anything you say or do. Would you like to use the bathroom first?"

She nodded and they began Day Four which, she reflected as she washed, would be exactly the same as Day Three and Day Five. Unless something changed or somebody came or she went mad. She looked round at him, lying on the bed, back to her, looking at an old magazine he had been reading the previous night and admired his stoicism. How did he keep this up day after day? He was truly a hero, or was he a little mad or was he both? She looked down at her pants and wondered how many more days she would have to wear them and she was almost overcome by an urge to take them off and throw them away. But she did nothing different that morning: pot, water drink, wash, clean teeth, help move bed round for him to do the same. Then together, they would trek round the room: empty pot, turn off light, open window, take it in turns to gaze out at the world beyond, something they could never do together or share. The morning promenade would end with them sitting on the bed to plan the day, the interminable day for two strangers who were fast exhausting the range of topics they had in common and whose relationship was defined by their forced enclosure and declining spirits.

*

Late that morning, Roger Southwark was developing his own unlikely alliance with Jocelyn Mandeville.

"Ah, Mr Southwark. What news?" asked Mandeville when he answered the telephone.

"Not much, so far," said Roger. "Not only have I been unable to contact any of Rob Grainger, Mark Harred or Mike Brompton, to help identify the other two lecturers at the party, but Harred has not been home since and has apparently disappeared for now."

"Good grief, how alarming!"

"He'll turn up, I'm sure. I shall have to speak to one or other of the students. I thought Antonia Mortimer; I know her quite well and she seems both intelligent and level-headed."

"Qualities rarely associated with our cadre of students. I have been unable to contact her but you might have more luck. I have her telephone number here. Have you a pen?"

Roger took down a number in Surrey, in a village near Reigate.

"I know you will be the soul of discretion, Mr Southwark; not too much detail in what you reveal to students or parents."

"Of course. Goodbye." He rang the number as soon as Mandeville had cleared the line and it was answered curtly by a woman with a cut-glass accent.

"Good morning. I am Roger Southwark, one of the teachers at Twirleston Academy. May I speak to Antonia, please?"

"Is there something wrong? She doesn't usually get contacted during the school holidays," she said impatiently.

"Not at all. She is a very good student. I just have an administrative query and I would appreciate Antonia's comments."

"I see. I'll get her for you." The woman put the phone down.

"Hello, Mr Southwark, how are you?"

"I'm fine, Antonia. Enjoying the holiday break?"

"Yes, thanks. I'm trying to plan out my revision for the exams."

"That's very creditable of you. I'm sorry to trouble you but there was a car accident after the party last Friday affecting James and Rory and the school has been asked by the parents what actually happened at the party."

"An accident? How terrible. Are they all right?"

"They are in hospital. I'm not sure how serious it is."

"That's so awful. I'll send them a get-well card. I didn't stay until the end so they were still there when I left."

"Who else was still at the party when you left?"

"Mr Harred, Mr Grainger, Mr Brompton. Jane, Suzy, James. Rory and Ursula. Fiona and one of the lecturers whose name I don't know left at the same time as me, and Mr Laycock gave us all a lift."

"What time did you leave?"

"About ten, or half past. Mr Laycock was leaving then and I asked him for a lift to Abigail's."

"Abigail?"

"Abigail Durrant. I don't think you know her; she is doing French, English and History. She lives in Twirleston Minor and she offered to put me up for the night so I didn't want to be too late and inconvenience her family."

"So, Tony Laycock was at the party?"

"Yes."

"The headmaster had been told the party finished at half past six or thereabouts. What happened to it after that?"

"We all went to the stable block and had some more drinks there until people gradually started to drift off."

"What was the atmosphere like when you left?"

"Well, it was like most parties towards the end; people had been drinking and some were slowing down while others were, you know."

"There weren't any drugs on offer, were there?"

"I don't know. I wasn't offered any. Why do you ask?"

"It might have affected how people behaved. Is there anything else you want to tell me about events at the party? Anything out of the ordinary?"

"No, I don't think so."

After he finished the call, Roger considered telephoning Mandeville again but there was not much to report yet. He chose instead to ring Gillian, as he'd said he would. He rang her at home.

"Not interrupting anything, am I?" he asked.

"No, my paper's nearly complete. You can come round for coffee, if you like?"

"Oh? OK, thanks."

Roger had been to her flat once before for a drinks party. It was in an apartment block less than ten minutes' drive from the college. He parked in one of the visitor parking spaces and walked up to the second floor to Flat C. He rang the doorbell and Gillian opened the lilac-coloured door.

"Hello, come in," she said, standing back. She was dressed in jeans and a tight white top but he thought she had taken some time with her hair and make-up. "Take a seat. I'll get the coffee."

Roger sat on an armchair and looked round the flat. It was decorated in the modern style in a large-patterned wallpaper with a mixture of the latest furniture and a couple of antique pieces. Two of Peter Blake's pop art prints decorated one wall and a copy of a Utrillo street scene hung over the tiled fireplace. A pile of notes lay on the coffee table, the top page decorated with a teacup ring. Gillian came in with a couple of mugs of coffee and a sugar bowl and spoons.

As she sat down opposite Roger she smiled. "Sugar?"

"No, thanks."

"I'm afraid just another of my weaknesses."

"Still, gives you strength," he said.

She smiled. "Now, what's the latest?"

"I know the name of one of the two unidentified lecturers: Tony Laycock."

"Tony? He is unlikely to have done anything to upset the apple cart; he is so quiet and diffident."

Roger shrugged. "Still waters and all that. Anyway, he will know who the other lecturer was, so worth a visit. Nice flat you've got here. Quite spacious."

"Yes, I was lucky to get this one. Two bedrooms and a corner plot. It was a bit run down when I bought it. I got it for just over £2,000."

"That was good."

"Yes, but flats never go up as much as houses; I don't know why. Anyway, suits a spinster with no ties."

Roger nodded. "May I use your phone?"

"Go ahead. It's over there, on the desk."

Roger telephoned the college to get Tony's number then phoned him.

A woman with a monotone voice answered, "Hello, 283."

"Mrs Laycock?"

"Yes."

"It's Roger Southwark here, from the college. Is Tony available please?"

"Yes, I'll get him. Tony, it's for you. Roger Southwark."

"Hello, Roger. What can I do for you?"

"It's about the party at the academy last Friday."

There was silence for a few seconds. "I can't speak here," said Tony, his voice even quieter than usual. "Can we meet somewhere?"

"Er, yes. How about the pub for a drink?"

"Yes, all right. Not one near me."

"How about my local, The Stag? It's got a private bar. You know the one?"

"Yes. All right, I'll see you there in half an hour."

Roger put the phone down. "That's strange," he said.

"What is?"

"Tony was a bit guarded. Didn't want to talk over the telephone. He has agreed to meet me at The Stag in half an hour."

"Sounds interesting. I don't suppose I can come along?"

"Might look odd, sorry."

"Never mind."

"Tell you what: give us an hour and come over yourself. I won't need that long."

"OK."

Roger finished his coffee and left soon after to arrive at The Stag a few minutes before Tony.

The landlord, Jack, smiled as he entered the saloon bar. "Morning, Roger."

"Morning, Jack. IPA, please."

He stood at the bar, engaging in idle chatter with the landlord and another man he knew by sight. After five minutes or so, Tony walked into the bar. Roger bought him a pint of light and bitter and they took their drinks into the empty private bar. Tony, dressed in his usual understated clothes, sat down in the bar and stared at his glass for several moments. Roger waited before speaking, a trick he had learnt in negotiating; let the other person start the conversation and you might learn something of interest.

"You wanted to talk to me about the party. Why?"

"Why do you think?"

"Nothing happened."

"How do you mean?"

"Well, nothing of importance."

"I wouldn't say that. Why did you want to talk to me privately, if nothing happened?"

"I didn't know what you'd heard. What's it got to do with you, anyway?"

"The headmaster asked me to look into it."

"What does he know?"

"I can't say. Why don't you tell me your side of the story?"

"You tell me who you have spoken to."

"Antonia Mortimer."

He nodded. "I thought so. Well, whatever she said, nothing happened."

"She said she got in your car."

"So did two others."

"You dropped them off first?"

"Yes, that was the way it worked out. Look, I gave her a lift. That was all. It was a mistake. I thought she was giving me the come-on but she wasn't. I didn't do anything."

"It all depends what you mean by anything."

"I didn't even touch her. Well, just her arm. When I went to kiss her, she turned away and I knew I'd been a fool. Surely she didn't say it was worse than that?"

"No."

"There won't be any further action?"

"No."

Tony visibly sighed with relief.

Roger leaned forward in his chair. "There were other events which need looking into."

Tony took a gulp of his beer. "Not to do with me?"

"Not directly. What happened at the end of the evening?"

"I don't know what happened after I left. That was some time after ten."

"With Antonia and who else?"

"John Knowles and a girl he had been chatting up. I think her name was Fiona."

"Did you drop them off together?"

Tony shook his head. "I dropped John at his house then I took the girl to the station. Antonia made sure she got her train."

"And then what?"

"I told you. I dropped her off where she was staying and went home."

"The others were still partying or about to leave as well?"

"There weren't many left. Mark Harred, Rob Grainger, Mike Brompton, three female students and two boys. Some of them were pretty drunk. They had started earlier than me. I left my last drink untouched. I took it steady driving home. You never know where you are with the breathalyser."

"Have you heard from Mike Brompton since the party?"

"No. I think he said he was going away, not last weekend but over the Easter weekend."

"What about Mark Harred?"

"No. What's all this about?"

"At some time after the party ended, two of the students, James and Rory, were involved in a car accident and both are in hospital, unable yet to say what happened. I have been unable to speak to anyone who was present when the party ended."

"I don't see what a car accident has to do with the party."

"The parents of the injured students have raised questions of teacher responsibility as our lecturers were at the party."

Tony shrugged his shoulders but said nothing.

"OK, Tony. Thanks for taking the trouble."

"I take it the college won't need to know about this?"

"Not as far as you are concerned, no."

"Thanks," said Tony. He got up and began to leave. Then he turned and said, "I paid for all the drinks for that part of the evening. Neither Mark nor John nor anybody else paid up." Then he walked off without saying any more.

It had been a shorter discussion than Roger had anticipated

and Gillian wouldn't arrive for half an hour. He looked at the list of people he couldn't yet account for: Harred, Grainger, Brompton, Suzy, Ursula and Jane. He thought this was all becoming a waste of time. Harred had probably gone off on one of his 'Lost Weekends', Brompton on holiday, Grainger nursing his constituency and the girls safely gone home or on holiday. The two boys, having failed to pull any of the girls, had taken to the road and a mixture of alcohol, high spirits and careless driving had ended up with them in the hospital. Hopefully they would be fine and they would have a tale to tell for the future. He related his assessment of the situation to Gillian when she arrived in the snug, a glass of Pils in her hand.

She nodded. "I see what you mean but don't you think you should keep going until you actually speak to somebody who was there when the party finished?"

"I think you are more interested in pursuing this than I am."

She smiled. "I don't like unsolved mysteries."

"I'll phone Mike Brompton after lunch and try Rob Grainger again."

"Do they serve decent food here?"

"Not bad. Better in the winter than in the summer months."

"How so?"

"Good on pies and fry-ups. Less good on poached salmon and salads."

"I'll get a menu."

She went into the saloon bar and came back with a plastic wallet containing a handwritten menu. She looked at it for a while and said. "I'll have the skate."

Roger looked at the menu a little longer then opted for the mixed grill. "I'll order. Another Pils?"

"Yes, please."

The lunch went on for an hour and more and the conversation drifted away from the night of the party to their common interests: economics, lecturing at college, reminiscences of college life, mostly of an amusing nature, their ambitions for the future, Roger's car. Neither appeared to be in any hurry to leave but then Jack called last orders and they looked at their watches.

"I had better get back to college and see if I can get hold of Mike Brompton. Are you interested?"

"Definitely. I'll see you there."

Roger was in the office first and, even before Gillian had arrived, he had tried, without much hope, to reach Mike Brompton.

"Any luck?" said Gillian as she came in.

"No, I should have tried after Tony told me Mike is going on holiday."

"It's only Wednesday. Perhaps they are going tomorrow."

"True. I'll try again this evening."

"You'll let me know?"

"Of course, if you want."

At six o'clock Roger arrived at Mike Brompton's house in the suburbs of the college town. He hadn't rung in advance. For no logical reason he could think of he felt that if he called unannounced, he would be more likely to catch Mike in. The house was a semi-detached late Georgian town house on three floors, a pediment along the top concealing the sloping roof behind. Lace curtains in the bottom halves of the sash windows prevented Roger seeing inside the ground floor. He rang the doorbell, which clanged like a Victorian bell and loud enough to wake the dead but nobody came to the door. He went over to the window and peered in. He could see nobody. He thought about walking round the back of the house but the side gate was locked.

"Can I help you?" asked a woman's voice from the front path of the attached house.

Roger smiled at the woman, a pleasant-looking person of about fifty who had just opened the front gate and was walking towards her front door. She returned the smile. He walked towards her. "Hello. I was hoping to see Mr Brompton before he went away."

The woman smiled again, this time apologetically. "Oh, I'm afraid they went after lunch. They thought they'd beat the big exit tomorrow: you know what the jams can be like. They have a long drive."

"Right," said Roger, cursing under his breath that he hadn't tried to get round earlier.

"Is it a very urgent matter?" she asked.

Roger shook his head. "No, not really. It can wait until…?"

"Tuesday, they'll be back on Tuesday."

"Thanks," he said and started to walk back to his car. Then he turned back. "I know this sounds like a silly question but are you sure they have actually left?"

The woman smiled. "Oh yes, Amanda dropped a note through the letterbox to tell me she had forgotten to cancel the milk and asked if I'd take it in."

"And Mike?"

"No, I didn't see him. I was out when they left, so I didn't see them go. Why do you ask?"

"No reason. Thanks again," he said.

As he drove off, not yet sure of his precise destination, he thought, *how tedious detective work must be. Missed contacts, one dead end after another, time wasted on pointless telephone calls and visits to people never there.* He toyed with the idea of ringing Mandeville to reveal his latest findings but decided against it. His information would be negligible; Mandeville would be disappointed and he would probably resign his role. He realised that he could no longer see the point of what was, after all, just a run-of-the-mill party and a car crash involving two, probably drunk, teenagers; hardly a rare occurrence and scarcely worth chasing up. He would sleep on it and decide tomorrow whether to continue with it or perhaps he would discuss it with Gillian. He found he had already been driving roughly in the direction of her apartment block and that decided it.

Gillian opened the door and looked at him quizzically. "Hello. I didn't expect to see you again so soon. Come in. Sit down, I'll just finish off something in the kitchen."

He sat down in an armchair and a few minutes later Gillian walked in, removing an apron. "How did you get on at Mike's?"

"I messed it up. I should have gone round to see him before lunch, rather than afterwards. He won't be back until Tuesday."

"Oh, well, a few days won't matter."

Roger shook his head. "You know, I'm beginning to think all this is a waste of time. The only real story is that James and Rory were injured in a car accident and, sooner or later, they will recover and explain what happened to their parents and anybody else who's interested; I'm certainly not."

Gillian laughed. "Poor old grump. There was me, hoping to be Dr Watson to your Sherlock Holmes and you don't want to play detectives anymore. Would you like a drink?"

"Yes please." He smiled.

"I've got most of the spirits or wine. I don't think I have any beer."

"A glass of wine, please."

Gillian went to the kitchen and came back with a bottle of white wine and two glasses. "Julian recommended this to me; I've no idea what it's like but it cost over four quid so it should be good." She poured them both a glass of Sancerre. "Would you like something to eat?"

"I don't want you to go to any trouble."

"It's no trouble. I'm not cooking this evening as we had lunch."

"Well, thanks."

She went out to the kitchen and returned with two plates of Caesar salad and some bread and topped up their glasses. "Why don't we go to the hospital and see how the boys are doing? Perhaps one or other of them are in a fit state to talk to us," she asked, an anchovy waving precariously on the end of her fork.

Roger smiled. "I'm sure Mandeville would have kept me informed."

"If the parents keep him informed. They will have other priorities."

"I doubt the hospital will let us see either of them."

She looked at her watch. "It's visiting time at the hospital now, I should think. Let's try tomorrow morning. Leave it to me. Oh! I can't do tomorrow. I've got this day in London booked with a couple of friends. Will it wait until Friday?"

"I don't see why not. Probably more likely we'll be able to see the boys. This is good," he added, gesturing to the Caesar salad.

"It's not much. I've got a cherry pie my mum made for dessert. Twenty-nine and my mother still worries in case I don't eat properly! Actually, she doesn't really, she just likes to keep me in the loop. I suppose it's even worse for you. Mothers and their sons?"

"She used to worry when I was at university but once I had my own flat and worked in London she decided not to, especially as I told her there was a lady who came in 'to do for me' whom she could assume did a bit of cooking, whereas I mostly ate out. Nowadays we are so far apart; my parents live in Dorset, that distance has made concern pointless."

After they had finished the salad, she took the plates out to the kitchen and returned with her mother's cherry pie, the pastry prettily decorated with the left-over pastry.

"It looks too good to cut into," said Roger.

"Well, my mother would say that eating it is the whole point, so tuck in."

Roger cut a slice for each of them and Gillian poured cream on the deep-red and golden pie.

"It's great," said Roger, taking a spoonful.

"Glad you like it; Mum will be pleased. That's why haut-cuisine food presented as art is so ridiculous; why spend so much time titivating something that has a transitory existence in that state, will be judged on its taste rather than its aesthetic value and will ultimately end up indistinguishable from even the ugliest food."

Roger nodded. "I suppose we are all affected by the appearance of our food to some extent but, of course, you are right." He smiled inwardly, enjoying her tendency to have forthright opinions about things which don't really matter, whereas he found it increasingly more difficult to get worked up about anything.

"You hadn't planned a holiday this Easter?" Gillian asked, putting down her empty plate.

"No, the break gives me the chance to catch up with friends and family. Why do you ask?"

"Mandeville's request to help didn't interfere with your plans then?"

"No, but I don't intend to chase around for him over the Easter weekend. I have got a couple of things on I don't want to miss."

"We shall have to sort out the mystery on Friday then."

"One last try, then we'll drop it," he said.

"Right."

"I ought to be going."

"No need, I'm not doing anything this evening. I'll make some coffee." She picked up the plates and went out to the kitchen.

A minute later, Roger heard the familiar noises of the kettle lid being taken off, the tap running, the kettle being plugged and the water starting to heat up. He had no particular desire to leave but wondered where this was going. This work colleagues' relationship, where you can have a coffee in the staff lounge without going for coffee together, or lunch in the staff restaurant or a drink over the Bellerephon, all without actually going out with that person. Now this meeting together because of the incident at the school, lunch at The Stag, coming round to her flat *twice* in one day. Was this slipping into something else without them noticing? Then all the complications and dangers of a relationship with someone from work: the whispering, the snatched moments of time alone, the danger of a falling out and then the awkwardness, the knowing looks, the embarrassment. He attempted to dismiss this flight of fancy, determining that this was just an interlude, a flurry of activity for two friendly colleagues and after tomorrow things would go back to normal. Or would it?

Gillian appeared with a tray and cups of coffee and milk and sugar. She was smiling but stopped as she noticed Roger's frowning expression. "Nothing wrong is there?"

"No, just thinking about the boys in the hospital and whether they will be all right."

"We'll soon know. Sorry, the coffee is instant, Bird's. I like it smoother."

"Me too," he replied, though not strictly truthfully.

After two cups of coffee, Roger did take his leave. Gillian did not attempt to dissuade him but suggested he pick her up at ten o'clock on Friday for the trip to the hospital. On the drive home he reassured himself that he was being silly with his worries about sliding into a relationship with Gillian. After all, he knew his own mind.

XI

FRIDAY

THE YOUNG WOMAN WOKE FIRST. SOME MORNINGS she lay awake but pretended to be asleep when he awoke so she could tell him she had slept well and he wouldn't worry about her. She was aware that sometimes he pretended to be asleep when she woke for the same reason. Today, she knew he was certainly asleep because his hand was on her leg and he would have removed it if he were aware. She didn't mind about the hand; she did not find him repulsive and anyway, it was innocent and sort of comforting. It was the seventh day of their imprisonment and she so wished to be comforted. She was sure she was going mad because she now regarded the daily routine of dragging the bed round and existing on a diet of slightly odd-tasting water as normal. If she were sane, she would surely scream and rave about their situation but she never did. She checked the bottom of her ribcage for signs of weight loss, as she always did. She was glad they didn't have a mirror so she might see her surely more prominent collar and hip bones and her shrinking breasts; not that it mattered: she was probably hideous now.

It was Friday now, Good Friday, she realised; the day that commemorated the death of Christ and the death of hope for his apostles. Although she fought against it, she felt her hope was dying too. Even though logic and common sense said that they would be rescued, her mind was constantly invaded by the same mad 'what-ifs'. Like the school not reopening after the holiday for some reason or nobody coming to the stable block for weeks as the classroom was not needed or the people that had done this meant them harm and would make sure nobody came for them. She dare not reveal her thoughts to her companion for fear her negativity should spread to him so she told herself she was stupid and had to have faith, but faith is hard without hope. Then she remembered the Spaghetti House siege in London the previous autumn and how people had been held hostage for nearly a week and how frightened they must have been. She told herself that was far worse than this and not to be so melodramatic. She wished he would wake and they could talk and he would make her feel more positive, as he always seemed to be able to. She waited patiently for the church clock to strike the hour or the half; it did not trouble the bells for the quarters. Then she recalled the stroke of luck the previous day and she smiled to herself.

After their agreement on Wednesday to try to invent some games, they found it difficult, due to a lack of equipment, to think of much other than word games. The more obvious ones like hangman or finding as many words as possible from a set of letters really needed pencil and paper so they fell back on spelling competitions and name games; going through the alphabet with names of painters or composers or mammals and so on. On Thursday evening, for no particular reason, they decided to do another check of the furniture in case they had missed something of use the first time. It was a fruitless task until they looked in the wardrobe and opened, with some difficulty, the locks on the suitcase, which they had not bothered to open before. It was empty, as they had thought, except for a couple of sheets of lined paper and Suzy felt something in the torn lining which turned out to be an HB pencil. They had reacted as if they had found a crock of gold, cheering and laughing. The pencil had a very short point so they decided to ration use of it and write in very small script. The man would have to do the writing as her writing hand was cuffed. Now, this morning they would be able to play hangman and all sorts of word games.

She felt much better now and waited patiently for him to wake.

But while she waited, he stirred.

"Good morning," he said, smiling at her.

"Good morning," she said, thinking it both idiosyncratic and yet sweet they maintained the formal pleasantries when all formality in their relationship was merely a charade, given that all the intimacies of life had been shared by them, bar one, of course.

They didn't talk; they had exhausted all the chatter over the past week and later, when boredom or a yearning to raise their spirits prompted it, the conversation would begin somewhere and roam over whatever subjects took their fancy that day.

He looked at her when she closed her eyes and thought how innocent and fragile she seemed. Although only technically old enough to be her father, his thoughts towards her were paternal, or were they avuncular? He had experience of neither in practice. He got out of bed and used the pot as quietly as he could. He looked back at her. "Breakfast?"

"Yes, please." She smiled. She wasn't ready to begin the ritual of the day.

He took one of the glasses used the previous day and turned on the tap. It spluttered a little then the water ran smoothly. He filled the first glass then began on the second and the water spluttered again and then stopped. He turned off the tap and turned it on again. Nothing.

"The water has stopped," he said.

"How could that have happened?"

"I'm sure it's not an airlock. It was probably from a different tank, not the mains and it's just run out. It hasn't rained for a while so that could be a factor."

The one 'what-if' she hadn't considered during her pessimistic musing that morning: the water supply. She felt grimly satisfied that she had not exaggerated her plight; her worst fears had been realised. In her imagination she had often pictured herself as the stalwart companion at the side of the hero as they made their escape. Instead, she was fated to suffer the ghastly death of a tragic heroine like Mimi in *La Boheme* or Violetta in *La Traviata*. Yet while she sat on the bed helpless, she saw the man pick up his piece of metal and begin working away on the other isolator screw, without a murmur. She thought his stoic perseverance was truly heroic and put her defeatism to shame and the tears ran silently down her cheeks.

He worked on the screw until the groove was large enough and then, slowly, he managed to turn the screw. He turned on the hot-water tap but there was no response. "If it was from the hot water supply it might not have been drinkable, anyway," he muttered. "Sorry."

She wanted to ask what they could do now but she was afraid her voice would sound hysterical, so she said nothing.

He sat on the bed and swung round to face her. "We are going to have to try something more adventurous, just in case we are stuck here for another week."

"Such as?"

"I'd like to try to get my arm free again."

"But how?" Alarm mixed with doubt in her voice.

"I have thought about it several times in case we reached this position. We have to find a way of breaking free the rail from the headboard so I can free myself while still wearing the handcuff."

"I don't think you will be strong enough, especially as you are bound to be run down without food."

"I know. I take your point, but my weight might do it. If we hang the bed out of the window my weight will pull down on the railing and it might weaken the rails."

"What if it doesn't? I won't be able to help you climb back in the room and you will be left hanging. You might be killed or injured. It's too frightening."

"It'll be all right. What have we got to lose?"

She nodded. What did they have to lose? Without water, it was all up for both of them. "When do you want to do it?"

"As soon as possible."

"I think I'd better do a pee."

"Don't empty the pot. We might need to drink it if this doesn't work."

She laughed at this newly discovered humiliation to add to all the others they had accepted. "How lovely to think my last drink will be my own urine. 'Those whom the gods would destroy, they first make mad.'"

"Do you know who said that?" he asked, by way of distraction.

"Er, no, Teacher, but I'm sure you'll tell me."

He smiled. "No, I don't know either. I think it's from Ancient Greece but who cares? I don't think it's from *Up Pompeii!*"

She laughed again and wondered at her ability to find so much amusing at the moment.

They did not drink the water from their one and a half glasses as they began to ration what little they had. They rested for a time to prepare for the expedition.

"Do you believe in God?" she asked suddenly.

"Sometimes, but I don't know if I do really," he answered. "Do you?"

"I think so. I want to. I suppose I can't face the idea I might be finished at eighteen."

He nodded. It occurred to him that, even if God did exist, there was no guarantee that He would give them both a passport to eternal life but he kept his views to himself. "We are not finished yet. Anyway, doesn't God help those who help themselves? Let's go through the plan."

She smiled and listened quietly, pretending to him and to herself that she believed in it.

"First, we drag the bed to the window. With both halves of the window opened, it will accommodate the bedhead. That's the easy bit. Next, we lift the bed as near we can to the bottom and the frame should lift up out of the base of the bed."

"Why are we doing that, even supposing we can?"

"It's to enable the bed to be weighed down at the bottom using the foot panel and legs for what comes next." He smiled and eventually drew a smile from her too.

"With the bottom legs detached, we turn the bed over and hang the headboard out the window upside down. Then we use the foot of the bed to weigh down on the frame and stop it tipping up. Once all this is done, I will climb down the headboard rails and hang on the headrail in the hope that will loosen the rail to which my handcuff is attached and I might be able to free it from its mounting. Then I will slip the cuff off the rail and either climb back up or drop down to the ground, whichever seems easier."

She stared at him in silence.

"Well, what do you think?" he asked.

"I don't know. So many things I'm not sure we can do. It's a tall order. Even if it all goes to plan you will end up hanging out of the window and anything could happen. You could be killed or at least badly injured and what if I couldn't help you? Where would we be? I'm frightened for you, and me," she admitted.

"If we don't get rescued in the next two or three days, without water we will probably die, especially as we have weakened reserves of energy. If we wait two days it may be too late. I have to try now."

She nodded in resignation rather than conviction. "OK, I'm ready when you are."

He did not tell her of his own doubts and trepidations about the success of this attempt to escape. He knew there could be no trial run, no practice, there would be one chance and, if it failed, the best he could hope for was to climb back up to the room in one piece to await their fate. He was afraid that he would fail for her sake and he dreaded the possibility that the last act of his life would be one of let-down, to fulfil a life of missed opportunities, also rans, wrong decisions and near successes to amount to nothing. He said nothing of this to her because there was still this one last chance to do something good that really mattered.

They took a sip of sour-tasting water and then set off, discarding the mattress to reduce the weight. The first stage, pulling and pushing the bed to the window, was something they had done many times before and they were soon at the window. The next part was more difficult. At full stretch her hand was not able to reach within six inches of the end of the bed. His hand was not at the end but he could lift the frame off the leg on his side.

"I can't lift enough," she said, "I'm sorry."

He thought she looked pitiful, her arm at full stretch, her mouth clenched with the strain and the handcuff biting into her stretched right hand. "Take your time, there's no hurry," he said. He waited, lifting as much as he could on his side but it didn't help.

Then he went to the other end of the bed, pulled it away from the window and leaned on the headrail until it moved a little backwards and the frame rose in the air. The girl tried again and, finally, the frame was free. They sat, tired from their efforts, on the sloping bed.

"Well done," he said, "That's the worst bit over." He patted her arm.

"Ready now," she said, after a few minutes.

They stood and slowly started to turn the bed upside down. First, they turned it on its side towards the girl, he lifting the frame with his free hand while holding onto the headrail with his cuffed hand. The strain of lifting the frame while his weight was leaning towards the bed took all his strength and produced a sweat on his brow he could ill afford to lose. The girl could only hold onto the frame to stop it shifting and countering his effort. At last, when he thought it hopeless, the frame reached an angle of thirty degrees and his weight began to play more in his favour and for a moment it became easier until, as the frame went higher to forty-five degrees, his feet were lifted off the floor and he was catapulted onto the bed and then down onto the girl who was trying to help pull the frame upright. Somehow, he had held onto the rail with his cuffed hand and, although he felt a painful jerk on his arm before it was left hanging above him, he thought he was none the worse for his fall. But then his fall had been cushioned when he landed on the girl.

Pulling on the frame, she had seen him above her but, with her cuffed hand restraining her, she could not dive out of the way. She ducked her head and yelped when his legs crashed into her back and knocked her naked upper body into the springs of the bedframe. Her cuffed hand twisted with force on the rail and she had an excruciating pain in her wrist. The bed had come to rest on its side, held upright by the now sideways headrail. His upper body had not hit her.

"Are you OK?" he asked hopefully as he moved a little nearer the headboard so he could sit a little more comfortably on the floor.

"Ooh," she groaned as she sat up. "Everything hurts. My back aches and my chest but most of all my wrist."

He looked at her wrist and hand. The cuff had cut into the bottom of the hand and it was bleeding slightly. "It's a cut. I think it will be all right. Try not to move it at the moment."

There was some bruising and minor cuts on her chest but nothing too serious and she could move her legs when he asked her to. "I'm sorry," he said, "I should have realised what would happen when the bed was lifted."

"It's not your fault," she said. She moved nearer to him to ease the pressure on her aching wrist, which she dared not look up at. Her back was leaning against his right arm, but her cuffed right arm was stretched over to the rail. "Hold me for a minute," she said.

They adjusted their position so he could put his free hand round her waist and she leaned against his chest. He could feel her relax against him and after a moment she put her left hand on his hand. It was the first time each had felt the warmth of the other against them and it seemed anomalous and yet also right at the same time.

"I know there is more to be done but can we stay like this for a little while?" she asked.

"Of course, there's no rush," he said softly. He looked behind him at her hand on the rail; it was becoming discoloured. "Is the pain any less yet?" he asked.

"A bit. My back's all right now. It's mainly the wrist."

They sat like that for perhaps ten minutes and then he took his hand from under hers and squeezed her arm.

"I know. We must get on," she said.

When they stood, she was facing away from the bed but

she slowly slid her cuffed hand along the now horizontal rail it was on so that she was not too restrained. She looked at her injured hand for a moment then said, "I won't be able to do much but I can pull downward on the end rail if you can lift it."

He had also slid his cuffed hand along the rail and he was able to use his full weight to lift and push the bed over, one hand on the rail and the other on the frame. With the girl unable to do much more than pull a little he could not quite believe he had managed it.

The two halves of the window bolted at the top and bottom and when they were opened the window went down to less than three feet from the floor. Standing at one side of the bed, he was able to lift his side of the headboard until it was balanced on the edge of the window. Then he pulled the other side up with her help until only a small part of the headrail remained in the room. He looked down at the paved ground below the window and thought how far it seemed and how this next move was probably madness.

"I am going to go soon. When I say, I want you to push the headrail out. For now, work the cuff up towards the top of the headrail as it is now and make sure you are as far as possible away from the bed so the frame doesn't hit you when the rail goes out the window."

She nodded, unable to speak because she was petrified at the thought of something happening to him but she did as he said.

He climbed up onto the upside-down headrail, his cuffed hand near the bottom and the other hand rather higher. He braced himself for the shock of the jolt and called out, "Now."

She made sure her cuffed hand was at the top as he had said then, using her shoulder she shoved the last part of headrail out while holding onto the windowsill. The immediate effect for her was that she was pulled towards the window and screamed as she was dragged down by her painful hand. Within a second the bedframe hit the windowsill and she was left hanging out the window with such pain in her hand that she thought she might faint. At the same time, the bedframe shot up from the floor and oscillated gently almost at right angles to the window. She held onto it with her uncuffed hand to avoid it sliding out of the window.

She looked down. Her scream had muffled his cry as the headboard swung towards the building and his back collided with the wall under the window. She could see his back was scratched and a red welt marked the place of impact. "Are you OK?" she asked, fighting back the urge to express her own pain.

"Not too bad," he called. "At least I am out. Can't see any movement in the rails yet. Perhaps my weight will eventually cause the headrail to bow, just a little. Is it stable at your end?"

"I'm having to hold the frame. If it tilts any more, I may not be able to stop it going out of the window."

"I had better not jump or move too much then."

"No!" she cried.

They stayed where they were, unmoving for some time, her in pain and him increasingly uncomfortable as he stood rigid, his feet on the headrail and his hands hanging on the headboard.

He considered the possibilities. One was to slide down the headboard rails and try to work the cuff round so that he hung on the outside. It might work but would it achieve anything? Another was to keep working at bending and breaking the rails until he was free. Finally, if all else failed, he might be able to climb back in the window but he thought it difficult; he would have only one hand to use and his weight, fixed to the headboard, would hold him back. He thought this might be the end. The sky was blue, no hope of rain. It was now just a case of hanging there till tomorrow, or the next day, or the next, until he passed out or his kidneys packed up or whatever else happened. He didn't pray, he didn't want to have hope. He just wished there was an afterlife so that whoever had done this to them might rot in hell.

"It's not going to work," he called eventually. "It's made of stronger stuff than I thought. Solid, Victorian metalwork rather than modern blown-together crap."

"What now?"

"There is no 'what now'. I'm sorry."

"Come back."

"I don't know if I can."

"Please."

"I'll try."

He stood up straight but he could barely move between the wall and the headboard. He could reach with his free hand into the room but he could not swing his legs nor use his cuffed arm to help him climb back in. She tried to push the bedframe a little to give him some space but it would not move and, as he pointed out, there was a danger the equilibrium of the bedframe and the headboard could be disturbed and she might not be able to hold onto it.

"I am going to try to get outside the frame. That will give me more movement and momentum," he said. "One more go."

Keeping his cuffed arm near where he stood, he slowly moved his free hand down towards the other. He shifted his knees so they were bending sideways and eventually he was crouched at the bottom of the hanging headboard. With both hands in position, he slowly and painfully managed to twist his cuffed hand round to the outside and now he hung down from his platform. His legs swung in the air and he could see his feet were only three or feet above the ground. Yet now, with his full weight pulling at the headboard, nothing was giving way. Eventually, tiring, he gave up.

He pulled himself back up onto the headboard and looked up at the girl. "Let's see if I can climb back in this way."

He couldn't get his cuffed hand into action and that held him back as he swung his legs up. They tried several times and she gave him what support she could but his legs felt leaden and he was tired and just could not get his foot onto the sill.

"Have a rest," she said. "Then we'll try again. We'll do it. You just need a rest."

They both called out for help but they were far from the rarely used back road and hidden from sight. He silently, reluctantly, surrendered and he leaned over the bedframe and held her hand.

XII

RESCUE

ROGER WAS RESTLESS. HE HAD BEEN UP FOR SOME time and over breakfast puzzling about his relationship with Gillian. When he had arrived home the previous night, he had, for an inexplicable reason, postponed a social engagement set for Saturday evening. He looked at the clock and it was still only ten minutes past nine. He thought there was no point in sitting around. He would get some petrol, buy a couple of Easter eggs if he needed them for random child relatives and then collect Gillian. He put on his newly purchased check jacket, looked in the mirror one more time and then went out to the car.

Temporarily delayed by a next-door neighbour eager to pass the time of day, Roger, after the completion of his visits to a shop and a garage, finally arrived at Gillian's just before ten.

"Hello," said Gillian. She had dressed in a suit, rather as she would for work, with perhaps a little more make-up than usual. She was aware that he noticed. "I thought I ought to dress more formally as we are going to represent the school."

"Yes, good idea. Perhaps I ought to have worn a tie."

"I should be able to find one." She disappeared into the bedroom and returned with a plain dark-blue tie. "This do?"

He nodded and put it on. "Do you think I ought to phone Mandeville?"

"I don't see why. He wants you to find out what happened in the crash and he hasn't kept you informed of any developments."

"That's true. Funny to go on Good Friday."

"It's a good time. I've got a friend who works in a hospital. Far fewer casualties and people reporting ill on bank holiday mornings; it's amazing how much holidays make people healthier."

Roger smiled. "Shall we go?"

The two male students had first been taken to the local cottage hospital to stabilise their conditions. Then, in view of the head injuries, they were taken to the county hospital, thirty-five miles away. It was an old hospital, some parts dating back to the turn of the century but it looked to be well-maintained as they drove up to the porter's lodge.

"Good morning. We are hoping to see two boys brought here with head injuries last Saturday," said Roger.

"What are the names?"

"James Newton and Rory Marnoch," said Roger.

He looked down a clipboard. "Well, they're not on the gate' so they are not critical. You'll have to wait till visiting time. As it's a bank holiday you can visit this afternoon."

"It's actually an official matter," said Gillian. "We are from their school and we have to make arrangements for next term and the students' return, if that's possible. I take it nobody has been from the school to date?"

"Not that I know of."

"Would you mind asking the ward sister if we could just see them for a few minutes?" Gillian persevered. "We have come a long way."

"What ward are they in?"

"The Howland, I believe," said Roger.

The porter blew out his cheeks. "I'll try." He picked up his telephone and rang a ward number.

"Hello, Sister. I have two people here who would like to speak to the boys who came in with head injuries. They are teachers from the school the boys go to and are making arrangements for next term. Righto, I'll send them up." He put the phone down. "You can have a word with the Sister and she'll decide what to do."

"Thank you," said Gillian sweetly.

The porter's gruffness softened and he pointed over to the new wing to his right. "It's the block over there with the blue doors. Take the stairs to the first floor."

They parked the car and walked over to the block which bore the title 'Russell Wing' and pushed open the doors. The smells of sanitation and cleanliness filled their nostrils as they mounted the polished stairs to the first floor. As they reached the Howland Ward, a nursing sister in a dark-blue uniform and white apron opened the doors and greeted them with a stern look.

"Are you from the school?" she asked.

"Yes," said Gillian. "We know it's unusual to trouble you at such short notice but we do have to produce a report on the accident; a matter of in loco parentis, you understand. As there was no crime involved, the police do not see it as their business, Sister…?"

"Mitchell. I'm afraid it is quite out of the question to see Rory Marnoch. He is out of the coma now but he cannot be disturbed. It will be some time before he is well enough to leave hospital."

"Is he mentally aware?" asked Roger.

"Yes, he is still improving but has some way to go."

"How is James Newton?" asked Gillian.

"Much improved. He had severe concussion but is well on the road to a full recovery."

"Might we see him for a few minutes?" asked Roger.

"Yes but keep it brief." She walked across the corridor and opened a door. "Take a seat in here and I'll bring him to you. You won't be disturbed."

The door was signed 'Visiting Lounge' and opened into a small room with three easy chairs. Gillian and Roger sat down and waited and a few minutes later a smiling young nurse knocked on the door and brought in James.

"Hello, Mr Southwark," he said, his eyes drawn to Gillian.

"Hello, James. This is Miss Trevis. How are you?"

"I'm all right, thank you."

Roger thought he looked a little worse for wear: bruising on the face and a cut on the forehead, one arm in a sling and a slight discomfort as he went to sit down, one leg appearing rather stiff.

"Mr Mandeville has asked me to check with you what happened in the accident. There are also some questions about the party going on for longer than it was supposed to and whether that had anything to do with the accident. I have spoken to Antonia Mortimer and Mr Laycock but they left the party before it finished."

"I have been expecting somebody to come and see me. I suppose I am in a lot of trouble with the school."

"Let's go through the events of the evening and then we'll discuss them," said Roger, not sure what James meant by that. "Tell us about the accident first."

"Rory was driving, it was his father's car. He was driving too fast, high spirits I suppose, and lost it at a bend. The car hit something and flipped when we left the road. Luckily, we had our seat belts on but we got knocked about a bit. He was worse than me."

"Just an accident," said Roger, "no blame attached to anyone. Now, about the party."

"Well, as you were probably told by Antonia, the party was nearly over when Mr Laycock and Mr Knowles turned up with some more booze and Max had the idea of moving the party to the stable block, out of the way of the caretaker. We all moved the cars down Back Lane and went in the back way. Everyone was drinking quite a bit and people started to, you know."

"I don't know."

"Well, getting a bit flirty. Two of the students, Ben and Samantha, were already an item and they were kissing and everything, then they slinked off somewhere and there were not many people left. Rory was very annoyed and uptight because all the girls were talking to the teachers and ignoring us. He had been hoping to get off with Antonia or Fiona but they only had eyes for the teachers and Jane was being monopolised by Mr Harred.

"He decided to play a joke on them all and drop some concoction he'd been experimenting with in the lab into their drinks. He went off to the loo and mixed some up then made sure he topped up all the glasses, except ours, of course. Nobody took much notice; they were all well away."

"What, is he mad? What sort of concoction?"

"Yeah, I was a bit worried. I told him it might be dangerous but he said they were only knock-out drops. He'd tried them himself and they had just made him sleepy and want to lie down. Basically, it was a mixture of tranquilisers, mostly diazepam, that sort of thing."

"What happened then?"

"Look, it was Rory's idea. It was just a joke and I sort of went along with it. Some of them, Antonia and some of the others, left without drinking the dodgy drink or much of it but those who stayed were soon very woozy. Something happened after that but I can't remember all the details. Although I hadn't taken any of Rory's knockout stuff, I was pretty drunk by then."

"Tell us what you do remember," said Gillian sympathetically.

"Rory got me to help two of the people up to the bedroom. He stripped them of their clothes and laid them on the bed, next to each other, to give them a fright the next morning. By this time, they didn't have a clue what was happening to them."

"That's a dreadful joke to play on somebody, James," said Roger.

"I know. I'm sorry now. I suppose someone reported us?"

"No, nobody has said anything. Who were the people you played the trick on?"

James shook his head. "I don't remember. It was only last night I remembered anything about the party and Rory's messing about with drugs. I guess the couple he played the joke on were embarrassed themselves and it didn't look good for them either."

"The couple *you* also played the joke on," said Gillian. "If we can't account for them, we cannot be sure they are all right. You must try to remember who they are."

His expression changed and he went as white as a sheet. "I've just remembered something else. As we were looking at them in the bedroom, Rory said something about, 'This will teach them' and he tied their hands to the bed   no, handcuffed them to it. He had a pair of handcuffs without the chain and tied them to the bed. I can't remember. Yes, that's it, we were going to go back at about midnight and undo the locks and that would be it and they would never know who played the trick on them."

"But you didn't go back because you had the accident." Gillian looked at Roger and the colour had drained from his face too.

"You mean nobody found them?" said James. "Oh, God, what have we done?" He put his head in his hands and started sobbing.

"Who are they?" asked Roger.

James looked blank. "I don't know, I still can't remember."

Roger went to the ward and opened the door.

The sister came over. "All finished?"

"Not exactly. Can I use your telephone? It's extremely urgent."

She took him to her office and he tried Mandeville's number and the caretaker's. Neither were answered. He went back to the lounge where Gillian was sitting with her arm round James. "Come on," he said and turned to James. "I'll see you later."

They told the sister that James had had a terrible shock and needed help and then ran down the stairs and out to the car.

"Don't you think we should have phoned the police?" asked Gillian.

"It'll take us thirty minutes to get to the school. By the time we'd have gone through all the cop's questions and all the rigmarole and they send somebody out, we'll be there."

He drove fast, speeding out into the country and then down towards the Twirlestons and to the academy. They parked where all the cars had parked the previous Friday and jumped out. "Are you ready for this?" he asked.

"No. Are you?" she replied as they ran across the long grass and through the slightly ajar gate.

They came to a sudden halt as they saw a man hanging from a window. He was naked, save for a pair of grubby underpants. His back was scratched and bruised with a welt across the middle, his legs and feet similarly marked and his hair unkempt, one hand was discoloured and was handcuffed to the bedhead, the other was raised up to the open window, holding somebody's hand. His head turned round when he heard them gasp; it was Rob Grainger.

They were rooted to the spot at first. A mixture of shock and relief prevented them saying anything. Rob's reaction was at first transfixed, then his body began to shake.

Roger and Gillian ran over to the door of the stable block. The door was not locked. The large room still bore the signs of the party of the previous weekend: the empty bottles, stained glasses, bottle openers, corks, a woman's earring on the table, a man's tie on a doorknob. They ran through the room and up the stairs. There were two rooms; one empty, the other a bedroom. Outside this second room, on a table and on the floor round it, was scattered mixed clothing and a small suitcase. As they entered the bedroom they saw, one arm on the frame of a bed, the hand holding that of Rob and the other cuffed to the headboard, Roger's female student, Suzy Plunkett, sobbing.

Gillian went to the pile of clothes, opened the suitcase and found a flowered shirt which she draped over the girl's shoulders.

Rob looked up. "Thank God you came. Can you get us some water, please? That tap has dried up."

Roger nodded, left the room and went downstairs. He found the toilets and filled a rinsed-out jug with water and took it upstairs with a couple of glasses. When he entered the bedroom Gillian was comforting the two prisoners with words of sympathy and encouragement. Roger poured some water in the glasses and Gillian gave one to Suzy and held the other to Rob's mouth.

"We'll get you out of those cuffs," said Roger.

He went out of the room and looked round the lobby area and in the drawer of the table but there was no sign of a key. He picked up the remainder of the clothes and took them into the bedroom and as he did so he heard a metallic noise as something fell on the floor. It was a small key. A minute later, he undid Suzy's cuff. He winced when he saw her hand. "We must get that seen to," he said.

He went back downstairs and out to the yard. "Can you hang on, Rob? I think it's too big a drop if I try to get you down."

Rob nodded and Roger went back into the stable block. There was a stepladder and he took it out to the yard where Rob had lowered himself to a crouching position on the bedhead. Standing on the stepladder, Roger unlocked the cuff and helped Rob down.

"Thanks, Roger." He walked unsteadily back into the stable block. "Fetch my clothes, mate. I suddenly feel inappropriately dressed."

Roger smiled and went back to the bedroom.

"Rob all right?" asked Gillian.

"Yes, just wants his clothes." He noticed Suzy had got her clothes on now. "How's the hand?"

Suzy flexed the hand and examined it carefully. It was very swollen by the wrist, where the deep cut was.

Gillian looked at it as well. "Is it very tender round the cut?" she asked.

Suzy shook her head. "It hurts but it feels better already."

Gillian put her hand on the girl's forehead. "You have a temperature. It may be infected. We shall have to go to the hospital later. First, we must get you both something to eat. You must be starving."

"Give us a couple of minutes," said Roger, gathering up Rob's clothes.

He rushed down and Rob dressed quickly and quietly. Then they heard the clump of shoes on the uncarpeted stairs and a smiling Suzy came into the room.

Rob smiled too and put his arms round Suzy and held her for a moment.

"Do you want to contact your parents, Suzy? They must be very worried about you," said Roger.

"They are on holiday so they won't have expected to see me until Monday."

"Let's get you some food and drink," said Gillian.

"I would love a cup of tea," said Rob.

Suzy nodded. "Me too."

Rob found his car keys in his jacket pocket and Gillian drove his car with him and Suzy back to her flat, while Roger followed on in his own car, stopping first at a supermarket to pick up some milk, soup, bread and ham and cheese and then at Rob's flat for some clean clothes for him. When he arrived at Gillian's flat, Suzy and Rob were drinking tea and they had eaten several biscuits each.

"It's only five whole days without food but I think you are supposed to build up slowly to get back to normal," said Gillian. "Perhaps some soup and maybe a sandwich for now, and something else later."

"Please, can I have a bath now? Then you can fumigate the place," said Suzy, finishing her tea.

Gillian smiled. "I'll run you one and then you can decide if there is anything of mine that isn't in the category of 'wouldn't be seen dead in.'"

When they had left the room Rob asked, "What did happen? Just a summary will do for now. That is, if you know most of the story."

"I know enough of the pieces to fit most of it together. It started quite simply as a practical, and rather nasty, joke that got out of hand. At the party your drinks and presumably those of some of the others were doctored by two of the students and you probably eventually passed out. While you were groggy, they took your clothes off and handcuffed you both to the bed. They intended to come back later and take the cuffs off so that you would either wake up in fright and then be relieved to have the key thrown to you or the cuffs would be off when you woke up and you would both be bewildered, embarrassed and perhaps feeling humiliated. Unfortunately, the two students were injured in a car crash and ended up in hospital. Mandeville asked me to see if I could find out what happened as the parents of the injured boys were kicking up a bit of a rumpus. Nobody knew that you had gone missing and it was only yesterday or possibly this morning that one of them remembered what had happened. He had assumed that someone would have rescued you by now. The other one has been in a coma and is still not right in the head."

Rob took another biscuit and stared at the wall for a while. "Bloody stupid joke; we could have died."

"I know. I thought you might already be dead. I didn't know there was water to the room."

"It finally ran out this morning. We would have been dead by Monday."

"Funny the water ran out."

"It was off at first but I managed to turn the isolator screw to on. It may have been in the tank for some time. Or perhaps was fed by rainwater and we haven't had much rain lately."

"Actually, I didn't know who we would find when we came to the stable block. James didn't remember and I hadn't been able to contact all the people there. I thought it might be Mike Brompton as I haven't been able to contact him or Mark Harred. He has disappeared apparently."

"Oh."

"Do you remember anything about the end of the party?"

"I don't remember going to bed. I think I saw Tony and John leave with two of the girls but after that, it's a bit of a blur."

"After they left, I believe Mike Brompton was still there and so was Mark Harred."

Rob rubbed his forehead. "That sounds about right. Mark was getting a bit physical with one of his students, I noticed. I think her name was Jane. Mike was chatting up another girl, I don't remember her name. I vaguely remember Rory topping up my drink; I was talking about politics with Suzy so didn't take much notice. I hadn't made a pass or anything at Suzy but I admit it did cross my mind that she was not my student as I no longer work at the school. That was all. I don't remember anything after that. Not going upstairs or being undressed or handcuffed. God, what sick bastards they must have been to do that."

"How did Suzy stand up to the ordeal?"

"She was brilliant. No hysterics or reproaches. When we first woke up, she thought I was party to the goings on and might have taken advantage of her but I swear I did nothing to her. We just had a conversation. Anyway, I was not in a fit state to do anything, even if I'd wanted to. I think she believed me but she didn't raise the subject again. I thought she was terrific the whole time. She put up with a lot. Imagine how difficult it was to keep even the most essential intimate actions private. Even if the practical joke had gone to plan, it was a pretty nasty thing to do; taking away what it means to be able to be civilised. That was the first thing the Nazis did when the Jews arrived at the camps, wasn't it? Taking away their clothes, their sense of self, their right to be treated with respect.

"Of course, she got upset at times, who wouldn't, with the privations and the challenges to dignity but she rarely complained. Whoever I had as a companion for that week couldn't have been better than her. She never let me down, she was never a burden." He took a handkerchief and blew his nose.

"Nor you to her, I'm sure."

"I hope not."

"You're right about what the boys did. It was not a joke; it was a despicable, vile act of assault and humiliation which could have resulted in the death of both of you. They deserve to have the book thrown at them."

"How did the one who told you about it react when you told him we were still not released?"

"James? He went as white as a sheet and seemed remorseful, I suppose."

"Remorse or fear of the reprisal to come?"

Roger smiled. "A bit of both, perhaps. How did you manage for a week tied to the bed? It's unthinkable."

Rob told Roger something of their existence in that bedroom: the laborious moving round the room for the simplest of tasks, the ancient magazines, the mental games to pass the time, the moments when they bolstered one another's spirit with humour and encouragement, the attempt to escape at the end when all seemed lost, but he didn't talk about the times when they were assailed, and nearly overcome, by fear and torment, or when Suzy cried.

Suzy returned from her bath, wearing a top and skirt of Gillian's. She smiled and Roger thought she was looking much better. Her damaged hand was bandaged and Gillian said she was taking her to casualty at the local hospital after she had had some food. Rob asked if Gillian minded if he had a bath too before he changed his clothes.

"Of course not," she said.

"Just a towel will do. I can look after myself," he said, picking up his change of clothing and following Gillian to the bathroom.

As Gillian made some sandwiches and heated soup, Roger told Suzy what he knew of the reasons for her ordeal.

"Gillian told me a little bit of it. Such a cruel thing to do, I don't think I can ever forgive them," she said, her eyes filling with tears.

"I think you have every right not to."

"What will happen to them?"

"The boys? I don't know. I think that will largely depend on you and Rob."

"You haven't reported this to the police?"

"Not yet. We were more concerned for you. Is that what you want?"

"I don't know, I think so. I have to mull it over and talk to Rob."

Gillian brought her over a bowl of chicken soup and a slice of plain bread. "Start with this and then we'll try a sandwich."

"Thanks," said Suzy. She picked up the spoon and stared at the soup. "Funny, isn't it, now that I can eat, I don't feel hungry."

"Body is still on starvation alert," said Gillian. "Try a little."

Suzy took a spoonful slowly, then another, more quickly, and soon she was clearly enjoying it. After she had finished, she accepted, without question, a cheese-and-cucumber sandwich, though she found she couldn't finish it.

"Don't worry, you'll soon be back to normal," said Gillian, taking away the plate. "Do you think you are up to going to the hospital to have your hand checked out?"

Suzy nodded. "I wish I could put it off but I suppose I should do it now."

"Yes, just in case there's a problem."

Rob rejoined them now, his curly hair washed and combed and with fresh clothes. He said he was now feeling more like his old self.

Gillian gave him the same meal she had served Suzy. "I'm going to take Suzy to the hospital to have this hand checked out. Make yourselves at home and have anything you want." She put a light jacket on Suzy and they were gone.

Rob took a spoonful of the soup and grunted approvingly. "The best food I've tasted since I don't know when. Ah! Yes, I do. I caught dysentery when I was six years old. I was sent to an isolation hospital with glass walls separating each bed from the next so I was effectively in my own ward. When my parents brought toys in for me, I was told that I wouldn't be able to take them home with me, they would have to be destroyed when I left. I couldn't fancy eating for day after day. Then one day, a nurse smiled at me and told me I was looking better and asked if I would like some bread and butter. It was the best bread and butter I ever ate but for the next few years I always wondered why it never tasted as good again." He smiled and ate more rapidly now.

When he finished, he put down the spoon. "Chicken soup will never taste as good again," he said.

Roger made another cup of coffee for them both and waited patiently while Rob finished eating his sandwich.

Eventually, he said, "I ought to go back to the hospital and tell James you survived. I know he deserves to suffer but he should know he hasn't actually killed anybody. Do you want to come with me?"

Rob smiled. "No thanks. My emotions might get the better of me."

"Will you be all right on your own?"

"Yes, you go ahead. I'm comfortable enough."

Roger drove back to the hospital and went to Howland Ward. It was now afternoon visiting time and the ward was packed with visitors at almost every bed. James was sitting on his bed while an attractive woman of about forty-five sat in a chair close to him. James was holding a handkerchief and occasionally touched his swollen eyes with it. The woman was patting his hand and smiling and talking earnestly to him. James ceased to give her his attention when he saw Roger come through the swing doors and approach his bed. The woman's head turned as she followed his gaze and her expression changed to one of fraught anticipation.

"Hello," said Roger.

Neither answered.

"You are James's mother?" asked Roger coldly, wondering whether it was nature or nurture that had given James his character; either way, she had played her part.

The woman nodded. "Yes, Patricia Newton."

"I think we should find somewhere private to talk," said Roger and he led them out of the ward to the corridor. They were followed by a nurse who asked where they were taking James and, when Roger said they needed to be able to talk in private, took them to the empty visiting lounge.

When they were seated, Roger introduced himself to Mrs Newton. "I'm Roger Southwark, one of James's teachers. Has James told you about the incident at the school?"

"Yes," said Mrs Newton, taking a deep breath. "Are they all right?"

"Recovering," replied Roger, determined not to make it too easy for either of them.

"Thank God," she said and patted her son's hand.

"When you say recovering, you mean they don't have to go to hospital?" asked James.

"Suzy has a serious cut on her hand and neither has eaten anything for over five days. Fortunately, they had access to drinking water otherwise they would have been dead by now."

Mrs Newton gasped. James was rather more phlegmatic.

"Thank goodness there's no harm done." A slight smile of relief had begun to creep across his expression.

"I wouldn't go that far," said Roger. "There will have to be an inquiry."

"At the school?" asked Mrs Newton.

"Yes, and perhaps the police might take an interest."

"Surely there has been no crime committed?" she exclaimed.

"Giving somebody a spiked drink, kidnapping, holding people against their will, depriving them of access to food and the basics of life. I'm not a lawyer but it smacks of criminality to me. Had they died, James would have been guilty of manslaughter at least."

James's smile disappeared. "Rory did all those things. I just went along with him. I was the one who said we should go back to the school."

"The car was going away from the school when it crashed," said Roger.

"Rory wasn't listening to me. He was high and driving like a maniac."

"How is Rory?" asked Roger.

"I don't know. I haven't seen him since he came out of the coma. I spoke to his parents briefly and they blame me for what happened to him."

"Why would they think that?" asked Mrs Newton.

"They think I shouldn't have let him drive if he was in no fit state."

"Perhaps that is why the police should be involved," observed Roger. "I have to go. I will be in touch." He left them staring at each other and asked the ward sister whether Rory was available to be seen by casual visitors yet. She said he wasn't, so he went back to his car and scribbled a few notes of the meeting before returning to Gillian's flat.

When Roger rang the doorbell, the door was opened by Rob. He looked less drawn now and even quite relaxed. He waved away Roger's apology for being left alone. "It was the first time I've been properly alone and without a sense of responsibility for a week, it's a pleasant change. How is James?"

"Relieved and anxious. Relieved that you and Suzy have come through but anxious that he might still be in trouble; not surprising, given what he has done. We will have to decide what to do."

"About what?"

"The repercussions of all this. I have to make some kind of report to Mandeville. The question of the involvement of the police will inevitably come up. How far do you think you would like this to go?"

Rob shrugged. "I don't know now. When I believed we were going to die, I wanted those responsible to be boiled in oil and to burn in hell. Now that we have come through this, I still want vengeance in the abstract but I don't yet have a view on the severity of the punishment. Suzy's views matter above anything else; she suffered more." He sipped a coffee he had made himself. "How did Gillian get involved in this business?"

"I bumped into her at the college the day Mandeville asked me to look into the accident. I told her that I was having trouble filling in the gaps at the end of the school party and had run into a series of dead ends and she started taking an interest and then sort of tagged along. She was really helpful, actually."

"And very kind today. I always thought she was a bit of a loner and not a very warm person. I misjudged her."

"You only ever really know what a person is like when you have to depend on them."

While they were talking about her, Gillian was arriving at the cottage hospital. She had assisted Suzy into her car and helped her again when they arrived at the hospital. The casualty department was the first area just after reception and Suzy and Gillian sat on hard plastic chairs along with only four other people.

"Nearly empty," whispered Suzy.

"Bank holiday weekend, always quiet," said Gillian. She added in a whisper, "Unless you are up to facing the police today, I think we should find a different reason for the injury to your hand."

"Oh God, yes. I'm not ready to start talking to anyone else yet, but what could I say?"

"I'm sure we can think of something: injury using a machine, playing a sport or game, as long as it was self-inflicted."

A voice called out, "Miss Suzanne Plunkett."

Suzy stood up, turning to say, "I'll think of something."

Twenty minutes or so later she was back, her hand rebandaged and a prescription in her uninjured hand.

"We have to go to the dispensary to get some cream and tablets," she said.

"How is it?" asked Gillian.

"Slight infection, nothing to worry about. The cut hasn't done any serious damage. He has put a couple of stitches in it. I'll have a scar but that's OK. He told me I should have come as soon as it happened."

"How did you say you did it?"

"I said I caught it in my father's electric vice when I was playing about with it. He seemed happy enough."

"Are there electric vices?"

"No idea but it's the first thing I thought of."

They both laughed, walking to the dispensary.

"Is it hurting much now?" asked Gillian, as they sat waiting for the prescription.

"Just aching a bit."

"I've got painkillers at home."

"You are being very kind to me."

"Do you think we should try to contact your parents?"

"They'll be back on Monday. I'll be home then. That will be soon enough for them to know; why spoil their holiday?"

Gillian nodded. "If your mother is anything like my mother, she'd come rushing back straight away."

Suzy smiled but didn't reply.

After they had received the prescription, Suzy asked if Gillian minded if she walked in the hospital grounds for a little while. "I just want to be outside for a bit. We were cooped up in that awful room all the time and it left me feeling claustrophobic. I can still smell the room now – and the blankets."

"Of course."

They walked for perhaps ten minutes or so, not talking much, just enjoying the burgeoning of spring in the trees and bushes and admiring the nodding daffodils. They stopped at one point and looked at the flowers for a while.

"It's the first time I looked at daffodils, really looked, since I was a child," said Suzy. "They are so perfect," she added as she gently touched the trumpet of one. "I really thought I'd never see a flower again." She stood up, a tear in her eye.

Gillian put an arm round her shoulder. "You've been through a lot. It must have been a terrible ordeal."

"At the moment I can't even think about it. I don't know how we coped."

"At least you weren't on your own."

"No, I wouldn't have made it without Rob. I doubt I could have moved the bed on my own and I certainly wouldn't have got the water running."

"I don't know Rob that well, but he seems a decent man."

"Yes. He was very kind and proper. At least I have no

horrible memories to deal with there. He was strong too; I mean strong mentally as well as physically. He never expressed his own fears or doubts we would make it. Not until today, when it did seem hopeless."

They walked in silence and then strolled to the car park. Suzy pointed to Gillian's Mini. "I love your car. Are you pleased with it?"

"Yes, it's reliable and cheap to run. Very hard to work on though, my father says. I wouldn't know. I just leave it to the garage. I'm not very mechanically minded."

"My father has promised me a car if I get into university and I'd like one of those. The same colour too."

"Have you thought of what you'll do tonight?"

"No. I can't face a long journey and I don't want to stay with a friend. Too many questions and too much drama. I could stay at a hotel."

"You are welcome to stay with me for a couple of nights."

"I don't want to be a burden; you've already done enough."

"No, really. I've got plenty of room."

"Thank you, that would be nice."

"What do you think you might like to eat tonight? I think something quite light would be better as your stomach may not be up to it quite yet."

"Yes, whatever you think. I couldn't face anything now. I feel a bit queasy. Although we had water, it had a funny taste and I wondered if it would make us ill but we didn't drink too much of it, just enough to keep going."

When they arrived at Gillian's flat, her two colleagues were sitting in silence, Roger reading a newspaper and Rob slumped in an armchair with his eyes closed.

Roger looked up when they came in. "Everything all right?"

"Nothing too serious," said Suzy. "It'll be fine."

Rob opened his eyes. "Thank goodness," he said.

"What have you been up to?" asked Gillian. "Taking it easy, I trust."

Roger put his newspaper to one side.

"I have been to the county hospital to see James. He was relieved to know you are both all right and I think he hoped, and his mother too, she was with him, that this would go no further. I warned him that this could become a police matter and that means that we have to make a decision. I know you are both tired and traumatised by everything that has happened and we can go into details later but we have to settle that issue; whether to go to the police or not. You see, I have to make a report to Mandeville before anyone else does and he will need to know. I think that decision lies with Suzy and Rob, don't you, Gillian?"

"Yes," she said.

Rob shrugged. "I don't know what to say. What they did was mischievous and stupid but they didn't mean it to end up like it did. Unfortunately, they would presumably be charged with kidnapping and imprisonment because lack of intention doesn't pardon the offence. If one of us had died, they could well have been charged with manslaughter. They must be held accountable in some way but I don't want revenge. I suppose I would wish to know the likely outcome before I brought the police in."

"Suzy?"

"I'm not sure either. James is not a bad boy and he was probably led astray by Rory who is quite a forceful person. Rory may have long-term consequences if he doesn't recover fully so he is already paying for it. I don't know what I think but if it hadn't been for Rob, I would be dead now so whatever he says is fine by me." She smiled at Rob.

"I'd like to know your views," said Rob, looking at his rescuers.

Roger didn't hesitate. "We should go to the police. What they did was nasty and unreasonable for the sake of a laugh at somebody else's expense. To make matters worse, they didn't consider what could go wrong, like making sure that somebody else was aware of what they had done. If James hadn't got his memory back in time, you two could have died."

Gillian nodded. "I agree. I was inclined to some kind of reprimand but it was you who changed my mind, Rob, when you mentioned that you might have died. Such reckless behaviour has to be shown to be criminal. If you drive a car that is not roadworthy, you don't have to kill somebody before the police charge you. It's what could have happened that matters and they are technically adults so they must be treated as responsible."

"What will happen to them?" asked Suzy.

"It won't be that bad because nobody died. Probably not even a prison sentence because there was no intention to do harm," said Roger.

"Perhaps just a magistrate's court rap over the knuckles," agreed Rob.

"I will speak to Mandeville about it tomorrow," said Roger. "I assume the school will want to take action of some kind."

They settled into a quiet late afternoon and evening. Suzy could hardly keep awake and Rob was preoccupied with his own thoughts.

Gillian had planned to cook dinner but the time seemed to whizz past and she hadn't even been shopping. Eventually, Roger went to the local fish-and-chip shop and bought enough for two adults and two children, everyone agreeing that the two former prisoners should have something tasty but not too much of it.

After the meal, accompanied by tea and bread and butter, Suzy said she was tired and would like to lie down and was not seen again that evening. Rob was also tired but declined the offer of a bed at Roger's and even refused the chance to be driven home. "I need to be normal now," he said, "and do normal things like driving home and watching some mindless rubbish on the telly and sleeping in my own bed."

"I'll see you in the morning after I have spoken to Mandeville," said Roger as Rob rose to leave. "You sure you want to drive yourself tonight?"

Rob smiled. "I'm sure." He embraced Gillian and then Roger. "Thank you both so much for your rescue; words are not enough to say how grateful I am and thanks for looking after us today. Where do you want to meet tomorrow?"

"Come round here at about eleven o'clock and we can all have a chat," said Gillian.

Rob nodded and he was gone.

Gillian went into the kitchen and Roger joined her. "I'll wash up. You've been on the go all day."

"Fancy a drink?" she asked. "I could certainly do with one."

"I think we deserve one," said Roger, declining the offer of a pair of Marigold gloves.

She took a bottle of Sauvignon Blanc out of the fridge, removed the cork and took the bottle and two glasses into the living room.

"Thanks for all you did today. It was amazing," said Roger.

"It was nothing really, just a single woman playing mother and nurse. Mind you, I feel quite shattered. I'll never forget that sight when first we saw them today. Him splayed out on the headboard and she reaching out to hold him and they were perfectly still. It was like something out of a late-medieval painting of a biblical or mythological scene. What actually was going on?"

"Their water had run out and Rob thought they must try to escape. He attempted to use his weight to break the rail out of position and free the handcuff. It didn't work and he was resting after several unsuccessful attempts to get back into the room. There were no other options left and they must have thought it was all over for them. He told me he was expecting to die."

"The poor things. Do you think he should have driven himself home, with all he's been through?"

"He'll be fine, he's in no hurry. He'll probably find it quite relaxing."

"Here's to the great escape," he said, raising his glass. "I am going to try to see Mandeville tomorrow. Do you want to come with me?"

"I'd like to but I think I should stay with Suzy."

He nodded. They sat back in their chairs, mimicking relaxation but actually exhausted. Their conversation retraced the events of the day and the one theme that dominated their exchanges was that of relief that they had been in time. Neither saw it as an achievement to be celebrated, the dreaded but averted alternative still plagued their reminiscences of the day. After a couple of drinks, Roger said it was time to go and though Gillian asked him, "Must you?" she did so without much conviction.

"See you tomorrow?" she asked at the door.

He nodded. "Thanks again for everything today. I couldn't have done this on my own."

He went to kiss her on the cheek but she was moving her head and their lips brushed. He went to move away but she maintained the kiss for a few moments. They smiled for a second before they bid each other goodnight.

Roger arrived home and slumped on a settee, intending to watch the television but finding himself suddenly washed out and unable even to go over the events of the day. He woke at about eleven o'clock with a stiff neck and dragged himself into the bathroom where he went through a truncated version of his nightly routine and found himself wide awake when he climbed into bed. He did go over the events of the day briefly but then found his mind oscillating between the horrors of a week chained to a bed without food and the challenge of deciding what action he would recommend to Mandeville that would be right in the circumstances. He did not fall asleep again till three o'clock.

Gillian had an equally troubled night, albeit following a different pattern. She had cleared away in the kitchen, as quietly as she could to avoid disturbing Suzy, then sat in her living room, listening to music turned down and polishing off the rest of the Sauvignon Blanc. She had not intended to kiss Roger but she was pleased that the incident had occurred and glad that she had made the most of the moment. Realising she had put down her marker, it was now up to him. He would be spared the dilemma of not knowing if she was interested and the risk of rejection which put some men off even asking for a date. She had seized the moment and she metaphorically raised her glass to that. After reading a novel for a while, without taking a single word in, and occasionally breaking off to mull over one or other of the events of the day, she finally went to bed at about eleven o'clock. Unable to sleep at first, bombarded by thoughts of 'what-if' in the imprisonment of Suzy and Rob, she eventually fell asleep only to wake again when she heard a sound in the flat. It was half past four according to her bedside clock and there was a light shining under her door. She assumed it was Suzy but put on her slippers and dressing gown and crept to the door, just in case. When she opened it, she heard the sound of a kettle boiling and smiled to herself: burglars didn't usually make themselves a cup of tea.

She called out, "Everything all right, Suzy?"

"Yes thanks. Sorry I woke you up. I couldn't sleep so I thought I'd get up for a bit. I was trying to be quiet."

"Not your fault, I'm a light sleeper. Is it the hand?"

"No, it doesn't hurt much. I just woke up and everything was going round in my head and I felt sort of as if nothing is real. Did last week really happen? Is this happening? I even pinched myself in case it's all a dream but that's stupid; if you pinch yourself in a dream, you won't *really* be pinching yourself, will you?" She suddenly started crying. "Then I started crying like this, silly tart." She reached over and took a sheet from a kitchen roll and blew her nose.

Gillian walked over and put her arm round Suzy's shoulder. "You've had a hell of a time and you're bound to be emotional about everything, it's so raw; it's not even a day since we found you. I'll make the tea. You look after your hand."

Suzy smiled and sat on a chair while Gillian pottered about. She made the tea and opened a cupboard to produce a pack of Anadin and another of Disprin. "Here, you can help yourself to the limit of my recreational drugs."

"Thanks, I have got a headache," said Suzy, reaching for the Anadin. "Would you mind if I stayed one more day?"

"No, of course not."

"Only I don't know whether I want to tell my parents about all this. My dad will go bonkers and start suing left, right and centre and my mum will make a fuss. I just want to forget about it, at least for a while."

"It will probably have to come out eventually."

"Yes, I know but if I feel calmer when I tell them it won't seem so bad and I can leave out the worst bits and maybe it won't come to a court case or anything."

Gillian nodded. "The only thing is, I have to see my parents on Sunday. I promised. I'm afraid I can't spend the day with you."

"I will have to be home by Monday myself so I will leave whenever you say."

"Do you want me to wash your clothes before you go?"

"No, thank you, I can do that when I get home. Perhaps just one thing to go home with; the cream top, if you don't mind."

"Of course."

One person who did sleep well that night was Rob. He drove home slowly, enjoying being on his own for the first time for a week, free of the responsibility, the fear, the hardship, the embarrassment, the claustrophobia that had haunted his time spent with Suzy. By the time he turned the key in his lock, all that was in his mind was the need to sleep. He resisted the temptation to look even cursorily at the pile of letters, newspapers and magazines on his doormat; he did not want any distraction to his one aim: sleep. He had a couple of shots of whisky and then climbed into his bed and went off straight away, having the first untroubled night for what seemed so long. He woke early without minding, experiencing for the first moment a strange feeling of something being missing and then seeing, lying on the bed cover, his left arm, no longer cuffed to the bedhead. He rolled over, smiling at the small freedom once lost and now recovered, and soon to be taken once again for granted. He lay there for half an hour or more, treasuring these moments of absolute freedom to do whatever he wished without hindrance or delay and promising himself he would never again get trivial or even important matters out of perspective. He had come close to death but had survived; only life mattered and he still possessed it. And yet! He pondered if ever he would feel again how precious life was as much as he had yesterday when it seemed about to end.

Finally, he got up and had breakfast, his favourite of tea and scrambled egg on toast, while looking through the headlines on the several copies of *The Guardian* and one each of the *Observer*, *Tribune* and *New Statesman*. Concluding that nothing earth-shattering had occurred, he turned to the post. Pushing obvious bills and the like to one side, he spotted an envelope bearing a Labour Party label and opened it, assuming it was a circular; it was a letter.

XIII

SATURDAY

ROGER AGREED TO MEET MANDEVILLE AT HIS home in Twirleston Combust, half a mile from the school and set away from the main road facing the green. It was an attractive Georgian house of grey brick, with wisteria climbing up the wall and a clematis clinging to the metal arch around the front door. Roger parked in the drive and walked up the gravel path. The bell clanged as he pressed the button and Mandeville opened the door with his usual jovial expression.

"Mr Southwark, do come in," he said.

Roger followed him down the hall, reflecting that Mandeville used the formal title not obsequiously but as a senior officer in the armed forces might refer to a junior one. Their destination was a reception room which Roger thought must be a study or library and they sat in comfortable moquette armchairs; a pot of coffee and cups already waiting for them.

"Coffee, just made. I like a man who values punctuality," said Mandeville, "'Punctuality, the politeness of kings', Louis XVIII, I believe."

He took a cigarette from the packet in front of him

and lit it, the first inhalation followed by a wheeze and the customary rumbling cough. "Marnoch's father telephoned me after you rang. The boy is responding slowly to treatment but the hospital fears there may be some permanent damage to his system. Too early to say for now. He still has no idea what happened on the fateful car journey. You said over the telephone you have some news?"

"Yes, but it's rather serious."

Roger recounted his findings concerning the party and its ending and how James and Rory had played their joke on Rob and Suzy with disastrous consequences.

Mandeville sat silently, listening intently, his expression gradually evolving from a questioning frown to a shocked open mouth. "Good God, thank goodness you found them. They will be forever grateful, I'm sure. A childish prank gone horribly wrong but no long-term harm done, fortunately." He poured some coffee into both cups and held the milk jug over one cup until Roger nodded and he added some before pushing the cup and saucer towards him.

"Rob Grainger and the girl may think otherwise," said Roger.

"Oh?" Mandeville added a little sugar to his coffee and stirred it slowly.

"Well, it might have been intended as a joke but it amounted to kidnapping, imprisonment and negligence. If they hadn't been rescued it would have been murder, or at least manslaughter."

Mandeville continued to stir his coffee, the tinkling sound reaching a crescendo before he suddenly stopped and took a deep drag on his cigarette. "I take it you haven't been to the police?"

"No, not yet."

"Good, no point in rushing to action. What do our victims wish to do about it?"

"They were sleeping on it. I haven't spoken to them today."

"And you?"

"I think we should report it to the police. Even if there is no long-term harm to Rob and Suzy, what Newton and Marnoch did to them is beyond a joke."

"On the other hand, the boys could well end up with a criminal record and this would have a profound effect on their lives."

"Actually, they did ask for it. Irresponsibility and malice deserve some retribution. What would you suggest we do?"

"The students will be expelled but permitted to sit their examinations. The welfare of Mr Grainger and Miss Plunkett are paramount, obviously. I suggest we sound them out and, if they are prepared to keep the matter out of the hands of the police, I will ensure the parents make good with some form of recompense."

"You think that will work?"

Mandeville smiled. "I can't guarantee it; the idea has only just come into my head. The fact is that if we go to the law, punishment will be meted out to the boys but the victims will have gained little except vengeance. They could sue but the boys have nothing worth suing and the only beneficiaries would be the lawyers. Whereas, if we find a solution involving compensation both sides win."

Roger rubbed his chin. He thought Mandeville had a point: a win-win solution beloved of negotiators. It was true that if James and Rory were prosecuted it would serve little purpose other than punishment. They were extremely unlikely to do something so stupid again and Rory appeared already to have paid a price of sorts.

"You may be right," he said, "but I think those who suffered should decide what happens next."

"Naturally," said Mandeville. "Will you see them again today?"

"Yes, I'll let you know what they say."

Mandeville nodded. "I am much obliged to you for everything you have done. It will not be forgotten."

Roger didn't answer. He felt his job was still unfinished. Much to his surprise, he really did believe the responsibility was his and he wanted to get to work straight away. He exchanged a few more pleasantries before leaving Mandeville and driving to Gillian's apartment.

He thought Gillian looked tired when she opened the door. "Everything all right?" he asked.

She nodded. "We had a bad night; Suzy couldn't sleep so we chatted for a while. She's getting dressed now."

"I'm not surprised she couldn't sleep after all that happened to her. Sorry you've had to take the brunt of it all." He put his hand on her arm.

She shook her head. "I asked to be involved and it's fine. How did you get on with Mandeville?"

"He wanted to keep things hushed up, leave the police out of it, but I said it is up to Rob and Suzy. Apparently, Rory may have long-term effects from the accident, they don't know yet. Not that it's relevant to what he did and must answer for."

They went into the lounge and Gillian made a pot of coffee while they waited for Suzy and Rob to appear. Suzy joined them in about ten minutes, looking washed out but cheerful but Rob did not arrive for nearly an hour.

"Sorry I'm late," he said. "I had a few things to see to with a week's post and so on."

He didn't offer any further explanation but the other three thought he seemed irritated and subdued, taking little part in the conversation reviewing the events of the previous day. The fact of the matter was that he was preoccupied with the contents of the letter he had opened that morning. He could remember every line.

Dear Rob,

I hope you are having a good Easter break. I had a meeting with Horace Blacklock and he tells me that he has decided to stay on after all for the next parliament. He says he has a good few years to go yet and thinks he will be able to chair his committee long enough to make his mark and pass it on when he is ready.

I realise this will be disappointing news for you after you have put so much time and energy into the constituency but we are all working for the greater good of the Party and your contribution will not go unnoticed. Another safe constituency is sure to come up for grabs as we near the next election and your time will come as the party needs candidates of your calibre.

We will always be pleased to see you here, anytime you are in the area and will undoubtedly see you at Conference and other events.

With all best wishes for the future.

Yours sincerely,

Fred Grayson, Constituency Party Chair.

When he first read the letter, he felt as if he had been kicked in the stomach. Now he was in numbed shock, unable to understand how fate had dealt him such a harsh blow so soon after his ordeal in the stable block. He knew it was nothing by comparison but he reasoned his resistance to bad news was lowered and his resolve to laugh off trivial disappointments would have to wait. At this moment, he could not even bring himself to talk of it, though he was unable to think of anything else, his career plans in tatters.

"Rob?"

He heard his name, as it seemed from afar. "Sorry?" he said.

"Your view as to whether we should go to the police?" repeated Roger, slightly tetchily.

"Er, not sure exactly. What do the rest of you think?"

Roger rolled his eyes and looked to the heavens.

"Are you all right, Rob?" asked Gillian. "We have just been round the table with our views."

"Sorry, I'm not quite myself today."

Gillian smiled sympathetically. "Perhaps it's delayed shock after what you have been through."

Rob nodded, smiling weakly.

"So far," said Roger, "Gillian reluctantly feels we should inform the police, Suzy is willing to forgive and forget but only if you are, I think it should be reported. I would be willing to accept the proposal of Mandeville that there should be a civil outcome with the parents, on behalf of the boys, offering some form of compensation. Your opinion will decide it."

The word 'compensation' pierced the fug of Rob's mind. Briefly, the thought of some kind of payment for his troubles came as a slightly soothing balm for his traumatising experience and the new anguish at lost ambition. "What sort of compensation?" he asked.

Roger shook his head. "I don't know yet. Mandeville is fully aware the decision can't be delayed. He will speak to the parents today and put them in the picture."

"Well, as Suzy is prepared to forgive them, I will not go to the police but I think we should both be compensated in some way. Often, people subjected to mental and physical torture suffer the effects long after the event and it could happen to us and involve therapy of some kind," said Rob, warming to the task.

"Like John Paul Getty III," said Gillian.

"And Patty Hearst," said Suzy, suddenly aware that a sum of money of her own might give her more financial freedom from her father.

"That settles it," said Roger. "I'll give Mandeville the go-ahead to set up a meeting between him and the parents."

"I think Suzy and Rob should be there in case Mandeville worries more about the school than them," said Gillian.

"You're right," said Roger.

A flurry of conversations followed this meeting. Mandeville reluctantly agreed to Roger's insistence that he, Rob and Suzy attend the conference with the parents which would take place the following Wednesday. Suzy had to explain to her parents that she had hurt her hand playing on a trampoline and that she would be returning to school for a tutorial which was not in any way disciplinary and Roger and Rob jointly agreed a strategy for the Wednesday meeting.

The Marnoch family lived near Moffat in the Scottish borders. Rory's mother had been staying in a hotel near the hospital since they had first become aware of the accident and her husband, having stayed with her over the Easter weekend, had prolonged the stay to be available for the meeting. Rory had definitely improved over the ten days since the accident. He was now described as 'out of danger'. Bodily, he would probably make a full recovery, though there were still concerns about his head injury and the full repossession of all his cognitive faculties. The Marnochs agreed to the meeting with Mandeville without hesitation, as Mandeville stressed the importance of a meeting to discuss his education, without even mentioning the matter of compensation, other than a vague reference to extra costs being incurred. On the other hand, James's parents were less amenable since James had convinced them that he had been an innocent stooge, dragged along by the forceful Rory. Mandeville had to hint at the possibility of police involvement initiated by Rob should they refuse to cooperate.

The meeting was held at the school, in the headmaster's study. Mrs Raglan, the school secretary, came in especially to take notes, Mandeville having given her a summary of the events of the previous week. Roger escorted Suzy and Rob to the meeting and they were early in case Mandeville had any late information for them. In fact, the headmaster was concise in his attitude to the meeting. "Just lay it on with a trowel: your suffering, hardship and near disaster and they will wilt before you. You've still got your hand bandaged, Miss Plunkett, excellent. Don't forget the handkerchief at appropriate moments. Mr Southwark, you play the advocate and I shall be the judge who applies the sentence."

"No black cap required these days," quipped Roger. Mandeville did not respond.

Mrs Raglan had coffee and biscuits prepared and sat with a brand-new shorthand pad and newly sharpened pencil next to Mandeville. Barely had they taken their seats when the Marnochs arrived.

Mr Marnoch was a large man in his fifties with grey, balding hair and he walked with a slight limp. He muttered a greeting and ignored the introductions made by Mandeville, merely giving a cursory nod to the group as a whole. His wife, ten years younger at least and a foot shorter than him, walked behind him until he ostentatiously drew a seat out from the table for her to sit on. Both were very well-dressed, not out of respect for the situation but because neither had clothes of any other kind.

"Daphne and George Marnoch," he barked at them as he took his seat. He looked at his watch and was about to say something when Mrs Raglan began serving his wife and himself with coffee and biscuits. While he began stirring a sugar cube into his coffee there was a knock on the door and, in response to Mandeville's call of, "Come," Mr and Mrs Newton entered the room. Roger recognised Mrs Newton from his trip to the hospital and today he thought her equally attractive, though now more sombrely dressed in a black dress with pearls. Her husband created less of a figure than Mr Marnoch, shorter and thinner and seemingly a little diffident as he fiddled with his tie and smoothed down his brown hair as he took the seat offered by Mandeville.

"Thank you all for coming," said Mandeville. I have invited Miss Plunkett and Mr Grainger, the two people trapped in the stable block, and Mr Southwark, one of our teachers, who fortunately tracked down Miss Plunkett and Mr Grainger and saved them from a ghastly situation. What happened on Friday, the last day of term, was extremely serious and, I have already explained to you, Mr and Mrs Newton and Mr and Mrs Marnoch, that your sons must be expelled. They will be permitted to sit their final exams in the summer, however."

"I hope you haven't brought me all the way down here to tell me that," said Mr Marnoch, slightly slopping his coffee as he involuntarily kicked the leg of the table.

Mandeville smiled. "No, Mr Marnoch. There is the matter of whether we should refer both your sons to the police for a criminal investigation."

"That's ridiculous," said Marnoch. "A stupid practical joke which went wrong and led to my son being severely injured. The two people were certainly inconvenienced and for that I am profoundly sorry but there was no intended crime."

"That would be a matter for the police to decide," said Mandeville, "but I don't think the word 'inconvenienced' adequately describes a situation in which they were handcuffed to the bed without most of their clothes, left with no access to food or water, other than from an old tank, for several days and may well have been dead by now as the water ran out last Friday."

"It was a cruel joke," said Suzy, reaching for her handkerchief, as she actually did feel a tear of anger form in her eye at this man's dismissal of all she and Rob had suffered as an 'inconvenience'.

Rob patted Suzy's hand and said, "I don't know if you have a daughter but how would you feel if she was forced to sleep, without clothes, in a bed with a man she did not know, without privacy of any kind."

Mrs Marnoch, who pictured her fifteen-year-old daughter in this predicament, visibly shuddered and Mr and Mrs Newton lowered their heads. Even Mr Marnoch seemed affected by Rob's intervention and ceased his protestations.

His wife said, "I am grateful to still have my son and am willing to make amends for what he did to you but please don't bring the police into this. He has suffered enough."

Her husband frowned for a second in response to his wife's apparent unwillingness to strike a hard bargain but he just shrugged.

Mrs Newton recovered her composure and in a lengthy plea for mercy said that her son had tried to restrain Rory from carrying out the escapade and should not be regarded as equally guilty.

Much to her surprise, her husband disagreed. "Irrespective of who played the greater part, he is still responsible. When he went out of the building, he left these two people to their fate until he chose to rescue them. Both our sons deserve punishment of some kind but if these two good people are willing to allow them to get on with their lives, perhaps we could make amends in a more productive way, acceptable to all."

Roger smiled benignly. "As in any civil matter, those who suffer loss rightly receive compensation and Suzy and Rob are willing to treat this as a purely civil matter."

"How do we know that they won't take the money and still report our sons to the police?" asked Mrs Newton, as much to her husband as anyone else.

"It would be their word against the boys without

independent witnesses and what would they gain?" said Roger, though he felt he was bluffing, as he didn't really know the answer to that one.

Mandeville had thought the meeting was going very well up to this moment: the righteous indignation of Suzy and Rob coupled with the measured arguments of Southwark, Mr Newton and himself were carrying the day. But now the fly in the ointment, or was it the wasp in this case, had arrived. He was temporarily lost for words and, from the total silence, he could tell he was not alone.

Eventually it was Suzy who spoke. "I never wanted the boys to be reported to the police and I promise that if you make an appropriate gesture to Rob and me, I will not report them and I will refuse to back any attempts to do so."

Mandeville smiled at Suzy. Her sincerity shone through and might yet win the day. Rob nodded his assent.

"How much?" asked Mr Marnoch.

Mandeville gave an expression of distaste. "Surely this is not a bargain to be haggled over," he said.

"What is it then?" asked Marnoch. "You will presumably come up with a figure and we will decide whether that is acceptable or make a counter offer. That sounds like bargaining to me."

"For goodness' sake, Leslie," said his wife, looking at him with a cold stare of contempt. "What did you have in mind by way of compensation, Mr Mandeville?"

Mandeville took a drag on his cigarette and let the smoke emerge slowly from his nose while he reflected on the question. "It is difficult to quantify a sum to make up for what Mr Grainger and Miss Plunkett have suffered. I suppose a very rough guide might be a sum which would enable them to enjoy a time of peace, enjoyment and relaxation which might in some way counter the extreme disturbance, struggle and ordeals which they went through in consequence of their incarceration for a week."

"Even if that were possible, it would hardly cancel the mental anguish they experienced when they struggled through those six days until they thought they were going to die," added Roger, concerned that Mandeville might be letting the miscreants off too lightly.

"Quite so," said Mandeville. "The biblical punishment of 'an eye for an eye', etc. would not match their experience as the culprits would know they would be released at the end of it," mused Mandeville, largely to himself.

"What a barbaric thought," said Mrs Newton.

Mr Marnoch folded his arms in disgust and Mrs Marnoch closed her eyes.

"Indeed," responded Mandeville, "but it does prove my point that adequate compensation is not to be taken lightly."

Mr Newton, who had maintained a calm, serene expression throughout the proceedings, smiled. "Perhaps Miss Plunkett and Mr Grainger would like to tell us what event or action might please them enough to take away or at least mitigate the hurt they feel as a consequence of the harm inflicted by the stupidity and recklessness of our two sons."

Mrs Newton looked perplexed at her husband's apparent surrender of their position but Mrs Marnoch nodded approvingly.

As he glanced at his wife a slight expression of amusement crossed Mr Marnoch's face. Newton had asked the same question as him, "How much?" but in a less aggressive way and now his wife approved. The bargaining had begun and Newton's question had the desired effect: Suzy visibly squirmed in her chair and Rob looked away from the inquisitive stare of Mr Newton.

Mandeville found himself considering the question from his own hypothetical perspective while he smiled benevolently at Suzy. "Do you have any thoughts on the matter, Miss Plunkett?"

"Two weeks ago, all I wanted was to pass my A levels well enough to go to university. In a way nothing has changed but after what happened to us that seems less important than it did. Yet if I don't pass the failure will now be harder to take. But there's not much we can do about that."

Roger thought there was something that could be done but kept his thoughts to himself.

"And you, Mr Grainger?" asked Mandeville.

Rob didn't want to say anything. Following the receipt of the letter from the constituency chairman he had sweated over the weekend, waiting for a chance to register his disappointment and plead his case and yesterday he had managed, after several failed attempts, to get in touch with the chairman. When the opportunity arose, he found he had no case to put. The chairman had said it was the sitting MP's right unless he was deselected by the constituency party and that would not happen. "That's life," as he put it. Since then, Rob had been seized by a mood of bitter frustration and self-loathing as his plans had come to nothing.

Now Rob was determined to maintain his dignity and say nothing. But, against his will, a tidal wave of sorrowful self-pity rose up in him and took over control of his mind, his mouth and his eyes. After a silence of a few seconds, the dam burst. "I am totally bereft," he said in a wavering voice, the tears jetting from his eyes and running down his cheeks. "Last week, I had to endure the most horrible humiliation and terrible ordeal with Suzy which left me utterly distressed," he sobbed, "and now I have learnt that all my plans for the future have been dashed by circumstances outside my control." He stopped; the fluency of his speech having come to a dead halt as the sobs picked up speed.

There he sat, the ruins of a man succumbing to the forces of his own nature.

As usual in such circumstances, this unexpected display of raw emotion led to a deathly hush as people looked away or at the ground, unsure what to say or do next. Only Suzy reacted. Her own eyes full of tears, she stood and walked over to Rob, putting a comforting arm round his shoulder and a hand on his.

"I'm sorry," muttered Rob, the tide of emotion receding and leaving behind a debris of embarrassment and withered self-respect. He reached in his pocket for a handkerchief and wiped his eyes and blew his nose while his surrogate nurse continued to comfort him. The sense that grew in him that he had 'made an exhibition of himself' was reluctantly shared by Mr Marnoch, Mr Mandeville and Mrs Newton, though none of them expressed as much as a shake of the head. Roger felt embarrassed pity and Mrs Marnoch nodded sympathetically with genuine sadness for Rob. Mr Newton sat impassively with his hands folded in front of him.

"Look what they did to us and you ask what it is worth," said Suzy as she looked at the assembled parents, her expression filled with contempt.

Mr Newton responded again, "May I have a few moments alone with Miss Plunkett and Mr Grainger?"

Marnoch looked at Newton suspiciously. "I think we should all be party to any discussions."

"I think it might be easier in a smaller group to understand their position." He gestured towards Suzy and Rob. "No decisions will be taken without your approval."

Mandeville nodded encouragingly. "I can see no harm and it may help to lower tensions. Would you be happy with that suggestion?" he asked, looking at the slightly quivering blob that was Rob and his soothing consoler. When they both nodded assent he turned to the rest of the room. "So, unless anyone has a strong objection to Mr Newton's proposal, I think we should adjourn for twenty minutes while Mr Newton confers with the injured parties." He stood up and the rest of the gathering followed suit, including Mr Marnoch, despite his reservations about the proposal.

When they were all gone, Newton smiled again. "Now, we can talk straightforwardly. I know what happened to you was despicable and we all owe you a great deal because of your forbearance and willingness to forgive. I am sure you know, but if you don't you will soon learn, that the old adage, 'It's not what you know but who you know', is undoubtedly true. The world is full of brilliant, capable and admirable people who failed to achieve their full potential because the right door remained closed to them for a lack of knowing someone who was willing to open it for them. I have influence and I have contacts. I may not be able to make a success of your life for you but I may be able to open the door that gives you an opportunity to make your own success."

Rob listened to Newton speak with barely concealed scepticism. He had heard this all before. The Svengalis, the miracle medicine salesmen and the share and horse tipsters who claim they can make you famous, cure your problems or make you rich but turn out to be charlatans, mountebanks and swindlers. Yet, in his fragile state, an egg without a shell, he wanted to believe this positive-sounding man with a pleasant, encouraging voice, benevolent smile and the intelligent, refined features one associated with a leader of men. Suzy was less suspicious. Her own father was a man of influence and he had the keys to many doors, though he was prone to open them only when he received something in return; he expected his children to achieve their own success as he had done. She listened but expected nothing.

"Tell me what you want that will help you achieve your ambitions and I will see what can be done." He looked at Suzy, his grey-blue eyes fixed on her until she felt she must speak.

"I want to pass my exams with decent enough grades to get into a good university."

Newton nodded. "Tell me the subjects and the examining board and I will see you have the exam papers and any necessary tuition three weeks before the examinations."

Suzy was astounded. No ifs nor buts; everything she had day-dreamed of offered to her without hesitation. To her surprise, she was reticent about accepting the offer and did not reply.

Newton smiled. "You are a good person, Suzy. Your resilience and the support you gave to Rob are testimony to that. You seem troubled by my offer. Perhaps you believe it's cheating of a sort?"

Suzy nodded.

"I don't think so. Every aspect of life is littered with examples of people getting an upper hand through good fortune: nepotism, favouritism, inside knowledge, hot tips, an examination paper which suits one student more than another and so on. You have been disadvantaged by a traumatic incident which might be expected to affect your composure and your concentration for months to come. We are merely trying to make up for that loss by giving you a little support. You will still have to write the answers to the examination questions well enough to get the good grades."

Suzy smiled. Newton had articulated her own thoughts better than she could have done and he had set her mind at peace. "Thank you," she said quietly.

Rob was impressed too. He looked at Suzy, now relaxed and smiling, and hoped this soothsayer could make matters better for him as well. He leaned forward in his chair.

"You said that your plans for the future had been dashed. May I ask what they were?"

For a moment Rob hesitated, aware that what was an ambition as important almost as life to him might not equate to much for most people. "I wish to have a career in politics and I was promised the opportunity of a safe seat at the next general election. This promise has now been withdrawn purely because the sitting MP has changed his mind, not for any failing on my part. I may not be able to get another chance."

If Newton thought Rob's tragedy as inconsequential as Rob feared he might, he gave no hint. He just nodded sagely. "So, you are in search of a safe seat. For which party? Hopefully not the Liberals."

"No, Labour."

"Leave it to me. It may take some months but I will find you a seat where you will have more than a fighting chance of being elected."

"You can really do that?" asked Rob.

"Yes, I have contacts. In the meantime, you can still try for a new seat yourself if you wish but you have my word."

Rob wasn't as confident as Newton but he took comfort from the conversation because he wanted to believe him. Before he could seek further reassurance, Newton continued.

"Now I suggest you both relax and perhaps book a luxury holiday during the Whitsun period or whenever and Mr Marnoch and I will be pleased to foot the bill with ample spending money plus a cash sum of £8,000. Alternatively, forego the holiday and we will give you each the sum of £10,000. There is just one other small matter. I know you are both trustworthy but I must have an assurance too. My solicitor will draw up the necessary paperwork for your signature to a confidentiality agreement that you will never divulge to any third parties the events of last week and will not press any legal claims against James and Rory."

Rob felt his reassurance ebbing slightly. "I have no objection to keeping quiet about everything but we have only your word too," he said.

Newton did not appear irritated by this challenge. "Quite right. I suggest that if I don't deliver my side of the bargain within a reasonable time, a month in Suzy's case and a year in Rob's, I will pay you each the sum of £25,000 in addition to what you have already received. I will put that in writing. I will expect you to pay the same sum to me if you break the contract."

"The only problem is that we can hardly sue you over breach of contract without Suzy admitting she was willing to cheat at the exam and me admitting that I was willing to be party to manipulation of party selection which would put paid to my political career," said Rob.

"We would all be in the mire so we must make this work."

Newton's rapid reply was enough to satisfy Suzy. "I am happy with the plan," she said.

Rob nodded after some hesitation and the deal was done.

Newton went off to get the others and the two injured parties looked at each other. "Are you happy with the arrangement?" asked Rob.

"Yes, very happy. I shall skip the holiday and take the money. I could buy a nice house round here for that."

"Just about. House prices have nearly tripled in the last six years. As long as he delivers on the deal."

"Rob, you don't mind me taking the easy path on the exams, do you?"

He shook his head. "No, of course not. You deserve a break. Anyway, lots of teachers give clues about the questions coming up if they see the papers beforehand. It's a corrupt world."

"When all this is settled, I suppose we won't meet again," she said.

"Would you like to?"

"Yes, it would be nice to say goodbye with a good memory rather than all the bad stuff we went through."

"You're right. We'll get the agreement done and have dinner or something when you have finished your exams."

"I'd like that."

"Actually, I have got some good memories from the bad time. The moment when we were rescued and knew we weren't going to die was pretty good."

She smiled as she thought of it, a memory that would surely never fade.

"There were odd moments, too, when we weren't shifting the bed round or trying to do something impossible when I enjoyed your company and we forgot what a nightmare it was. I will always remember those moments too."

She nodded and the tears began. "God, I've become such a weeping Minnie lately," she said, momentarily laughing.

He stood up and put his arm round her for the first time since they had been freed and they shared a quiet moment together before the door swung open and the others began filing in.

Mandeville invited them to talk among themselves while they waited for Messrs Marnoch and Newton who were, he said, 'finalising the arrangements'. There was some small talk between Mandeville and Roger and between Mrs Marnoch and Mrs Newton. Suzy and Rob sat quietly, the former hoping Marnoch would approve the plan, the latter wondering if they should have asked for a bigger cash payout.

The two fathers walked into the room and sat down. Newton was smiling; Marnoch had his usual expression, somewhere between a scowl and a sneer.

"Welcome back, everyone," said Mandeville. "I believe that Messrs Newton and Marnoch have made an offer of compensation to Miss Plunkett and Mr Grainger which both have found acceptable: a sum of £10,000 each. A very generous and, I think, appropriate offer. The matter will go no further outside these four walls." Naturally, Mandeville made no reference to the additional favours offered by Newton.

The two wives looked a little surprised but passed no comment. Mrs Raglan paused for a moment with raised eyebrows and Mandeville beamed, his beloved school saved from bad publicity and an official investigation.

Roger smiled and thought it generous, to a point. He assumed Newton and Marnoch paid the top rate of income tax at eighty-three per cent and as their accountants would find a way to register the payment as a loss of some sort, they would pay only seventeen per cent of the £10,000, just £1,700 each. Not bad for getting your son off the hook and burying the embarrassing bad news but not terrible for Suzy and Rob either. The only loss was to the Treasury and through it the taxpayers but they had no say and knew nothing about it anyway. A success all round. His thoughts were interrupted by the mention of his name as Mandeville continued.

"I wish to place on record all our thanks to Mr Roger Southwark, whose sterling work in investigating the events of last Friday week and finding out exactly what happened undoubtedly ensured that lives were not lost." Mandeville nodded towards Roger and led the applause by everyone present.

The group began to disperse. Mr and Mrs Marnoch left first, Mrs Marnoch stopping to shake hands with Suzy and Rob and her husband doing his best to smile in the background. Mr Newton then spoke to them, tying up a few loose ends of the arrangements, exchanging telephone numbers and so on.

Roger waited to talk to those he had rescued and, when the Newtons had gone, he walked over to them.

"I hope you are reasonably happy with the agreement," he said. "No money could compensate for what you went through but the horrors will fade to some extent and this will help."

"Thanks, Rog," said Rob. "You were great and you and Gillian were so kind. The deal is fine. We can't speak to the police or the press but I just want to forget about it and move on. I'm going away now for a few days. I'd be grateful if you don't mention all this in college."

"My lips are sealed."

"Thanks. See you next week."

"That goes for me too," said Suzy, feeling slightly guilty that he didn't have the whole story. She kissed him on the cheek. "I am going home for a few days before term starts. See you in class?"

Roger nodded and shook hands with them both.

"Let me buy you a drink," said Rob.

"Thanks, but no, I've got a few things to do."

They headed for the car park. "Let's have a drink to celebrate," whispered Rob as they came out of the front door.

Roger went into the secretary's empty office to check his mail and, as he came out empty-handed, almost bumped into Mandeville.

"Ah, Mr Southwark, glad you are still here. Come back to my office, please."

Mandeville picked up an envelope from his desk and gave it to Roger.

"What's this?"

"I suggested to Messrs Newton and Marnoch that a little gesture of thanks to you would not be amiss."

Roger opened the envelope. Inside were two cheques for £1,000 each.

"That's very generous, thank you."

"It's the least I could do. I think you saved all our bacons, as it were. Will you join me in a glass of port?" He went over to the glass cabinet and took out two glasses and a bottle of Sandeman and poured out two large glasses of the deep-red fortified wine. "*All's Well That Ends Well*, as Shakespeare might put it," he said, raising his glass.

"All's well that ends well," said Roger.

XIV

GILLIAN

AFTER THE MEETING, ROGER DROVE OVER TO SEE Gillian and keep her updated on events. On the way he stopped at the wine merchants and bought a bottle of Veuve Clicquot. She answered the door and he presented her with the bottle.

She nodded approvingly. "For me? How lovely!" She kissed him. "All went well then?"

"Yes, I think everyone was happy with the outcome." He told her about the tentative conversation around compensation and then Newton's takeover of the situation and his private talk with Suzy and Rob which culminated in an offer of £10,000 to each of them. "Whether or not he added any other sweeteners I have no idea, because the parents insisted on a confidentiality agreement so the story will not appear in the press and there will be no contact with the police. Mandeville was very pleased about that."

"And you are pleased too, if you decided to celebrate?"

"I am pleased but I also have cause to celebrate." He took the envelope out of his inside pocket and produced the two cheques. "My reward for our efforts. I think one of these belongs to you."

"Don't be silly. You did all the work; I just came along for the ride."

"More than that. You were a great help, especially with the idea of visiting James at the hospital which led to us finding them in time."

"No, honestly, Roger. I am pleased they did recognise our efforts but I think you deserve it all. I enjoyed getting involved in the rescue and helping you a little, it was great. I'll settle for a glass of bubbly and if you want to take me out to dinner or something, that would be more than enough of a reward."

"You're on," he said.

She took the bottle out to the kitchen, "I'll put it in the fridge for a bit. Not quite cold enough, unless you are in a hurry?"

"No, nothing else I have to do today."

"That's good, nor have I." She sat down next to him on the sofa.

"I don't suppose you've heard from Mark Harred or his wife yet?" she asked.

"No. I don't want to go around there again in case things are still up in the air. We'll see what happens with the start of the new term."

She nodded in agreement and she asked him about some of the details of the meeting and what the parents were like. "How is Rory?" she asked.

"Still recovering. Didn't get a real update but he's not going to be left a physical wreck or anything." He had noticed how attractive she looked when he arrived but now he was aware of how good she smelt too, whatever perfume she was wearing.

After ten minutes, she went out to the kitchen and came back with the bottle and glasses. "Are you hungry?" she asked. "It's nearly lunchtime."

"Bit peckish, but not very."

She went out again and came back with some crisps, olives and Ritz crackers on a platter, with cocktail sticks for the black olives. "This OK?"

"Just right," he said, easing the cork from the bottle with a gentle pop. He poured the champagne in the glasses in a short burst so the bubbles stopped teasingly at the top of the glass without running over. A second, slower pour took the drink almost to the top.

She smiled. "You are well-practised," she said.

"Years in the City," he said. "Everyone gets good at something. Here's to Rob and Suzy and a better future."

They clinked their glasses. "And to us for finding them," she added. "Mm, this is good," she said. She offered him the plate and he took some crisps. "Olive?" she asked, harpooning one with a cocktail stick and holding it up to his lips. He accepted it with his lips and was pleased to find it was stoneless. She put the plate down, after taking a cracker and an olive for herself. They stood in silence, enjoying the drink and smiling at each other.

When is free will just that and when is it subjugated by a form of compulsion, our actions forced on us by another or something compelling from within? There is a tendency to claim free will for our virtuous actions and compulsion for those we are less proud of. But when virtue is not the issue, who is to say? These were questions which whirled through Roger's mind much later but at this moment only Gillian could answer these conundrums. She was quite sure she was acting of her own free will, whether or not her will was being driven by circumstances and feelings outside her control. Of course, the situation was amenable: a happy day, success in their venture, celebration and reward and champagne, a drink which has connotations of excitement and gratification in a way that a pint of stout or a glass of Advocaat don't quite conjure up. She was not interested in analysis, only that the moment was right and should not be missed nor blown by a mishap or an ill-judged move which resulted in clumsiness or, worse, farce and the moment be lost, perhaps lost forever.

She put down her glass and put her arms round his waist. "What a lovely surprise, a champagne lunch, and what a lovely day." She was sure of her ground; she had kissed him before and he had not demurred, there had been no hint of recoil from her embrace and his expression had remained affectionate. She kissed him now and held him close to her and when they parted, he returned the kiss with as much warmth.

He put his glass down and they held hands for a moment or two. Then he kissed her again and topped up their glasses. He sat down on the sofa and she joined him. They sat in silence, taking a drink and picking at items on the platter. After a couple of minutes, she leaned over and kissed him, this time for longer and thinking of the next step. "Do you want this?" she asked.

He smiled but there were mixed emotions in his expression. "Yes, but is it wise?"

"Wise?"

"Sensible, you know, with us working together."

She winced. "I have thought about it myself. If we worked in a factory, there would be the two weeks of teasing, mickey-taking and mild or worse off-colour wisecracks and then everybody would accept it and forget about it. But, in our supposedly more refined atmosphere there will be the superficial silence and underneath the comments behind our backs, the sniggers and the innuendo and the gossip that we never hear. Can we bear it? Well, I can. I don't give a toss about what other people think. What they get up to in their private lives is nothing to do with me and what I do is none of their business. It just shows how boring their lives must be."

Roger laughed. "I agree entirely. Actually, I was thinking about how awkward it might be for us if it doesn't work out and we are still working together."

It was Gillian's turn to laugh. "We haven't even got going yet and you are worried about the break up."

Roger smiled sheepishly.

"We're not teenagers," continued Gillian. "Surely, we can at least act grown up if it all goes to pot. Anyway, for the time being we will just carry on as before, acting at work as if we are just colleagues and nobody will take much notice, unless you are caught dragging me behind the filing cabinets for a ravishing."

Roger laughed. "Is that an invitation? No, you're right. I get a bit over-protective of my private life."

"I don't expect you to change your life for me."

"Nor I you, but people always say that then expectations develop and after that demands."

"Well, if and when that happens, we will review the situation, as people always do."

"Yes." He was conscious that he had already begun to contemplate cutting back on his weekend trips to London. He topped up their glasses.

"I hope you are trying to get me drunk," said Gillian, giving him a knowing wink as she picked up her glass and took a few more sips.

XV

SUMMER

On the following Monday, the new term began, both at college and the academy. For most of the staff in both institutions, nothing of interest had occurred during the Easter break, especially as all of those at the academy and most of those at the college had not strayed near the place for the duration of the fortnight's holiday. For those in the know at college: Roger, Gillian and Rob, there was the fairly muted anticipation of waiting for the return or not of Mark Harred and an answer to the question over Mike Brompton. None of them particularly cared; Rob had his own concerns and Roger and Gillian had each other as objects of preoccupation, but they were all curious to know.

At quarter to nine, Mark Harred arrived for his nine o'clock class with HNC Year One and his arrival was noted by Rob, who shared the same staff room.

"Morning, Mark. Have a good break?" asked Rob.

"Morning, Rob. Eventful."

"Get away?"

"'Get away' as in 'go on holiday' or as in *The Likely Lads*, meaning disbelief or scepticism?" said Mark in a slightly prickly way.

Rob smiled. "The former."

"Not exactly. Domestic matters took up a lot of my time. What about you?"

"Nothing special."

"I suppose you were nursing the constituency?"

"No. The sitting MP has decided to stay on."

Mark shook his head. "Politicians rarely go quietly. Bit of a bugger for you, though."

Rob shrugged. "Hopefully something will turn up."

Mark hurried about his business, getting his notes ready and the right register for the class.

Rob watched, noting that Mark's shirt and tie looked uncreased, his face cleanly shaven and his demeanour untroubled. He waited until there were no other lecturers in the room and said, "Quite a party last day of term at the academy."

Mark did not react. "Yes."

"Especially in the stable block. How's Jane?"

Mark was ready for his class and heading for the door. He stopped in his tracks and said nothing for a few moments. "Don't know. Haven't see her since that night. How's Suzy?" he retorted, as he bustled off to the classroom.

Rob's response of, "She's fine," ringing in his ears.

Mike Brompton was equally taciturn about events at the party. He arrived as usual at lunchtime since he had evening classes to take and appeared completely at ease with life. Rob, at the urging of Roger, who wanted to tidy the loose ends up, casually mentioned the party in passing to him but Mike responded as if he had merely dropped in for a short while and said nothing about the problems at the end of the evening. Rob reported the same back to Roger who shrugged, satisfied he had nothing else to report to Mandeville.

That was the last time the academy party was mentioned in the lecturers' offices at the college.

Not so at the academy. There, at the speed of a bushfire, the news that the party had stretched on and ended with the car crash involving James and Rory, spread throughout the school half an hour into the new term. The car crash incident had made the semi-exiled James something of a hero as he related his attempt to save them both when Rory lost control of the car and then, refusing to care for his own safety, insisted on attending to his more seriously injured friend till help came. This story could neither be verified nor disputed by Rory as his memory of the event was completely absent. James, for obvious reasons, did not mention the matter of spiked drinks and what happened afterwards. With Suzy also keeping silent and saying she went home as usual, news of that kind was virtually non-existent. Except for a few wisps of smoke from a rumour about Jane.

Jane had spent the evening, in her own opinion, on cloud nine. She would like to have gone as far as calling it cloud ten but, as a geography student interested in weather patterns, she knew the categorisation of clouds only went as high as nine. She had been in rapture when Mark Harred, for whom she had an unannounced adoration, had chosen her, rather than Antonia, his usual favourite, to spend time with at the party.

Having spent the first two hours or so in mild flirtation, Mark turned up the volume once those that remained decamped to the stable block. Years before, he had read somewhere the adage, 'Make a married woman laugh and a single woman cry, to win their hearts', and he brought this into play often with young women whom he sought to conquer; Jane was no exception. Now, he not only told Jane how attractive she was with a cascade of carefully constructed compliments. He also revealed how in his life he had experienced a series of unrequited or unhappy affairs, culminating in the tragic history of his marriage. He painted his sad story of a young couple, madly infatuated who had married too young and then gradually grown apart. Neither was to blame and they were unwilling to break up for the sake of the children so they were locked into a loveless marriage. The tragedy was that in Jane he realised he had found someone who could make him truly happy. By this he was not referring to a sexual relationship but a union of souls. Unfortunately, it could never be.

Mark expounded his well-honed lament with such perfection on this occasion that, though he thought it strange, he began to believe there was some truth in his soulful ballad. That occasional ennui with his life of deceits and the never-ending pursuit of young women returned. Here was the opportunity for a new, pure start. He even dismissed thoughts of a sexual conquest and pondered an elopement, however mad that might be. He discreetly took her hand in his and proclaimed his honourable thoughts towards her, even using his adaption of the Prayer of St Ignatius, which he reserved for the coup de grace for all his conquests.

"Take, Jane, receive all my love, my liberty, my understanding, my whole will, all that I have and all that I possess. Do with it as you will, according to your good pleasure."

To his surprise he was able to conjure up a tear in his eye, which was swiftly reciprocated by Jane and all was moving towards an unknown but sure to be a moving outcome when Rory topped up their drinks. Jane barely touched her drink again as she was too excited and thought any more alcohol was bound to make her lose all control of herself. She had been touched beyond words at the thought that as she felt for him, so did he for her and she saw herself as Eloise to his Abelard, Elizabeth Barratt to Robert Browning, Beatrice to Dante.

Mark did try a little of Rory's concoction but thought the taste odd and decided he'd had enough. He suggested they go somewhere they could be alone. He led her out of the large room past the toilets to a storeroom full of stacked boxes and a load of junk and shook his head. Then he led her upstairs; there was no resistance from the hand he was holding. At the top of the landing, he saw the bedroom and the bed and his pulse quickened for a moment but he thought it unacceptable for a tryst. He led her back down stairs and out of the back door and they walked towards the gate.

"What time do you have to be back?" he asked.

"No time."

They walked briskly across the rough grass, the wet stalks rough against her legs, when Mark stopped and put his hand to his head.

"Are you all right?" Jane asked, holding his arm.

He shook his head, as if to clear it. "I feel a bit peculiar," he said.

"Shall we go back?"

"No, I just need a moment."

They walked slowly to the car, only a few yards away and he leaned against it for a few minutes.

"Can you drive?" he asked.

"Yes, I passed my test in January."

He gave her the keys and climbed rather unsteadily into the passenger seat.

Jane started the engine and looked at him. "Where do you want to go?"

"Anywhere you like," he said, his eyes closed.

She set off towards the market town of Franglid, a forty-minute drive away, occasionally looking over at Mark and thinking what a sad end to the evening and not what she had hoped.

After about ten minutes, Mark opened his eyes. "I'm feeling a bit better now. Stop the car, please."

She pulled over by a farmgate. He got out and vomited

onto the verge then got back into the car and wiped his face with a handkerchief. "I apologise for that but I think that last drink I had was dodgy."

"Dodgy?"

"It tasted weird; I think someone might have put something in it. I'm all right now."

"Do you want me to drive you home?"

"Not unless you are fed up with me."

She smiled. Not even his sickness had weakened her attraction to him. She was now Fanny Brawne to his John Keats. "No. Where then?"

"The Moon Hotel in Franglid."

She nodded.

They pulled up in the virtually empty car park and Mark jumped out of the car and went round to hold Jane's door open for her. He felt so much better.

They walked through the main door and into the lounge bar, where he ordered a brandy and soda for himself and a Babycham for her.

"Cheers," he said and took a drink from his glass. "That's better."

"How are you now?" she asked.

"Fine. I just felt very woozy for a few minutes. Probably have a headache in the morning."

"Who would want to spike your drink?"

"One of those immature male students, I suppose. Silly tosser. I hope it hasn't spoiled things?" he asked.

"No, not in the least," she replied, reassuring both of them.

He looked round the bar: nobody he knew, just an elderly couple talking quietly and two men at the bar discussing the football results. "Shall we get a room?" he asked.

She nodded.

They went over to the door opposite the bar with the

word 'Reception' emblazoned on the glass. Jane was trying to look nonchalant but guessed she probably seemed clueless or gauche. She could feel her heart pumping.

The porter said, "Good evening, sir. Can I help you?" without looking up."

"We would like a room for tonight, a double please," said Mark.

The porter looked up and cast his eyes from Mark to Jane. "Have you any luggage, sir?"

"No, we didn't expect to stay here tonight but the car needs attention so I shall have to sort it out in the morning."

"Good thing you managed to get as far as the hotel, sir," said the porter. He looked at his empty register as if assessing the availability of rooms. "Very good," said the porter, "a double room for this evening. I'm sure you won't mind paying in advance, sir, but it's the rule with late bookings and no luggage." A slight smile crossed his face.

"How much is that?" asked Mark.

"That will be £6.50, sir, including full English breakfast, of course."

Mark opened his wallet and produced £7. "Keep the change," he said.

"Thank you, sir," said the porter. "We are quiet this evening, I can offer you one of our best rooms with full ensuite facilities, at no extra charge."

"Thank you," said Mark.

Jane felt there was some kind of ritual going on, to which she was not really party. "Have you a toothbrush and toothpaste, please?" she asked.

"With our compliments," said the man, handing over a toothbrush and toy-sized tube of Colgate.

"Thank you," replied Jane.

Putting the items in her bag and taking Mark by the arm,

she walked with him slowly up the stairs to the room. She had seen better halls, this one had certainly seen better days, and she was not expecting much of their room, but she was pleasantly surprised. It had been quite recently decorated with a William Morris style wallpaper in a subtle blue with complimentary-coloured satin paint. The furniture was of a faux regency style; creamy white with gold highlighting and the floral carpet was pale and clean. In the bathroom she could see a pampas-coloured suite.

Mark invited her to sit with him on the small two-seater sofa and she happily did.

He looked at her earnestly for a moment. "I meant what I said, earlier. I do care about you and I don't want to take advantage of you. I wanted to be alone with you so that we can share our thoughts and hopes without the attention of others and without a sense of imposed shame." He kissed her hand and held it in his.

"I believe you," she said. "I want that too."

He leaned over and kissed her chastely to which she responded with enthusiasm. After a minute or so they separated, enjoying that delicious junction when all options were available but none yet engaged, and neither failure nor disappointment even considered.

Mark ordered coffee from the porter and it was brought up to their room by an elderly waitress, who poured the coffee courteously and was pleased with Mark's generous tip. Jane was also pleased as she had been advised by her mother that a generous tip reflected a generous soul.

Over coffee and into the night they talked a great deal of their unexpectedly rapid discovery of their love for each other, which Jane surmised was proof of its truth while Mark could only put down to the result of a rebirth of some kind. Eventually, the exchange of romantic plaudits exhausted, a move could no longer be delayed.

Jane ran a bath and used the free, if dubious, toiletries, then emerged from the bathroom, a towel maintaining her modesty. Mark smiled and went into the bathroom to share the bathwater. Jane, aware that there was nothing for it but to sleep in their clothes or to go naked, had already made up her mind and slipped out of the towel under the cool sheets. She waited, listening to the splash of the bath, the brushing of the teeth, the flushing of the toilet, the opening of the door. Then watched the well-built figure in a small towel, the turning off of the light and the discarding of the towel, before the slight movement of the mattress as he climbed in the bed and she felt his body next to hers. She had already made up her mind about the next move. This was not her first time. Her first lover had been an inexperienced, cumbersome boy the same age as her who had been overcome by nerves the first time and was brisk to the point of almost instantaneous relief, the second and mercifully last time. She was confident that this time it would be a more fulfilling experience as she turned towards him and kissed him while her hand ran over his chest.

Jane was not disappointed. A man of many first nights, Mark made love to Jane with tenderness and enthusiasm and just as much with proficiency and perfect timing. As they lay back in tired contentment, Mark was not disappointed either. His new-found emotions had not, as can often happen, interfered with his performance, indeed, he had hardly been aware of his emotions while they had been locked together, until now. "I love you," he whispered tenderly, as they held hands. Then he fell asleep.

The next morning, they had a full cooked breakfast, which Mark pronounced rather good. Jane, wondering whether, having had time to sleep on it, Mark would feel differently, was encouraged by his not creeping off to the telephone and his talk of going shopping to equip them for a trip away. She did telephone her mother to say she was staying at the school for another weekend as she wanted to plan her revision for the following term and then have a couple of days camping with two of her friends. Her mother was very pleased with her industriousness and that she had saved enough from her allowance to have a short holiday.

They drove the car supposedly to a garage but in fact to the town car park and then went to the shops for underwear, a couple of shirts for him and a dress and top for her and some toiletries. He then went to a barber and had a shave while she had a coffee. Just before he collected Jane, he went into a jeweller and bought a diamond-and-sapphire bracelet for Jane and a silver neckless with an amethyst stone for his wife, each to be given at an appropriate time. Then they were off.

For three days, they drove around Rutland, recently and reluctantly no longer a county, and the surrounding parts of Leicestershire, staying at commercial hotels and taking in the sights of wherever they stopped. Visits to Melton Mowbray, Belvoir Castle and Oakham Great Hall decorated with its large horseshoes, alternated with trips in the country, notably Hambleton and Rutland Water, and lazy afternoons in the hotel. The evenings were spent with dinner followed by early nights. It was on Tuesday evening that, for the first time, the conversation dragged a little and each of them seemed to the other preoccupied.

As they came up the stairs, Jane asked, "What are we doing tomorrow?"

Mark replied, "We need to talk about that."

"I know, I have to let my mother know what I am doing."

They sat together on the sofa and Mark looked down for a few seconds. "I told you I love you and I do, but I have to think about the future for both of us. I am nearly twice your age and in twenty years you will still be a young woman while I will be galloping towards retirement. I don't want you to be wasting your best years on me. In any case, you are bound to see things differently when you are older and you will probably tire of me long before then."

"But..."

"Please, let me go on. It's hard enough to do as it is. There is also the question of my children. I don't know if I could leave them and I certainly cannot abandon them. I would still want to support them and you would be deprived of me caring for you as *I* would wish until they are grown, which will be many years." Mark was suddenly aware that he sounded like Edward VIII making his abdication speech. He cleared his throat and continued, "I have to go back. I'm sorry."

Jane held his hand. "I understand," she said.

"You do?"

"It was a dream but it's too much to go on."

Mark hugged her. "You are a wonderful person," he said. "Will you keep this as our secret? Our own love story, unsullied by public knowledge?"

"Yes, of course."

For Mark and Jane it was not the deadly nightshade and the knife of *Romeo and Juliet* that ended their tragic love story, but glasses of Cointreau and off to bed for a last sexual hurrah.

The next morning, after breakfast, Mark gave Jane the silver necklace with the amethyst stone. "As a reminder that I shall never forget you but always love you."

With tears in her eyes, Jane accepted the gift and reciprocated his statement of fidelity and they had one last passionate kiss. Mark dropped Jane off at Franglid Station and waved at her from the platform as she leaned out of the window. He sat in his car, a weight off his mind, a plan already forming for the trial to come and optimism for the future. He turned on the radio and the station was playing 'December

63' by the Four Seasons. Mark's face broke into a smile and he swept out of the station car park, joining in with the band as they sang the chorus.

Mark arrived at his house and as the car pulled up, he caught a twitch of the net curtains in the sitting room. He opened the front door and was greeted by his two children running into the hall.

"Daddy, you're back," said the elder one, a seven-year-old with plaits. "Where have you been? Mummy was so worried."

Mark picked them both up in his arms and gave them each a kiss. "It's a long story, but I'm back now, that's the main thing." He was aware that his wife was standing behind him and looked round. "I'm sorry," he said.

His wife turned on her heels and went into the kitchen. He put the children down and followed her.

She was at the sink, pretending to wash up but the same plate was being scrubbed over and over. "Why didn't you have the decency to ring me?" she asked, finally rinsing the plate and placing it in the rack."

"I should have done but I was not thinking straight; I had a lot on my mind."

"Were you with a woman?"

"For all that time? Of course not. Look, I went to the party at the school and had a few drinks and I was talking to some of the girls and I thought about my tendencies and how it has to stop but I needed time to work through it. When I left the party, I'd had a few drinks; I thought I'd stay the night in a hotel. The next morning, I made my mind up; I needed time to sort myself out. I drove up to Leicestershire and walked a lot and thought a lot."

"But why not phone me and let me know you were all right?"

"I meant to but I seemed to be in a bit of a fug. I'm sorry."

"Luckily, I know you well enough not to worry until you've been gone at least a week."

"Believe me, I wanted to change but I had to be sure I could before I came back and I have changed. I've let you down so often in the past but I will be better in the future, you will see."

"Is that the truth, really the truth?"

He nodded.

Five years before she would have embraced him, perhaps three years before, but now she merely smiled. "We shall see."

He produced a box from his pocket and opened it to reveal an exquisite bracelet of diamonds and sapphires. "A token of my love for you," he said.

"It is beautiful," she said. "Thank you."

Mark walked into the sitting room and put upright the photograph of himself on the baby grand.

*

Jane told nobody of her adventure, certainly not her parents, nor her sister. When she returned to the academy, she kept her silence while the other students at the party recounted their conversations and petty flirtations with the teachers. Then, one of her closer friends, Fiona, who had also been at the party, asked her about the recurring rumour she was having an affair with Mark Harred.

"Apparently, the two of you were seen holding hands at the party and then going off together upstairs."

Jane smiled. "We left the stable block together by the back door."

"What happened after that?"

The vivid memory of that brief liaison flooded her mind and the determination never to speak of it collapsed in the might of the joyful reminiscence of it. "Will you keep a secret?"

"Yes."

Jane told the story of her brief fling with Mark: the falling in love with each other, the rapturous elopement, the wonderful lovemaking, the realisation that their love was doomed by circumstances and their noble self-sacrifice. By the end, the tears ran down her face as she was overcome by this articulation of the principled acceptance of her loss.

Fiona, too, shed a tear on hearing this tragic tale. Despite her promise, she was so touched by the true nature of Jane's brief relationship with Mark that she felt she must put the record straight with the sordid gossip she heard from others. To two or three reliable friends able to hold their tongues, she revealed the uplifting story of Jane's brief affair with Mark and a few days later every female student at the academy knew the story of a love story, nearly blighted by a strange trick played by someone unknown, but then brought to its fullness, only to be lost in a mutual act of selfless courage. Most liked the story enough to take it at face value. A few were more cynical.

One of the earliest to hear the story was the normally extrovert and confident Ursula. She had never known what had happened to her at the party. When she and Mike Brompton had drunk Rory's concoction, she had remarked to him that she felt unwell and he had taken her outside. The fresh air had not done the trick so, before the drinks had taken their full effect, he had half-walked, half-carried her to his car. The next either of them remembered was waking up at five o'clock in the morning and he driving her home. On the journey they had agreed that nothing had happened and decided, for both their sakes and the avoidance of interminable speculation by others, to say that he had driven her home at the end of the party. His wife had not been impressed by his late arrival home but, as they were going away that morning, decided to leave the interrogation and any consequent reprisal until they arrived at their destination. Meanwhile, Ursula had reflected on the matter but, with no one to share her vague worries, had tried to put it all behind her. Now that she had learnt of the spiking of drinks at the party, she found her vexation return as her vivid imagination and tendency to colour in grey, imperfect memories nurtured and stimulated this little worm of a worry as to what had happened to her that night. *Where had his hands been when he carried her to the car? Had he fallen asleep at the same time as her? He had woken before her, why didn't he wake her straight away? What was he doing while she still slept? Why did he make a point of them agreeing that nothing had happened?* All these thoughts bobbed to the surface of her mind from time to time and she could not quell them but she did not share them because nobody would have the answer.

So, despite the lurid rumours about the party, the silence of Ursula and Suzy, not to mention James, and the absence of Rory meant that there was little for the gossipmongers to feed on. Obviously, the revelations of Jane stoked the fires of interest for a few days but the story was already over and, after a few more days of frenzied inquisitiveness by the odd keen stirrer, the excitement rapidly dissipated and the nearness of the A level examinations dominated the interest of the students.

Roger noted a remarkable change in his British constitution class, notably in the changed attitudes of James and Suzy. James, who attended the revision classes, was much quieter and less full of himself and was the model of the conscientious, attentive student. Suzy, without necessarily changing her beliefs or opinions, was the epitome of the star pupil, answering the questions posed by Roger warmly and intelligently, seeking compromise and understanding and resisting any opportunity to criticise the views of either her teacher or her fellow students. In the less-belligerent environment, others in the group were emboldened to participate more and express their views. After a week or so, Suzy also took to spending less time in the company of those at the school, going out during free periods and in the evening to meet 'a friend' as she put it and 'a boyfriend' as her peers suspected. In class she would often speculate whether a particular topic might be in the exam and, despite Roger's refusal to be drawn, raised that area's profile in the minds of the rest of the class. When the final sessions of private revision took place, she led the sessions and encouraged them to concentrate on those areas Roger had thought paramount, adding her own 'hunches'. The whole group appeared pleased when they came out from the last exam paper. A similar pattern followed the other subjects taken by Suzy and those that paid attention to her mild shepherding were not disappointed when they saw the papers. Heartfelt were the thanks she received from her fellow students for her perceptive research into past papers, together with an intuitive judgement which amounted to little less than prophetic.

XVI

THE PROMOTION

In the Department of Business and Management Studies, the summer start-of-term staff meeting was usually a light-hearted affair. The Institute of Banking courses were virtually finished and the other courses would follow a gentle winding down of activity in this first part of term as examinations signalled the end of each course, a process reaching its climax with the few weeks left after the Whitsun break before the great summer migration. The meeting was dominated with exam-invigilation arrangements and the visit of external moderators but was given a frisson of excitement by one important announcement from Dr Frost.

One of the principal lecturers in the department had decided to retire at the end of the summer term and there would be an internal promotion among existing senior lecturers to fill the vacancy. The news led to a general buzz of interest at the meeting and afterwards in the various staff rooms several conversations took place, assessing the likely runners and their odds of success. Naturally, all the senior lecturers were silent on their likelihood of entering the race except for those who were nearing retirement themselves or for some other reason did not wish to put their names forward and were prepared to say so.

In one room, Julian Wesley was already marking examination papers, looking up occasionally to contribute his views to a discussion about the rumbles in the press about Jeremy Thorpe, the Liberal Party leader and the strange business of the Norman Scott affair. There was general agreement that the only person who did not realise he had to resign was Jeremy Thorpe himself.

"Changing the subject," said Julian, "any news on the candidates for the new PL? A bit early, I suppose."

"Not really," said Una, who was always the first to know everything of interest. "Frost wants names by the end of the month to prevent people from prevaricating about whether to throw their hats in or not. I've heard there will probably be no more than three on the shortlist: Vic Stone, Michael Brompton and Don Coppice will definitely go for it."

"I thought Frost wanted someone on the business studies side," said Javeed. "Vic is law and Mike is accounts but isn't Don management?"

"Not according to Don," said Una. "Although his students are often studying subjects containing the word 'management', he claims his teaching is in areas such as freight forwarding, shipping and marketing, which are about trade and running a business rather than the principles of management. I think I see his point. Certainly, Dr Frost has accepted that argument," she added.

Javeed looked sceptical. "These bods always twist the rules whenever it suits them. I teach management accounting: does that make me a management lecturer?"

There was silence for a few minutes while everyone in the room processed this information and decided to treat the question as rhetorical, except for Bill who shrugged his shoulders and said, "There you are."

"I hope Vic gets it," said Gillian. "He's always fair and plays straight."

"True," said Bill. "I wouldn't mind him but I'm bound to support an accountant."

"I don't see why," said Javeed. "It should be the best person for the job."

"There it is," replied Bill.

When the list closed, only the three candidates Una had identified put their names forward. Peggy White, the head of the secretarial section, considered applying but eventually decided she didn't have enough experience of the whole range of business studies subjects and chose not to, a great disappointment among her team. One or two others, whose ambition had outgrown their self-awareness, were gently advised not to bother by Dr Frost and the interviews were set for the third week in May. Fortuitously, this would permit the three candidates to attend a meeting with a member of HM Inspectorate of Education who was visiting the college on Thursday the 5th of May to give a talk to the principal, vice-principal and head of business and management on the future of business education in colleges.

The day arrived and the attendees convened in the boardroom for coffee and shortbread biscuits, baked by students from the Catering Department. Dr Frost, his hair a lustrous gold in the bright sun which came through the windows on the landing, led his three colleagues up to the boardroom just as the trolley with coffee and biscuits arrived. They stood to semi-attention while waiting for the arrival of the senior staff and their important guest.

Don Coppice was a fifty-year old, medium-height, slim man of a sallow complexion and black hair, greying at the temples. He wore a well-cut navy suit with a pocket handkerchief of a blue-and-crimson paisley pattern. He did not enter the light conversation of his colleagues; he was here to listen, not to talk. He checked his propelling pencil was fully functional and opened his new, blank notepad.

Vic Stone had just turned fifty-two and had lately felt increasingly that his best years were behind him. He regarded the forthcoming interview panel as his last opportunity to reach the top of the lecturer grade ladder. He was looking forward to hearing about the future but knew, and certainly hoped, that the education wheels ground sufficiently slowly that he would be nearing retirement before any major changes were implemented. His love was for his subject and that subject, with its roots deep in natural law, civilisation and justice, would outlive the comings and goings of educational fashion. He patted down his wayward, curly brown hair and adjusted his blue tie, the knot of which was forever sagging to leave a gap under his collar. He looked at the drinks trolley and contemplated whether he should have a biscuit after he'd had some difficulty doing up the trousers of his best suit that morning.

The youngest of the three was Mike Brompton, the senior lecturer in accountancy. Though he would welcome the promotion on offer, in truth his ambition was not in further education. He would return to his profession eventually, his background and image fortified by experience and public service in the vocation of teaching, which he enjoyed. With his CV quiver full of beautifully honed, varied arrows, he could aspire to great rewards in his future career, whether he received this appointment or not. He did not wait to be invited but took one of the shortbread biscuits and had just finished consuming it when the principal, vice-principal and HM inspector came into the boardroom.

The inspector was a thin man in his mid-forties, dressed smartly in a grey suit with a red tie. His dark hair was receding a little and he wore black-framed glasses which he pushed up his nose as he nodded to the candidates for promotion, who watched him intently for clues to his character as he took his seat.

"Good morning, gentlemen," said Professor Dunmore breezily. "I am grateful to you for attending this presentation. Some of you may know Mr Howard Proctor from previous visits. Shall we serve coffee and biscuits first?" He looked over at the tea lady standing by the trolley and smiled and she sprang into action, serving everyone with coffee and placing a large plate of the shortbread biscuits on the table.

Most took a biscuit as the plate was passed round. When it was offered to Mr Proctor he recoiled slightly theatrically. "No, thank you. I doubtless have enough cholesterol chugging round my system without adding more from a butter and sugar time bomb."

Vic Stone looked at his biscuit for a moment and tentatively took a bite from it. One or two at the table laughed. Mr Proctor did not laugh; he was readying himself to speak. He took a sheaf of papers from his case and placed them carefully on the table. After thanking the principal for holding the meeting, he introduced himself and pointed to the papers.

"Copies of this will be available afterwards but I should like to present a summary of its theme now to paint a broad picture of the underlying ethos and I shall be pleased to take any questions." He took his rather fine wristwatch off and placed it on the table, perhaps conscious that he should not take up too much of the time of these busy people or possibly that his own time was vitally important. He glanced at the time on his watch, pushed his glasses up his nose, and began.

"My paper is entitled *A Holistic Approach to Business Education.* As you will all know, education is always in a process of evolution but, at times, we see something of a quickening in the pace of evolution brought on by the need for a new strategy; what one might term a 'quantum leap in educational evolution.'" He paused for a moment, a smile skirting his lips, the listeners responding with polite smiles and chuckles. He resumed. "Such a change is demanded by the rapid developments in the workplace brought about by the advent of information technology and computerisation. In 1974, the Business Education Council was established to drive that forward and we shall soon see a new range of courses in business education. This is not a name-changing exercise but new courses delivered by a new, vibrant approach and it is this which I would like to outline now.

"To educate young people for the business world of the future we must first put the student, not the teacher nor the subject, at the centre of the learning process. Individual subjects must be subsumed within an integrated learning which reflects all the needs of the person going into the world of work, hence the holistic approach. The courses must allow for the metacognition of each student, we should strive for mastery learning for he or she in each unit of work and relate these units to the organisational climate within which the student operates. Schemas and semantic mapping might well be considered in setting out the planned course profile.

"Each student should be viewed as an individual pacing machine requiring their own differentiated supervision, pointing us to disciplined inquiry and guided discovery. This necessitates flexible assignments and an individualistic education for every single student. This is nothing new; the Winnetka Plan was formulated just after the First World War. So, teaching styles must adapt to accommodate these changes.

No more reliance on subject-based essays but the embrace of a new world of content mediated instruction, computer aided teaching, inter-curricular exercises and differentiated supervision, feedforward and the raising of horizons. A bright future we must be prepared to embrace and I am sure you will. Do you have any questions?"

The group was totally silent. The senior management, rarely involved in teaching of any sort for several years past, were grateful that they would merely have to direct change rather than actually deliver it. They were reticent lest any question might betray their shaky understanding of what was being envisaged and their failure to digest the plethora of advisory documents and planning materials which had landed in their in-trays in the past year. The principal, feeling it incumbent to take the lead, asked one of his standard questions which he found were suitable for any occasion. "Thank you, Mr Proctor, an interesting and, may I say, an enlightening, résumé of the future direction of business education. What is the anticipated take-up of this new range of BEC courses?"

While Mr Proctor expounded his vision of the future, the candidates for promotion, those who would be delivering this brave new world, were still mulling over the content of the presentation. After the first few moments of the talk, they had understood most of the words taken in isolation but not always in the phrases and sentences in which they were presented. For Vic Stone, the one clear consequence of the changes envisaged was that, within business education, his subject, law, would lose its stature as an independent area of study and be submerged in a hotchpotch of vaguely business-sounding, grandiose-titled modules which he thought amounted to gobbledygook. Aspects of law as they affected businesses would be referred to but their essence would rarely be considered. He looked over at his two fellow candidates,

Coppice scribbling furiously and Brompton staring at the HMI, his left thumb on his lower lip, and knew he didn't want the promotion and they were welcome to it.

The HMI had finished answering Professor Dunmore's question and out of the brief silence which followed came the pleasant drawl of Mike Brompton. "From what you say about disciplined inquiry and guided discovery, Mr Proctor, there will be much more scope for students to undertake their own research and to work in teams with other students?"

The HMI nodded encouragingly, almost warmly. "Precisely," he said.

There were a few other questions, another of them by Mike Brompton and then Mr Proctor looked at his watch, looked over at the principal and Professor Dunmore drew the meeting to a close.

Already both sceptical and ambivalent about his own chances of getting the principal lecturer post, Vic thought that Mike had drawn ahead of Don Coppice in the race through his informed questioning at the meeting with the HMI while Don had appeared rather dumbstruck. The interviews were a couple of weeks away, however, and Vic was aware that frontrunners are always vulnerable to the fast finisher.

The following week and ten days before the interviews, Mike Brompton was asked by Dr Frost to meet him in his office. Mike assumed it was to be a business meeting about planning for a new course or a query about a student. He left the door open when he walked into his line manager's office but Dr Frost asked him to close it.

"Take a seat, Mike," he said.

Mike felt slightly uneasy but couldn't think of any reason why he should. What Dr Frost said next came as a bolt out of the blue.

"There has been a complaint against you by one of your HNC students."

"Oh? About what?" asked Mike, in his usual calm voice, though inside his mind was in a whirl as he tried to think how this could possibly have happened.

"One of the female students claims that you have made racist and misogynistic comments during your classes."

"What? I can't believe that," Mike replied, at a loss to think of anything he could have said which would have been interpreted as either racism or misogyny.

"I must investigate. You understand?"

"Yes, of course; I don't believe I have anything to hide. Am I allowed to know my accuser's name?"

"Pauline Coppice."

A picture of Pauline Coppice sprang into Mike's mind: the wife of Don Coppice and herself a part-time lecturer in geography and history. As a member of the lecturing staff she was permitted to sit in on classes with the permission of the class teacher but as to why she had attended his course he had only the vaguest idea. When he had asked her, she had said that some knowledge of accounts could be helpful in some of the classes she taught. She had never once asked a question nor made a comment throughout the year. Nor had she submitted any of the eight optional pieces of homework Mike had set the group. Apart from making the occasional note, she had passively sat in the classroom, staring forward at the roller board and now the course was about to end.

Mike flushed. "Pauline Coppice? I can't believe it. If I did say anything she found offensive, why did she not speak to me about it?"

"Perhaps she was uncomfortable; you and her husband being colleagues."

Mike, now regaining his equilibrium, was more assertive.

"Be that as it may, I cannot recall ever saying anything that might have been construed as racist or sexist in the class, to her or anybody else."

Dr Frost smiled sympathetically. "I know this must be upsetting for you. I have not yet mentioned it to the principal as it could be a misunderstanding of some kind and I don't want to prejudice your application for promotion if there is nothing to it. I will investigate the matter thoroughly and decide whether to refer the matter to the principal after I have completed my enquiries."

"I appreciate that, thank you," said Mike.

"I will take your class this week for the first fifteen minutes."

Mike nodded and left the meeting to go straight home. Though sure of his innocence, he still felt vaguely guilty, as if he had done something wrong without realising it, perhaps through a lack of insight on his part or a misunderstanding of some sort. He felt unable to talk about it to anyone at the moment, not even to his wife.

The management structure in the college, as it was in most colleges in the sector, delegated considerable authority to the heads of department, notably in matters of discipline of both staff and students, though a decision regarding a serious matter involving possible dismissal would be referred to the principal and, for a member of staff, also to the local authority. Dr Frost had decided that this case, with the very limited detail he had at present, did not yet justify referral to the principal without further clarification on his part. His reserve on the matter was due more to what had been said by Mrs Coppice than his conversation with Mike Brompton.

Pauline Coppice had been to see him two days earlier and made allegations of a vague nature. When pressed for examples she had spoken of insinuation, double entendre and discriminatory comments disguised as humour or banter. The one thing she claimed to be sure of was that she had been aware of a prejudice against women and people of other races and that Michael Brompton made her feel uncomfortable. When she had indicated that she wished to see the principal, Dr Frost had agreed to arrange this and advised that he would come back to her within a week. He did not mention his own intended investigation; he would be sure to conduct it before the week was up.

Dr Frost had spoken to nobody about this matter, apart from Pauline Coppice and Mike Brompton. Like everybody else, he said he believed that a person is innocent until proven guilty. Unlike many of those who expressed that belief, he actually meant it. An accusation, however detached from reality, brings forth a chorus of prejudice and doubt from those whose ability to keep an open mind evaporates on the first mention of an impropriety. Almost immediately the hackneyed phrases of prejudgement are proclaimed: 'There's no smoke without fire', 'I always thought there was something odd about him', 'Well, who'd have thought it, there's no telling with people', 'It's always the ones you'd least expect' and so on and so on. For this reason, Dr Frost would tell nobody of the accusation until he had some notion of the truth. Nor would he make the well-meaning mistake of dismissing the accusation out of hand, trusting to his own judgement. That way leads to talk of a cover-up, to whispers behind hands, conversations behind closed doors and a smouldering fire of suspicion which never quite goes out and which might at any time flare up again when doused with the petrol of conspiracy theory or the flares of unsubstantiated fresh evidence. Dr Frost would act only when he had as much hard evidence as possible from those who witnessed the supposed incidents.

On Thursday afternoon, the head of department walked into the HNC second-year group who were expecting Mike

Brompton. All nine of them stopped talking when they saw him come in. Pauline Coppice, who had not spoken to anyone else in the group since taking her seat, sat in the front row of desks, facing the roller board.

Dr Frost took his place at the front of the class and addressed the students. "Good afternoon, I am Dr Frost, the head of department. I should like to have a few words with you. Mrs Coppice, would you mind leaving the room and waiting in my office? I will join you in a few minutes."

Pauline did not move for a few moments and Frost thought she might refuse. "Thank you," he said and walked over to the door, opening it for her.

Pauline hesitated for just one more moment before she rose from her seat and slowly walked out of the room. As he returned to his position, Frost was aware that the tenor of the group had changed. Formerly, merely curious at his arrival, now they were watching him in anticipation.

"I have a question to put to you and I would appreciate a candid and full answer. Have any of you heard Mr Brompton make what you would regard as racist or misogynistic comments during his weekly classes with you or anywhere else in the surrounds of the college?"

The members of the group looked around at each other, some with blank expressions, others questioningly at their neighbour. One young man asked, "Sir, what does misogynistic mean?" which drew a rolling of eyes from one of his female colleagues and a snigger from another.

"It means strongly prejudiced against women and this might include disparaging or insulting, perhaps even suggestive, remarks to or about a specific woman or women in general related to the fact of them being women," replied Dr Frost.

One of the young men older than the others, perhaps twenty-four or five, spoke up. "I can honestly say that I never heard Mr Brompton mention coloured people in the class, let alone anything bad about them."

Another added, "This is an accounts class so we rarely mention other countries, let alone the people that live there." His fellow students mumbled support for both these statements.

The young woman who had rolled her eyes earlier put her hand up and Frost nodded.

"As far as I'm concerned, Mr Brompton treats us all the same: if he makes a joke or amusing comment it's never anything to do with the person's sex and he's never patronising towards women or anything like that."

Another female member of the group nodded. "What's this all about? Is Mr Brompton in trouble?"

Frost didn't answer directly. "A member of this class has complained that Mr Brompton did make racist and misogynistic comments and I have to look into it. I gather from what you have said that none of you are aware of this."

They all shook their heads.

"You would be prepared to make a statement to that effect?"

They all nodded.

The young woman who had asked if Mike was in trouble raised her hand. "Mr Brompton never said anything bad to Mrs Coppice either, at least not in front of us."

"I'm very grateful for your assistance," said Frost. "Mr Brompton will join you shortly."

Frost went to Mike Brompton's office where Mike had sat alone, waiting to be called. Frost told him he could take his class now and asked him to come to Frost's office when it was finished. He then went back to his own office where Pauline was sitting, clutching her handbag on her lap. As he took his seat, he was aware of her eyes fixed on him. She did not blink as his eyes met her stare. He found her a most unattractive woman: a figure he could only describe as stodgy; heavy, rather masculine facial features; rather frightening, flaring framed black glasses and greying, dark hair in a style that not been fashionable since the 1950s. It crossed his mind that the fact he disliked her, now more than he had twenty minutes before, made her appear less attractive, just as the woman he had recently fallen in love with he found more attractive every day.

"Pauline, could you be more specific about the racist and inappropriate comments about women that you have told me were made by Mike Brompton?"

Pauline's expression did not change. "He said he didn't like teaching black people as they were not very intelligent and he said that women are useless at accounting and should stick to female subjects or, better still, stick to getting married and bringing up children. He laughed when he said that."

"To whom did he make these comments?"

"I overheard him talking to another teacher."

"Who?"

"I don't know his name."

"What does he look like?"

"I can't remember."

"Did he make both these comments at the same time?"

"No, different times."

"But to the same person each time?"

"Yes. No. I'm not sure."

"When did he make these comments?"

"Once before Christmas and the other time last week."

"So, he didn't actually make comments directly to students as far as you know?"

"No, not as far as I know."

"Of course, you may have overhead something said out of context or even misheard what was said."

"I can't say."

"As a colleague, could you not have spoken to Mike Brompton about your dislike of his language? After all, you had not heard him say these things to you or any student and you were listening to what was presumably a private conversation. I would have thought that a reasonable thing to do, especially as the second comment at least could have been a joke in poor taste and an apology would have been the most apposite outcome."

"I might have felt intimidated or threatened if I had gone to him directly."

Frost looked at Pauline closely again. *Surely people would find this woman more intimidating than Mike Brompton?* he thought. He kept his conjecture to himself and responded to her last statement. "Really? He has always seemed to me a polite, reasonable person, certainly not someone inclined to put the fear of God into anyone? I suppose it's all a matter of opinion. Tell me, why did you decide to come and see me at this particular time?"

"Whereas I had reluctantly been willing to let his previous remark pass, this latest comment about women showed a pattern of behaviour. I felt I must speak to somebody in authority."

"It had nothing to do with the fact that your husband and Mike Brompton have both applied for the vacancy of Principal Lecturer and that accusations of this sort could affect Mike's hopes of preferment?"

"That didn't cross my mind."

"To be frank, Pauline, I don't believe you. I have spoken to your fellow students in the accounts class and not one of them supports your complaint. To the contrary, the female students spoke up for Mike Brompton. Your new statement, which you did not bring up before, is unsubstantiated and will almost certainly not be corroborated by any of your colleagues. I do not quite understand the motive for your complaint against him but can only assume it is to damage his reputation for your own purposes. Whatever your reasons, I am inclined to the view that your statement is a calumny and I shall advise the principal appropriately."

For the first time in the interview, Pauline looked less composed. Her face paled and she fiddled with the clasp on her handbag. "I suppose it was too much to expect a man, especially a man in authority, to take a woman's side against another man."

Frost did not respond to her challenge. "If you still wish to proceed, I will take the matter to the principal and he will investigate it fully and transparently as he always does. In that case, I am confident that your dragging Mr Brompton's reputation through the mud will serve no purpose and he may well be justified in suing you for slander. I suggest you sleep on the matter and let me know tomorrow if you wish to proceed. If I don't hear from you by Monday, I will assume you have dropped your complaint. You may go back to your class if you wish to do so."

Pauline shook her head slightly but said nothing. After a second or two she stood up and left Dr Frost's office. She did not go back to her accounts class that day or ever again.

After Pauline had left, Frost sat back in his chair and lit a cheroot, a habit he had recently taken up to go with his change of image. He had surprised himself at the forcefulness of his statement to her but did not regret it; indeed, he felt he had experienced a moment of righteous anger. He liked to think he took seriously accusations of racist language or disparaging remarks against women but he had seen before that it is all too easy to throw the mud of vague suggestions around which stuck on the victims of such slander and this he felt could quite easily have happened here.

What to do now? he thought. A one-time project manager by profession, he took a piece of paper from his desk drawer and began to sketch a simple flow chart.

Did Don know Pauline made a complaint? – If No, No Further Action.

If Yes, did he approve? If No, No Further Action.

If Yes, did he connive with her? If No, No Further Action, but advise him of poor judgement.

If Yes, Take Action (but what action?).

He looked at his effort and was satisfied with it as an exercise but could not see how he would get an answer to any of the questions. Don would almost certainly deny knowledge of the actions of his wife and even if he did own up that he knew, he would not admit to any part in it. There was no point in interviewing him about the matter. He would wait to see whether Pauline continued with her complaint before deciding what action to take with them. He did some paperwork on staff-student ratios and student fallout numbers while waiting to see Mike at five o'clock.

Not surprisingly, Mike finished his class a little early and knocked on Frost's door at ten to five. He looked pale and anxious when he came in the room and sat opposite Frost.

"How did the class go?" asked Frost.

Mike smiled. "The students looked as worried as I did when I walked into the room. They were keen to tell me they had nothing to do with the complaint and they were generally supportive, which I thought was kind."

"I'm not surprised; I got the impression they liked you. I have spoken to Pauline Coppice and I would like your comments on the two specific examples of prejudice she claims you made when talking to somebody else." Frost repeated the example of racial prejudice.

Mike shook his head. "I have no recollection of making

that statement to anyone. That would be a ridiculous thing to say, as well as offensive."

Frost repeated the sexist statement Pauline had attributed to Mike.

Mike laughed. "I do remember saying that a week or so ago to Bill Rendell. I was actually telling him what my first boss had said about women applying to become chartered accountants; he was very old-fashioned about women. Bill and I both laughed about what a dinosaur he was; he wouldn't have got away with it these days." He looked relieved.

"So, it doesn't reflect your own opinion?"

"Hardly; you may remember my wife is a chartered accountant and she earns a lot more than I do."

Frost smiled. "As far as I am concerned, you have nothing to worry about. I have asked Pauline Coppice to reconsider her complaint and she has until Monday to let me know if she wishes to go ahead. I doubt very much we will hear any more of it."

"Thanks for investigating this business properly. The rumours are probably circulating already and before you know where you are they have become the default truth."

Frost nodded. "I've seen the rumour machine at work myself too many times to let it go. At my previous college I was promoted internally and some joker or malicious bastard started a story that I only got the job because I was the principal's nephew. A literal case of nepotism. Within a fortnight of my getting the job, it had become an established fact throughout the college even though the principal and I had never met before I worked at the college and he was a Scot with Irish connections while I am English with a Canadian mother. I challenged one person who I knew had spread the rumour and he had nothing to say. Rumours thrive on silence."

Mike managed a smile but in truth he felt quite sick and had already thought about throwing in the towel and going back into professional practice.

As Frost had expected, Pauline did not pursue her complaint but let it lapse. Neither Pauline nor Don Coppice came to see Frost about it. So, whether Don knew about the complaint, Frost was unable to say. He chose to take no action now. There would be time enough when the repercussions came.

A week later, he put forward two names to the principal as a shortlist to be interviewed for the principal lecturer post: Mike Brompton and Vic Stone. They were the two names he had always intended to put forward, provided he learnt nothing to the detriment of either, which he had not. The news of the omission of Don Coppice's name from the list went round the department close to the speed of light and, that afternoon Don Coppice knocked on his door, closing it behind him.

"Yes, Don?"

"I am not on the shortlist for the PL, I see."

"That's right. I did say I wanted to appoint someone on the business studies side; we already have four PLs in management, all for very good reasons but I want a rebalance."

"But I *am* in business studies. Look at the courses I teach."

Frost looked at a copy of Don's timetable he happened to have on his desk. "Marketing management, freight forwarding and shipping management, principles of management, etc., etc."

"Yes, but the courses are not pure management, they are commercial subjects I teach in the main."

"I seem to remember you were keen to teach management subjects specifically to get enough higher-grade work. It's about perception, Don. You would be seen as another management lecturer by most people in the department."

Don frowned but he knew Frost wasn't budging. He turned way but then stopped and looked round at Frost again. "Is this anything to do with Pauline's complaint against Mike Brompton?"

"No, why should it be?"

"I had nothing to do with it."

"I'm glad to hear it but, as I've said, it had no bearing on the shortlisting." Frost had rehearsed this interview and had the answers to the likely questions off pat. He looked down at his paperwork and Don turned his back and left the room, shutting the door more noisily than was strictly necessary.

Ten days after that, Vic Stone and Mike Brompton were interviewed by a small panel of senior managers, including the principal and Dr Frost. Mike was interviewed first and then Vic. While the panel deliberated, Mike and Vic sat in the waiting room. Mike looked agitated and didn't say much.

Vic smiled at Mike. "You'll be appointed. You're the right man for the job. I haven't got the energy or the stomach to implement change and I have a feeling that once they start messing about with things, they won't stop till they've changed everything. I would have seen my time out to get a bigger pension and delegated all the work to the ambitious section heads."

Mike smiled weakly. The interview had been strange and disconcerting. He had been asked pretty straightforward questions and had answered them well enough but there was a strangely dead atmosphere. There were no follow-up questions, no comments on what he said; it was as if they were not listening to his answers. He tried to convince himself that they had already made up their minds and were going through the formalities but he was uneasy. Then he was called back into the boardroom and he relaxed a little for a moment until the smile was wiped off his face by the expressions of those on the interview panel.

"Mr Brompton, I'm afraid we are unable to offer you this post, despite your obvious strengths," said Professor Dunmore. He picked up a letter from his desk and tapped it with his hand. "Apparently, for the last year and a half you have engaged in part-time teaching at Twirleston Academy."

"It was in my own time and I believe it is not considered unacceptable for lecturers to have outside teaching or other academic work."

"It is not, you are quite right. However, you also attended a party held at the school at the end of last term and when the official party was ended you drank alcohol with some of the students without their parents or their teachers present. That was inadvisable, even if they are over eighteen, as you could be placed in a compromising situation. More seriously, one of the students has written to the school and to the college with a complaint that you may have taken advantage of her while she was unconscious."

Mike felt as if a wild animal had just clawed at his innards. "I refute the claim entirely," he said. "There is an explanation."

"No doubt, and you will have the opportunity to address this matter in due course but you understand that it is impossible to prefer you for promotion at this time."

"Could not the panel have been postponed until it is sorted out?" asked Mike, desperately, looking over at Dr Frost.

Frost shook his head. "I'm afraid you attract trouble, Mike. First the accusations by Mrs Copping and now this. It won't do for a senior member of staff to be attracting trouble. In any case, you did make a professional error of judgement."

"But I know nothing of this. Surely I should have been notified."

"The headmaster did not wish to write to your home address for obvious reasons, so the letter is waiting for you at the school. The headmaster sent a letter to me as a matter of courtesy; it arrived yesterday. I am sorry this happened; very unfortunate," said Professor Dunmore. "I know it's a shock for you, but we thought it better to go through the process rather than eliminate you before the interview stage, which would inevitably be more embarrassing. You are innocent until proved guilty and any investigation is a matter for the school so you are not suspended by the college."

Mike came out of the boardroom and his despondent expression surprised Vic but before he had a chance to ask what happened, he was asked to go back into the boardroom to be offered the post. Bewildered but flattered, Vic accepted, partly out of pride but primarily for the increase in salary and the significant effect on his pension. When he came out of the boardroom, Mike had already left. He was relieved beyond measure that he had no further teaching commitments that day and went home to tell his wife the news that what had been in the bank was now on the scrap heap. What made the situation even worse was that he was then grilled by his wife about the events at the school party and why he had come home so late that night. She believed his story but called him a bloody fool for getting in such a predicament. "You should have known better than to be around at the end of a drinks party when things can go off the rails and nobody remembers exactly what happens and everybody is prepared to believe anything could have happened and you are the fall guy. I hope it will be a lesson to you."

Equally in a state of shock, Vic took his wife out to dinner that evening and the next morning he started to draw up his plans for the business studies sections of the department. Suddenly, from nowhere, he was abuzz with ideas.

EPILOGUE

Whether Don Coppice felt any resentment at not getting the promotion, he didn't tell anyone in the department. His take on it to those who, out of curiosity or schadenfreude, broached the subject was that Frost had taken a narrow view of what constituted business studies and didn't want someone with his professional expertise across both areas. Of necessity, he would reconsider his career opportunities. Don's disappointment was not alleviated by Mike Brompton failing to get the job; rather it was multiplied. While he had seen Mike as a rival, he had discounted Vic entirely and to lose even to him was more than his pride could bear. He never spoke directly to Vic Stone, Mike Brompton or Dr Frost again.

Later that term, Pauline gave in her notice and, as a part-time lecturer, could leave at a few weeks' notice so that the Humanities Department had to manage her classes in the summer. Don gave notice that he would quit at the end of the summer term at the very last moment to make finding a successor as difficult as possible. At his farewell, on his last day, he informed everyone that he was looking forward to going back into the City and the Baltic Exchange. He said he would be on a salary commensurate with the one he'd given up when he became a lecturer and more than twice what he was currently earning. His colleagues smiled and took what he said with a pinch of salt, as they had done when he regaled them with stories of his past successes through all the years they had known him. One young lecturer standing behind Don made a rude gesture with his hand which summed up what many of them were thinking but he did not notice the smirks.

Mike Brompton endured a week of torture before the inquiry at the academy. His wife did not accompany him to the school as she considered it would add credence to the claims if he thought them serious enough to drag along the loyal wife to stand beside him. She assured him that she knew him well enough to be sure there was nothing to worry about. He was certain there was nothing in the accusations but was not as confident as she that he would be exonerated.

Mr Mandeville was, as usual, keen to keep publicity to a minimum and, assuring Mike that all would be well, prevailed on him not to bring in a union official from The National Association of Teachers in Further and Higher Education at this stage. Ursula, on the other hand, was accompanied by her parents and their solicitor and Mike's fears turned to alarm. However, he successfully defended himself against Ursula's complaint of possible assault because there was no evidence provided from Ursula, merely a suspicion. When quietly questioned by Mandeville, she admitted that she was troubled by the possibility that something could have happened while she was unconscious but agreed she had seen Mike Brompton's drink interfered with as well. The only witness was James Newton who saw Mike Brompton drink the tampered-with drink and later, when he and Rory went to their car, he had seen Mike in the car unconscious, a state which would have persisted for several hours.

Mike said that he bore Ursula no grudge but that the rumour had been enough to lead to his losing his opportunity for promotion at the college and that he, though the accused, had become the principal victim of this sorry state of affairs.

Mandeville opined that there was no proof whatsoever that Ursula had been assaulted in any way and said the school would take no further action. The solicitor, after consulting with the parents, said that they did not intend to pursue the matter further and regretted that Mr Brompton's career had been adversely affected by this matter. Ursula wept and left the court most distressed but afterwards found that she could convince herself that no harm had come to her just as easily as she had convinced herself that it had.

Afterwards, Mike handed in his notice, finished his year at college and then accepted a post with a major accounting firm at a salary three times that of his senior lecturer post. Javeed, Bill and the other accounting lecturers continued to help accounting students to pass their examinations and thereby earn significantly more than their teachers.

Vic Stone took his new role of Principal Lecturer in charge of business studies very seriously. He established a management system in which empowerment and delegation were the keys. All members of staff were encouraged to be proactive in putting forward new ideas involving the development of the curriculum and new teaching techniques. Such ideas were given a fair hearing and if adopted passed to section heads or course tutors to implement. Vic concentrated on his role of leadership, notably in the teaching of his beloved law and on those courses where it retained its splendid isolation as a subject.

Gillian Trevis and Roger Southwark slowly became a couple over the summer term and nobody minded or particularly cared. Roger's weekends in London became few and far between and when he did go, he took Gillian with him. At first, they maintained all three homes but eventually the flat in London went but Gillian kept her flat 'just in case', as she put it. They had no desire to marry yet but they announced their engagement after they moved in together during the summer to finish off probing questions. Roger found that his savings and investments stopped dwindling as rapidly as before and the complications in life which he always shirked were reduced rather than increased when he settled into their relationship. He was more than content with his life. Gillian's interest in solving the question of the missing lecturers had partly arisen out of her enjoyment of mystery novels and a few years later, she wrote one herself about a couple trapped in a building with no means of escape.

Mark Harred was true to his word to his wife, up to a point. He stopped teaching at Twirleston so he wouldn't be tempted so easily. There remained the matter of the college but nobody was asked to act as chaperone during the whole of the autumn term. His wife, who understood him better than anybody else, even himself, forgave him for the umpteenth time. His colleagues were pleased to see the end of the chaperone role but were unable to account for this dramatic change of character, cynically assuming his wife must have read him the Riot Act. Unfortunately, he fell off the wagon, as it were, just before Christmas and was found in flagrante delicto with a relatively mature student, in the medical rest room. Fortunately, he was discovered by one of the caretaking staff who let him off with a warning and, to maintain his discretion, arranged for Mark to sort out a legal problem for him pro bono.

Mr Manville was relieved and somewhat surprised that the academy, as he put it, "Sailed successfully between Scylla and Charybdis and went over the Niagara Falls without disaster." He managed to keep all the inquiries in-house and out of the newspapers and was able to secure a generous donation to the school from the families of James and Rory, in addition to their payments to Suzy and Rob. All future social gatherings would end with a personal inspection of the premises by the caretaker and himself.

Later, when the A level results came out in August, Suzy Plunkett would achieve three A's and confirm a conditional place at Somerville College, Oxford, to read philosophy, politics and economics. Her father was delighted at her success and gave her a significant increase in her allowance. She never told her parents about the ordeal in the stable block nor the compensation received from the Newtons and the Marnochs. She opened a savings account and let it grow slowly for the rainy day she was sure would come when she lost the approval of her father. James Newton achieved good, if not spectacular, A level results and also went to university to please his father, though James found it hard to concentrate on his studies. Fortunately, he was assured of a career in banking through his father's connections and his grandfather was over eighty so a generous bequest was certain as long as he kept his nose clean. In any case, he was able to reflect that at least he could concentrate on some aspects of his life unlike Rory, whose concentration span had been severely, and probably irreparably shortened to little more than Planck time, since the accident.

Suzy and Rob had exchanged telephone numbers and addresses after the meeting at the school to fix a compensation package but they had not seen each other since. Even the business of signing the confidentiality agreement had been done separately. It wasn't that their feelings for each other had weakened; both remembered the other with affection and loyalty, and they shared a bond forged in an experience few had endured. Perhaps it was the rawness of the memory that neither wished to revisit that prevented contact. Or perhaps the realisation they had little in common but the extreme events of that week. It may have been they didn't even attempt to find a reason: it was just the way it was. Suzy decided to make the move. While sitting at home, looking once again at her A level results and feeling just a little bit guilty because of the help she had received, she remembered their agreement to meet for a celebration dinner and realised how much she wanted that to happen.

After a great deal of deliberation, she picked up the phone and rang Rob's home number. It rang for four times and she began to get cold feet. As she took the receiver away from her ear, she heard him answer.

"Hello, 348221."

"Hello, Rob, it's Suzy."

"Suzy! What a nice surprise. How are you?"

"I'm fine. I received my A level results yesterday."

"Yes, I thought about you. How did you get on?"

"Straight As."

"That's great. You'll have no trouble getting a place anywhere you like."

"I have one at Oxford, Somerville."

"Excellent, well done. Have you decided what you'll read yet?"

"Yes, PPE."

"I thought you might. I'm sure you'll love it."

"I'd like to take you out to dinner. We said we would do it to celebrate my results."

There was a pause and she wondered if he'd changed his mind.

"I'd like to but I'm old-fashioned enough to think the man should pay, at least the first time."

She laughed. "Well, I won't argue with you about it."

With Suzy at home in Bosworth and Rob at his flat near the college, a meeting needed some planning. Rob offered to drive up to Bosworth but Suzy thought that might lead to awkward questions as her parents knew nothing of the week they had spent together and she couldn't think of suitable answers to the questions her mother was bound to raise. Eventually, she suggested she would meet him in Hinckley and they could take it from there.

Rob drove the hour and twenty minutes or so from his flat and met Suzy outside Hinckley station. It had been a stifling, hot day in a very warm August and he was glad they were meeting in the cooler evening. It was the first time he had seen Suzy wearing a dress and she looked very pretty. He had made an effort too, the first time he'd worn a suit for months. They embraced and kissed briefly on the cheek. It was the right thing, they both felt, yet were surprised they felt a little gauche in each other's company when they had slept in the same bed, near naked. But that was then and this was now.

They took a trip out into the country and had dinner in a hotel where Suzy had eaten before; the menu was classical and the dining room airy, even if there was no air conditioning. She was sure it would be fine.

As they were offered the menus, Rob said, "This is a celebration in lots of ways; let's have a glass of champagne."

When the champagne arrived, Rob raised his glass. "Well done in the exams and here's to a happy and prosperous future to you."

"It should be 'well done' to you for getting us through our trial and tribulation so we *can* celebrate now," she said, despite his hand raised in protestation. "You know, I had a lot of help in the exams. I feel a bit of a fraud really," she added in a whisper.

He shook his head. "You still had to do the work and, anyway, you deserved a good break."

They talked about her going to Oxford. "Not too far if you need to go home but far enough that you can't be expected to pop round to the parents too often," said Rob.

She smiled. "What about you? Has Mr Newton kept his promise?"

He shrugged and shook his head. "Not so far but I'm over it now. I was very disappointed at first, the news coming just after what happened to us, but it's not the end of the world. After all, life is meant to be a lottery, win some lose some. Hopefully, I'll get another chance but if not, sod it."

She raised her glass to him and smiled. "Here's to you and I still think Mr Newton will come up with something."

He thought she was being kind and responded with a hopeful expression.

Over dinner, they talked about going to university and he told her a little about his time at a polytechnic in London. "Not much of a comparison though. You'll be in the refined atmosphere of the very bright and the very well-connected; all *Brideshead Revisited* and a touch of *Lucky Jim*."

She smiled. "I definitely count among the well-connected, rather than the other category."

Eventually, the conversation drifted into the subject that was at the back of both their minds but so far unspoken. Rob asked Suzy if she had been left with any after-effects of their ordeal.

She raised her hand and showed the red scar. "I think people assume this is a bodged suicide attempt because they never ask."

He smiled. "Do you get any pain from it now?"

"Not really. Only a constant reminder of painful times."

Rob nodded. "Hopefully nothing serious mentally?"

"You mean a tendency to wake up screaming or sweating in the night or dreaming of being dragged round the room on a bed being chased by a chamber pot? No, nothing like that, at least not at first. I think my mind blocked it all out. Lately, I have had some strange dreams with reminders of some of the awfulness of it. Claustrophobia, that kind of thing, but nothing terrible. Perhaps the memories would have been worse if our captors had been around, goading or torturing us. It was just us two, surviving. Do you remember that plane crash in the Andes a few years ago and those not killed in the crash managing to survive, at least some of them, even though it was horrendous? I thought about that when we were trapped and it kept me going because it was never that bad. That and you."

They were both silent for a while and Rob felt a lump in his throat.

Suzy smiled. "What about you? I hope you had no physical problems? You hit the wall with a mighty crash and your back looked so bad then."

"I'm fine. Not many after-effects at all. It was not a very long time and it would have stuck with us more had it gone on and on. Sometimes, it hardly seems real."

She nodded, saying nothing, but then her thoughts hit a nerve and she reached for the handkerchief.

Rob topped up her glass and she drank a little, unable to speak. A woman walked past their table, stared momentarily at Suzy wiping a tear and then gave a look at Rob which signified 'You swine'.

"I'm sorry, Suzy. I promised myself I wouldn't raise that business; I didn't want to upset you. I couldn't stop myself."

"Don't apologise. We should be able to talk about it. After all, we shall never forget it, and it didn't end badly. I get emotional because it was so awful but you were so good. I was pretty useless."

He put his hand on hers. "Actually, you were great. You didn't go to pieces or blame me or make it more difficult than it was. You got me through it as much as I did you."

She held his hand for a moment. "Thanks," she said. "For everything."

After dinner he offered to take her home but she refused. "My father will pick me up from the station, but thanks anyway." He took her to Hinckley Station and saw her off.

"I hope we don't lose contact," she said, as they waited for her train.

"No. I hope so too."

They kissed and embraced. She got on the train and they waved as the train pulled away. They parted with their bond intact. Yet, though they sent each other Christmas cards and the odd update on how they were and what they were doing, they never saw each other again.

Rob triumphed over the human tendency to forget immediately about the good things to come one's way and to concentrate on the strokes of ill fortune. He always reminded himself of that Good Friday when everything seemed up and death was at most a day away. He enjoyed his teaching more and resumed his activism for the Party, accepting that promotion in politics from spear-holder to leading actor would probably never come. He even forgave Mr Newton for failing to meet his promise to him and decided not to press the matter of the £25,000, thinking, *he probably did his best.*

In the new autumn term, he returned to his teaching with vigour and commitment and barely thought about any other career. Then, in the first week of December, the Labour MP for a Derbyshire constituency resigned his seat to take up a post with the United Nations and a week later he received a letter from the Constituency Party Chair inviting him to be on the shortlist as she had heard such good things about his work for the Party. He duly attended the interviews on the set day where he made the final two. He was then adopted ahead of a middle-aged man, a former factory worker and union representative who had worked for the party for thirty years but wasn't able to match Rob's grasp of political theory nor his analysis of the government's recent white paper, *An Approach to Industrial Strategy*.

After his selection, Rob wrote to James Newton's father a carefully worded letter, thanking him for the support he had received in his career. He received a letter back, congratulating him on his success but assuring him that everything he had achieved was entirely due to his own efforts and strength of character. Rob smiled at the contents of the letter but that was as far as he got in understanding quite what had happened in his quest for a parliamentary seat. In due course, he held the safe seat at the 1979 election and settled into his career as a prominent backbencher who preferred fighting for causes he was interested in rather than seeking membership of the shadow or any other cabinet.

The college rolled over into another new year, always the same but always different. Dr Dunmore decided that year to become an emeritus professor at his old university to leave the college to new blood. The new principal was a man from a vague social science background and numerous educational qualifications who impressed the Board of Governors with his plans for the future. He envisaged the end of stale, inward-searching departments led by all-powerful heads of department. Instead, 'a matrix of interacting heads of resources, courses and staff would lead to a dynamic and creative search for excellence in a three-dimensional interface'. Naturally, there would be far more managers than before and he suggested the title of director for himself as he had so much more to administer and to lead. Once the new management structure began working, there were far more people the staff had to report to but no one who could actually take responsibility for a decision or provide a way out when the sides of the matrix were unable to agree. The flow chart of decision-making appeared to be designed by Maurits Escher and nobody in the management chart could find anything to say against it. It was a new era.